Also in this series:

Savannah Martin has always been a good girl, doing what was expected and fully expecting life to fall into place in its turn. But when her perfect husband turns out to be a lying, cheating slimeball—and bad in bed to boot—Savannah kicks the jerk to the curb and embarks on life on her own terms. With a new apartment, a new career, and a brand new outlook on life, she's all set to take the world by storm. If only the world would stop throwing her curveballs...

They say absence makes the heart grow fonder, and Savannah is certainly learning the truth of that statement.

It's been a month and a half since Rafael Collier left town, and although Savannah knows it would be hideously inappropriate—not to mention supremely stupid—to miss him, she wishes he'd come back soon. His grandmother's ailing, the nurse he hired to take care of her has disappeared, and somebody is watching the house and following Savannah as she goes about the business of bringing her first real estate transaction to a close.

But when Rafe comes back, things only go from bad to worse. Resident nurse Marquita Johnson is found murdered, and Metro Nashville Homicide Detective Tamara Grimaldi is asked to handle the case. It doesn't take long for her to focus her interest, once again, on Rafe.

Now Savannah has to make the choice between staying safe by accepting her old flame Todd's proposal, or taking a chance on losing her heart and her life by trying to help Rafe, as the term 'contract pending' takes on a whole new meaning.

CONTRACT PENDING

Jenna Bennett

CONTRACT PENDING
SAVANNAH MARTIN MYSTERY #3

This is a work of fiction. Names, characters, places and incidents either are the product of the author's imagination or are used fictitiously, and any resemblance to actual persons, living or dead, business establishments, events or locales is entirely coincidental.

Interior design: April Martinez, GraphicFantastic.com

ISBN: 978-0-9899434-0-6

MAGPIE INK

One

A bsence makes the heart grow fonder, they say, and there must be something to it, because I started missing Rafael Collier pretty much the minute his taillight disappeared around the corner at the end of the block. As the weeks went by with no sign of life, I only missed him more.

Or maybe missed isn't exactly the right word. I mean, I'm not stupid, and missing Rafe would be just that. Stupid. We weren't involved, and it wasn't like I cared that I might never see him again. Not really. Not much, anyway.

Or maybe I cared a little. When a man saves your life, you tend to feel a little sentimental about him afterwards, and the fact that Rafe is drop-dead gorgeous and has made no secret of finding me somewhat attractive as well, didn't exactly hurt, either. Nor did the fact that he was the only man I had ever met who could, quite literally, leave me breathless and weak in the knees with no more than a look.

So yes, I might have been just a mite disappointed that he hadn't decided to take advantage of me before he left town. The idea that he might never come back, and that I'd missed my chance to indulge in one night of wild passion before I settled down and married my old boyfriend Todd Satterfield, was irksome, to say the least. I'd gotten used to having Rafe around, his cheerful attempts to talk me into bed gave my ego a much-needed boost after I leaving my cheating husband two years ago, and, to be honest, I felt safe knowing Rafe had my back. I'd gotten myself mixed up with two different murderers in the past few months—something of a record for someone who's not looking for trouble—and just in case it happened again, I'd feel better knowing that Rafe was in reach. Except he wasn't, and now something was brewing that caused my want of him to spike into something close to desperation.

It all started over dinner with Todd at Fidelio's Restaurant.

Todd Satterfield is my brother's best friend and my mother's choice of second husband for me. He's also someone I dated for a year in high school. When I married Bradley Ferguson, Todd married a girl named Jolynn because she reminded him of me, and when I divorced Bradley, Todd divorced Jolynn. Now he wants to get back together. He hasn't come out and proposed yet, but he's come pretty close. And when he eventually gets around to it, I don't see what I can do, other than accept. He's everything a well-brought-up Southern Belle should want in a husband: normal, healthy, and good-looking, at least if one's tastes should happen to run to the fair-haired and blue-eyed all-American type. He is also nice, honest, attentive, unfailingly polite, loyal to a fault, and flatteringly devoted. Oh yes, and well-off. More than capable of providing for me in the manner to which I was born, and to which I would like to become accustomed again, once I don't have to support myself. He can trace his antecedents back to the War Against Northern Aggression—that's the Civil War to you Yankees—and he has a brilliant future ahead of him in the district attorney's office in Columbia, and probably—if I know him—in politics. In short, he's perfect. Or would be, if it weren't for one thing.

"Have you heard anything from Collier?" Todd asked. His voice sounded strained.

I shook my head. "Not a word."

Todd smirked. "I always told you he was trouble."

He had. Repeatedly. He was absolutely convinced that Rafe was a threat to my virtue—correct as far as it went—and he kept giving me reasons why I shouldn't have anything to do with him. He—Todd— had even gone so far as to hire a private investigator to follow Rafe around, just so he could prove to me that Rafe was involved in illegal activities. Since this was something I'd already suspected anyway, the news didn't come as a big shock.

"I know you have," I said docilely.

"I gave the police those pictures I showed you, you know. The ones of Collier and those three men who were involved in those open house robberies last month. The police seemed quite interested in them."

"I'm sure they were," I said. Rafe had been involved in last month's robberies up to his eyebrows, and considering that he's at least six three, that's pretty high up. "They're all languishing in jail already. Detective Grimaldi told me."

Tamara Grimaldi with the Metropolitan Nashville Police Department's homicide unit is by way of being a friend of mine. Or at least a close acquaintance, if that isn't a contradiction in terms. We met a couple of months ago, after Rafe and I stumbled over my colleague Brenda Puckett's butchered body in an empty house in East Nashville, and the detective dragged both of us to Police Plaza for questioning. She turned up her nose at my delicate constitution and ladylike vapors, but over time we buried the hatchet and arrived at an uneasy sort of truce. The detective tolerated me and made no attempt to hide her interest in Rafe, although I've never been entirely sure whether that interest is professional or personal in nature. On the one hand, he has done plenty in his life that might interest a police detective. On the other, he has attributes that might interest any halfway conscious woman, too.

"I met your Detective Grimaldi," Todd said. "When I dropped the pictures off."

I didn't see the sense in explaining that the detective isn't actually mine. "What did you think of her?"

"She seems competent enough," Todd said. "And she was very complimentary of you. Although she said something I didn't understand. Something about your terrible ordeal and a DVD…?"

I grimaced. "Oh. That."

Todd looked politely inquiring, and after an uncomfortable pause, which I tried to fill with sips of wine while I avoided his eyes, I gave up. "I told you about what happened last month. With Perry Fortunato, the man who raped and strangled Lila Vaughn, and who raped and strangled his wife, and who would have strangled me too, if Rafe hadn't killed him first."

A shadow crossed Todd's even features. He didn't like to be reminded of the fact that I—and he—owed Rafe Collier my life. "Yes."

"Well, I didn't mention the fact that he liked to film things. Like sexual encounters. His own and other people's. And that he tied me to his bed and was going to film me. Except he ended up filming his own death instead."

Todd went very still. "He tied you to the bed?"

I nodded.

"Naked?"

"Well… almost naked." I'd been wearing a bra, panties, and a pair of shoes, to be exact. And earrings and a watch.

"Collier was there?"

"He killed Perry. I told you that."

Todd had taken to breathing through his nose. Somehow, the fact that Rafe had seen me in my skivvies seemed to upset him more than my almost being raped and murdered. "Did he touch you?"

"Perry? No, he didn't get a chance to. Other than when he undressed me and tied me to the bed in the first place. But I was unconscious then, so I don't really know what he did."

"Collier!" Todd clarified, between gritted teeth.

"Oh. No. Of course not." Other than a teasing stroke up my arm that had almost made me jump out of my skin, but there was no need to mention that. "He's not like that."

"Hah!" Todd said. He grabbed his glass of Merlot and tossed back the dregs. I took another ladylike sip of my Chardonnay in lieu of remonstrating. It was difficult not to try to explain why he was wrong, but I knew from experience that it wouldn't make any difference. Todd was convinced that he knew what Rafe was like, and there was nothing I could say or do to change his mind. And therein lay the problem. Todd loved me, but he was obsessively concerned about my relationship with Rafe, and he would go to almost any lengths to make sure nothing happened between us. As evidenced by his giving his photographs to Detective Grimaldi in an attempt to get Rafe arrested. And as evidenced by his showing the photographs to me in the first place. He'd even turned me on to a woman named Elspeth Caulfield, who—Todd claimed—had been compromised by Rafe in high school. We'd all gone to Columbia High together, a few years apart, and Todd claimed Elspeth had had either a nervous breakdown or an abortion as a result of her encounter with Rafe. I had tried to ask Elspeth about it, but she refused to talk to me, explaining sweetly that we were ladies and didn't discuss things like that. When I'd asked Rafe, however, he'd said she'd been a more than willing participant, and that she'd kept hounding him for months afterwards to continue the liaison. If she'd had a nervous breakdown or an abortion, she sure hadn't mentioned either to him.

"Have you seen anything of Elspeth lately?" I asked now, in an attempt to play tit for tat.

"As a matter of fact," Todd said, totally oblivious, "I have. She contacted me last week sometime, looking for you."

For me? "Why? Last time I tried to talk to her, she wouldn't tell me anything."

"Maybe she has changed her mind," Todd said. "Maybe she has realized that nothing good can come from continuing to protect him, and she has decided to tell the truth."

"Or maybe she has realized that it isn't fair to keep quiet about it when nothing happened between them—nothing worse than a couple of kids making out, anyway—and she's decided to go ahead and come clean."

Todd is far too well-bred to roll his eyes, but he looked like he wanted to. "Sometimes I really don't understand you, Savannah."

"I don't understand what's so difficult to understand," I retorted. "He said he didn't force her, and I believe him. Why would he? There were plenty of girls who would have been happy to have him."

This time Todd really did do a tiny eye-roll. "Who?"

"Yvonne McCoy, for one." Yvonne was someone else I'd gone to high school with, who had told me that she and Rafe had had a fling once upon a time. Unlike Elspeth, Yvonne had had no problem talking about it. At length. Todd's smile was patronizing.

"Yvonne McCoy would have been happy to have anyone, Savannah."

Unfortunately, this was true. Yvonne wasn't a bad person, but she didn't know the first thing about keeping her legs together. I added, "And Marquita Johnson. Or whatever her name was back then."

"Cletus Johnson's ex-wife? Yes, I remember that. She drove poor Cletus crazy, the way she was always hanging around Collier. Of course, she still is." I could have sworn I saw an unbecoming smirk on his face.

"She's taking care of Mrs. Jenkins," I said.

Tondalia Jenkins is Rafe's grandmother on his father's side, and she's old and slightly dotty and needs constant supervision so she doesn't wander off and get lost. Rafe is too busy with his life of crime to be available 24/7, so he hired Marquita to be a live-in caretaker. Needless to say, Cletus—who is a deputy sheriff in Sweetwater, working under Todd's daddy, Sheriff Bob Satterfield—isn't too happy about that. I think Marquita had probably left him before Rafe came back into the picture, but considering the history between the three of them, I could understand Cletus's feelings.

"Are you still going over there regularly?" Todd asked.

"To the house? Of course. He asked me to keep an eye on Mrs. Jenkins while he was gone, so I stop by every few days. I was there on Sunday afternoon."

"And how was everything?"

I was well aware that Todd couldn't care less, but maybe he was just as tired of talking to me about Rafe as I was of listening.

"Everything was fine," I said. "Mrs. Jenkins was napping and Marquita slammed the door in my face. Just as usual." I had asked the nurse if she'd heard from Rafe, and she'd been so chagrined at having to tell me no that she'd lost any vestige of self control. "I'm planning to go back tomorrow."

Todd nodded. "You'll be careful, right?"

"Of course. Not that there's any reason to worry. The neighborhood may not be the best, but Mrs. Jenkins's no bigger than a mosquito, and although Marquita doesn't like me, she's not going to hurt me."

"Not even if she thinks you're trying to cut her out with Collier?"

"Don't be silly," I answered. "Normal people don't go around hurting other people just because the man they like is paying a little too much attention to someone else."

"So you agree he's been paying you too much attention?"

Todd's an attorney, did I mention that? Note the instant leap into hostile witness cross-examination.

"That depends on what you think is too much," I answered, unwisely. Since divorcing Bradley and living on my own for the first time in my life, I've had to learn to stand up for myself in ways unbecoming a well-bred Southern Belle, and it's beginning to show. Todd's blue eyes narrowed. I added, "He hasn't paid me any attention for the past five weeks, remember? He hasn't called, he hasn't written, he hasn't tried to contact me in any way whatsoever. He may even be dead by now."

I hoped he wasn't, but I knew it wasn't impossible. Rafe had left town because the police were getting ready to arrest him, but he had also gotten on the wrong side of some bad people over the past ten years, and they might be after him to settle the score. He had told me there was a chance he might not come back. I was prepared that I might never see him again. I wasn't exactly happy about it, I suppose, but I was prepared. Or so I thought, anyway.

"Do you really think so?" Todd had what I can only describe as a hopeful lilt in his voice.

"Anything's possible. Don't get your hopes up, though. He'll probably show up sometime around Christmas and explain that he spent the past few months in jail. Don't worry about him, Todd."

"I'm not worried about *him*," Todd said.

"You know what I mean. I've told you before, I'm not involved with him. I just don't want him to end up dead. He saved my life. I can't do anything to save his, but at least I can pray."

"You pray for him?"

"It was a figure of speech." And yes, I do. I added, "Let it go, Todd. My God, what will it take for you to believe that nothing is going on between us?"

Todd looked like he wanted to answer, but he thought better of it. "Where did you say he went, again?" he asked instead. "Memphis, wasn't it? Didn't the Tennessee Bureau of Investigation just roll up a big gang of cargo thieves out there?"

"I believe they did." It had been all over the news for the past couple of days.

Todd smirked. "What are the chances that Collier was a part of that, do you think? It wouldn't be the first time the TBI showed an interest in something he was doing. Maybe they finally got him this time." He rubbed his hands together.

"I'll ask Mrs. Jenkins tomorrow," I said. "She's his closest—his only—relative, so I guess they'd notify her if anything happened to him."

"I'm sure they would." Todd signaled the waiter. "Are you ready to go, Savannah?"

He insisted on driving me home, in spite of my assurance that it would be OK to just put me in a cab. My apartment was twenty minutes in the opposite direction, and he had an hour's drive to get home to Sweetwater after dropping me off. He wouldn't hear of it, though, so we sat side by side in the front seat of the SUV as he maneuvered through the darkened streets over to Nashville's east side, where I rent a one bedroom apartment in a multi-use development on the corner of Fifth Street and East Main. Todd parked on the street and walked me up to the second floor, again disregarding my assurance that I was perfectly capable of fitting the key in the lock on my own and that he had a long drive ahead of him.

"You know, Savannah," he said when we stood face to face in the hallway outside my apartment, "if you're so concerned about my driving home in the dark, you could invite me to stay. I could get up early and drive down tomorrow morning instead. My first appointment isn't until nine."

I stared at him. Was he serious? Was he insane?! "I can't ask you to spend the night. What would people think?"

"That we're involved?" Todd suggested.

Well... yes. "You know as well as I do that in our circles, that means marriage is next."

"And you don't want to get married? Remarried?"

I took a fractional step backwards, distancing myself emotionally as well as physically. "I'm sure I'll end up getting remarried one day. I'm only 27; it's not like I want to spend the rest of my life alone. But I'm not ready yet. I'm still carrying baggage from being Mrs. Ferguson, and... um... there are things I want to do."

I didn't want to think too deeply about that last statement, but I knew that Rafe had told me to hold off on marrying Todd until he came back to town, because he had plans for me, and if I were married, that would seriously cramp his style.

"I see," Todd said. He was staring intently at me, in a way that suggested that he might be trying to read my mind. I didn't think he could, but I also didn't want to take any chances. So I looked away, down the hall.

"You should go. It's a long drive."

"You've mentioned that," Todd nodded. "All right. How about Tuesday? Are we still on?"

We'd had what pretty much amounted to a standing dinner date every Tuesday and Friday for the past five weeks. When Rafe left, Todd had decided he'd better take advantage of this time without—as he perceived it—competition, and he had been wining and dining me every chance he got. Which was twice a week. I didn't want to go out with him any more frequently than that. First because I didn't want to give him the idea that I was waiting for him to pop the question, but also because mother has brought my sister Catherine and myself up never to give any gentleman the impression that we are too available. Occasionally, he'd get us tickets to the opera or the theatre on a Saturday or Sunday instead, and we'd skip one of the other nights, but I never went out with him more than twice in the same week.

"Sure," I said.

"I'll pick you up at the usual time." He leaned in to kiss my cheek.

I nodded. He'd pick me up at the usual time and we'd go to the usual place and eat the usual dinner. Not that there was anything wrong with that—I knew exactly what I'd get, and had the assurance of knowing that it would be excellent—but just once in a while it would be nice to try something different. Especially since I had personal reasons for wanting to avoid Fidelio's. My ex-husband had taken me there on our first (and last) wedding anniversary and invited his mistress to join us, under pretext of talking business. Needless to say, I didn't have good feelings about the place. I was also concerned that one of these days, I'd run into Bradley and the new Mrs. Ferguson celebrating *their* anniversary at Fidelio's. But I knew better than to question Todd's choice of restaurant, and I suppose there's something to be said for tradition and continuity. It's safe and comfortable, if nothing else.

"Good night, Savannah." He squeezed my hand. I smiled.

"Good night, Todd. Thanks for dinner." I went up on my toes to kiss his cheek. At the last moment he turned sideways, and I ended up kissing his lips instead. They were cool and tasted faintly of red wine.

The kiss went on for a few seconds, and when I pulled away, Todd had what I can only describe as a triumphant smirk on his face. He had a spring in his step as he walked down the hallway toward the stairs to the first floor. I let myself into my apartment and locked the door behind me.

TWO

Mrs. Jenkins's house on Potsdam Street—the house where Brenda Puckett met her untimely end, and where I'd met Rafe two months ago, for the first time since high school—is a big run-down Victorian with an overgrown yard and a tower on one corner. Before he left town, Rafe had done his best to fix it, but there's a limit to how much one man can do in a few weeks, so when I drove up the circular drive the next afternoon, the place still looked pretty dismal. The grass was dry and dead from the summer heat, and yellow leaves had started to fall from the trees onto the lawn, but no one had made any attempt to rake them. The porch swing was still peeling and the boards in the porch creaked under my feet as I made my way up to the front door.

The door bell had long since given up the ghost, so I banged on the glass instead. And waited while shuffling footsteps made their way toward me, agonizingly slowly. "Who is it?" Mrs. Jenkins's quavery voice asked.

"It's me, Mr. Jenkins. Savannah Martin. I just wanted to see how you were."

I heard the rattling of chains and the sound of the security bolt being pulled back, and then the heavy oak door opened. "C'mon in, baby."

Mrs. Jenkins's wrinkled raisin-face beamed up at me. As usual, she was dressed in a flowery housecoat and fuzzy slippers. She'd been wearing the same thing every single time I'd seen her, although these days, at least both dress and slippers were neat and clean. Her steel-gray kinky hair was carefully tamed and slicked back against her head, and she looked reasonable healthy, happy and alert. At least I thought so, until she glanced at my midsection and added, "How's my grandbaby this mornin'?"

It was actually early afternoon, but that was the least of my concerns. "Your grandbaby is thirty years old, Mrs. Jenkins, and somewhere in Memphis. I'm Savannah, remember? Rafe's... um... well, I'm not sure what I am—I don't think I'm Rafe's anything, really—but I know I'm not pregnant."

Mrs. Jenkins's eyes turned vague for a few seconds while she processed this information. I held my breath. Sometimes she believes me, sometimes she doesn't. Sometimes she has no idea who I am. She forgets me between visits, and the past is a lot more vivid to her than the present, so she mistakes me for LaDonna Collier. LaDonna was Rafe's mother, and she had gotten pregnant by Tyrell Jenkins more than thirty years ago. Old Jim Collier, LaDonna's daddy, had then shot Tyrell because he didn't want his daughter involved with a black man. All three of them were dead now: Tyrell while LaDonna was still pregnant, Old Jim when Rafe was twelve, and LaDonna most recently, this summer. Her death was the reason Rafe had come back to the Middle Tennessee area in the first place.

Eventually, Mrs. Jenkins's eyes cleared. "Oh. Hi, baby. It's you."

I nodded. "I brought you some cookies and lemonade. Would you like to go inside and sit down?"

"Sure, baby." She shuffled down the hall, leaving me to close and lock the door behind me.

The first time I'd been in this house, there had been debris and mouse droppings on the floor and cobwebs draping the ceiling. Today, it looked better. Not as fabulous as it could look, with an influx of a few hundred thousand dollars and a lot of elbow-grease, but not bad. Rafe had refinished the floors and taken down the tattered wallpaper, although the plaster walls in the hall still needed a coat of paint to come into their own. He'd expended more money and effort on the kitchen. A new bank of cabinets stood against the wall, topped by a new Corian counter, and a new refrigerator hummed in the corner, instead of the avocado-green 1970s relic that had been here before. The old, cracked vinyl had been replaced by new, and someone— probably Marquita—had taken the time to cover the kitchen table with a pristine, yellow-checkered tablecloth. I didn't like the woman any better than she liked me, but I had to admit she wasn't bad at her job. Except...

"Where is Marquita today?" I asked, opening the cabinets above the counter to look for glasses and something to put the cookies on.

Mrs. Jenkins looked around, vaguely, as if she expected to see Marquita pop up from behind the microwave. Fat chance of that, no pun intended. Marquita was two years older than me, two inches shorter, and approximately twice my weight. She might be able to hide behind the side-by-side refrigerator, but not behind anything smaller.

"Did she run an errand? Go to the grocery store, maybe?"

Mrs. Jenkins's face cleared. "Gotta phone call," she said. "Took the afternoon off."

"Really?" I placed a plate of gourmet chocolate chip and oatmeal raisin cookies on the table before I turned around to pick up two glasses of lemonade. "Does that happen often?"

Mrs. Jenkins shrugged her birdlike shoulders, a cookie already halfway to her mouth. "Girl's gotta have free time, you know. Can't always stay here with me." She bit into the treat greedily, scattering crumbs on the tablecloth and the front of her dress.

"She's *supposed* to be here with you," I said, sitting down opposite. "That's the point of paying her. You're not supposed to be alone."

"Marquita's gotta couple kids, you know, baby. They was here visitin' last week."

"No," I said, "I didn't know that. Where are they now?"

"Livin' with that ex-husband of hers down south, I guess. Or maybe with her mama. They's in school down there, so she only gets to see 'em weekends. And not all the time, neither."

"Is that where she went? To Sweetwater to see her children?"

Mrs. Jenkins shrugged again. "Can't rightly say, baby. But she'll be back tonight. And meantime, I get to eat what I want and see what I want on the TV." She winked. I smiled back.

"So how is everything going? When Marquita is here, does she take good care of you?"

Mrs. Jenkins nodded, her mouth full of raisin and oatmeal. When she had swallowed, she assured me that yes, Marquita took very good care of her. We sat and chatted for another fifteen or twenty minutes, and then I got up to take my leave. Mrs. Jenkins shuffled with me out to the front door, and I told her I'd stand outside to make sure she put the chain back on after I'd gone out.

"By the way," I added, just as I was about to leave, to give the impression that the question wasn't of much consequence, "I don't suppose you've heard from Rafe, have you?"

Mrs. Jenkins looked blank for a second, like she had no idea who Rafe was. Then she shook her head. "Can't say as I have, baby. Why?"

"Oh, no reason. I was just thinking… if Marquita doesn't come back…"

"She'll be back. Ain't the first time she's gone home to see her babies." She looked at me, shrewdly, for a moment, and then added, "You miss him, huh, baby?"

"I guess I do." I might as well admit it. It wasn't like Mrs. Jenkins would tell anyone—no one who mattered, like my mother—and it was nice to be able to say it to someone. Especially someone who'd likely have forgotten by the time I drove away. Plus, I was worried. I had expected him to be back by now. I'd even taken to checking the Memphis newspapers online while I was at the office every morning. That was how I'd found out about the TBI arresting all those people in the hijackings of those cargo containers Todd had mentioned yesterday. I wasn't so far gone that I read the obituaries yet, but I did skim headlines, and if I came across anything about shootings or arrests or the unrolling of criminal syndicates, I read the article to make sure Rafe's name wasn't mentioned. So far I had refrained from calling the Memphis justice system to inquire whether they had him locked up somewhere—I didn't want to turn them on to him if they didn't—but I figured it was only a matter of time before I gave in to temptation and picked up the phone.

Mrs. Jenkins patted me sympathetically on the arm. "He'll be back, baby. Don't you worry; he can take care of himself."

I nodded. "Thank you, Mrs. Jenkins. I'd better be on my way. Do you need anything else while I'm here?"

Mrs. Jenkins shook her head. "Marquita'll take care of me when she gets back tonight, baby. Meantime, I'll just eat cookies and watch the TV." She closed one of her little black bird-eyes in a wink. I smiled back.

"Have a good time. I'll stop by again in a few days. Just to make sure you're all right."

Mrs. Jenkins said that that would be fine, and I headed back home, where I spent the rest of the night curled up on the sofa with a romance novel and a bottle of wine. Let Mrs. Jenkins have her cookies and her TV; I'd take a bottle of Chardonnay and the florid prose of my favorite author Barbara Botticelli any day.

Barbara writes what is affectionately known as bodice rippers, and in this latest release, the blonde and beautiful Lady Serena—Barbara Botticelli's heroines are always blonde and beautiful—was doing her best to avoid being kidnapped and put in the harem of the dastardly Sayid Pasha, while falling hard for the dark and dangerous Sheik Hasan al-Kalaal, who was out to bring Sayid down. The Egyptian setting was exciting, and Sheik Hasan was equally so, with his melting, dark eyes and to-die-for physique. When he rode off into the sunset on his Arabian stallion, his robes flapping in the wind, my girlish heart went pitter-patter.

I continued the book the next afternoon, while hosting an open house for Timothy Briggs. Tim was my boss now that my former boss, Walker Lamont, languished in prison. I had put him there, and sometimes I wondered if it might not be better for me to go to work at a different real estate company. But Lamont, Briggs & Associates was located right down the street from my apartment, and nobody seemed to hold it against me that I'd been responsible for getting Walker arrested. The two women he killed had worked for what used to be Walker Lamont Realty, too; that may have had something to do with it. Anyway, Tim was far too busy to host his own open houses these days, and since I wasn't busy at all most of the time, he often asked me to stand in.

This week's open house was a small and uninspiring mid-century ranch in a settled area full of old people and unmarried spinsters, and it was a rainy day to boot. Hardly anybody came, and I had plenty of time to read. I stayed by the front window, ready to hide the book whenever anybody pulled to a stop outside, but although a few people came by, nobody seemed to want to buy the house, at least not right at the moment. I had my hopes pinned on a small white car, a Honda or Toyota, that drove by a few times, slowing down to a crawl whenever it got alongside the house, but whoever was inside never actually pulled up to the curb and stopped.

At 4 o'clock, I closed up shop and headed home. On the way I stopped at the grocery store and did my shopping for the next couple of days, and then I headed to my apartment to cook dinner.

Ten minutes after I walked in, the phone rang. I picked it up with one hand and tucked it under my chin while I continued to chop tomatoes. "This is Savannah."

For a second I couldn't hear anything, then I became aware of breathing. Not heavy breathing; just the usual kind.

"Can I help you?" I added. Maybe he or she hadn't heard me the first time. Sometimes there's a second or two of lag-time on cell phones.

A pause, and then a muffled voice whispered, "Look out the window."

"I beg your pardon?"

Was this some kind of joke? I didn't recognize the voice; couldn't even tell whether it was male or female. High-pitched man, low-pitched woman, someone hiding his or her voice behind a handkerchief...

"Who is this?"

I got no answer, but the breathing continued. Eventually I gave in to curiosity and wandered over to the double doors to the balcony. Maybe something exciting was going on outside. Maybe Todd had hired a mariachi-band and a dancing bear and a stretch limousine with the words '*Will you marry me?*' spray-painted on the roof. Or a hot-air balloon or a blimp or at least a megaphone with which to serenade me.

Or maybe, a treacherous voice in my head suggested, *it isn't Todd at all.*

Maybe Rafe was back, and was waiting downstairs. There was no reason why he wouldn't have come upstairs to the door, or why he'd bother to disguise his voice when he called, but what the heck, I was in the mood to be hopeful. I opened the doors and stepped onto the balcony.

In my ear, the phone clicked off, and outside, nothing at all was happening. There was no balloon, no blimp, no limo, and no mariachi-band. Certainly no dancing bear. Nor did I see anyone I knew. Rafe's Harley-Davidson wasn't anywhere on the street below, and Todd's green SUV wasn't there, either. There were cars parked at the curb, sure—a shiny, black Cadillac with tinted windows, a white compact, a lemon yellow VW Beetle with a sunroof, and a red pickup truck with a load of mulch in the bed—but they didn't belong to anyone I knew.

Nothing happened—nobody waved, or shot at me, or made themselves known in any other way—so after a few seconds I went back inside the apartment and back to my tomatoes. Unless it was a prank call, someone yanking my chain for the fun of it, they'd call back and tell me what they wanted.

By nine the next morning, nobody had called, and I had put the whole incident out of my mind. I was on my way to the office for our weekly staff meeting, and then I was planning to check the Memphis papers online, just in case something big had broken in West Tennessee since Saturday morning.

Every Monday at 10 o'clock sharp, the sales staff at Lamont, Briggs & Associates gets together for a meeting. We discuss our new listings, our new sales, any new buyer prospects under contract, how successful our open houses were the day before, and so on and so forth. I very rarely have anything to contribute, unless I just happened to have hosted an open house for Tim or someone else the previous day. In my almost four months in business, I'd only had one client—actually two, but they were a couple, buying the same house—and at the moment, we were waiting to close. In other words, they had found a house they liked, I had negotiated a contract acceptable to both buyers and sellers, and now the sale was pending. After I had detailed my experiences at the open house yesterday—minus the fact that I had spent most of my time vicariously enjoying Sheik Hasan al-Kalaal—Tim looked from me to Heidi Hoppenfeldt. "When is the appraisal for the townhouse scheduled?"

Heidi looked at me, chewing. Tim had brought in a box of donuts, and she was working her way through them.

"As far as I know it's tomorrow," I said.

Tim and Heidi were co-listing the townhouse Gary Lee and Charlene Hodges were trying to buy. It was Brenda Puckett's originally, and when she died, all her listings got divided between the two remaining members of the Brenda Puckett real estate team: Tim and Heidi. Tim got all the high end, expensive stuff and Heidi the smaller, cheaper starter homes. But when Walker went to jail and Tim took over as broker, he got so busy running the office he couldn't keep up with his work, and so he talked Heidi into becoming his assistant, the way she'd been Brenda's.

"Excellent!" Tim said, showing all his capped teeth in a blinding smile. Before coming back to Nashville to become a Realtor, Tim spent a couple of years in New York City, trying to get on Broadway as a song-and-dance-man. He's light in the loafers and has a brassy tenor voice, and although I doubted it, he might have been the person who called me yesterday and told me to look out the window of my apartment.

No reason why he would have, of course; plus, I hadn't seen his car down below. And seeing as he's driving an eye-catching convertible Jaguar in baby blue with matching leather interior, I think I would have noticed.

When the meeting was over, I headed into my office, a converted coat closet just off the reception area. There's not much room there; just enough for a desk, a chair and a standing lamp in the corner. While I waited for my computer to boot up, I looked through the mail that Brittany, the receptionist, had put in my box. A circular from Hewlett-Packard offered special discounts on office equipment to NAR-members; NAR being the National Association of Realtors. A circular from Dell did the same thing. There was a reminder that I hadn't paid my office fees yet this month, which Brittany had snuck in among the real mail. A couple of postcards from other agents showcased their new listings or sales. Following that was this month's edition of Realtor Magazine, with a cover story about mortgage scams.

The Memphis *Daily News* had nothing new about the unrolling of the cargo gang, but a whole slew of other crimes had taken place over the weekend. Shootings, robberies, rapes, burglaries; you name it. I was scowling at a sidebar of statistics—Memphis and Nashville both have twice the crime of New York City, proportionally—when I felt someone looking over my shoulder. When I turned around, I got a heady whiff of Tim's aftershave, and felt my head spin. After a moment, I managed to croak out a question. "What's that you're wearing?"

"This old thing?" Tim flicked a manicured finger at his emerald green satin shirt.

"I was thinking of your aftershave. Or cologne."

"Shower-gel, darling." He told me the name and added, coyly, "Remind you of someone?"

"I'm not sure. Maybe." I turned back to the computer.

Tim glanced from me to the screen and back. "Any word from the scrumptious Mr. Collier?"

Tim has a crush on Rafe, and since Rafe is happy to flirt with anyone, man or woman, they get along famously. The fact that Rafe doesn't bat for Tim's team doesn't seem to bother either of them, nor does my presence slow them down at all.

I said no, I hadn't heard from Rafe.

Tim added, "You know, Savannah, you could go buy yourself a bottle of gel and take a shower." He waggled his perfectly plucked eyebrows. I'd gotten so used to his suggestive remarks by now that I didn't even blush.

"No thanks. And I didn't say that's who it reminded me of."

"You forget," Tim said, "I've had the pleasure of smelling your boyfriend, too."

"He's not my boyfriend. And for all you know, I may have lots of friends who use that same shower-gel."

Tim giggled. "Your other boyfriend doesn't. Not that he smells bad, of course. Or looks bad, either. He's more your type anyway, isn't he?"

"Todd? I suppose he is." Loyal, devoted, flatteringly attentive, not to mention gainfully employed in a legitimate profession. And if he can't quite claim to have Rafe's knock'em-dead sex-appeal, he's certainly handsome enough in his well-dressed, well-coiffed, professional way.

"Although he doesn't have much of a sense of humor," Tim added.

Tim and Todd had met for the first time last week, at Fidelio's. Tim had stopped by our table to say hello, as was his wont when we crossed paths outside the office. He'd done it before too, when I'd been there with Rafe. Except this time, my date wasn't into playing games with Tim. When Tim batted his eyelashes, Todd just stared blankly at him, and Tim's sly reference to Rafe had been remarkably ill-received by Todd. It had taken the rest of the night for me to calm him down, and he still wasn't entirely settled in his mind, as evidenced by him bringing it up again on our next date.

"He wants to marry me," I said. "It's understandable that he wouldn't think it's funny when you ask me suggestive questions about other men."

"There was nothing suggestive about it," Tim retorted. "I just wanted to know when that megalicious hunk of manhood is coming back to town."

"And you didn't think the words megalicious hunk of manhood— if megalicious is even a word—might be offensive?"

"I thought it might offend *you*," Tim said innocently, "since it isn't every woman who can handle it when we confirmed bachelors look at her man, but I had no idea it would offend your date."

"Yes, well, Todd is touchy when it comes to Rafe."

"And you're not?"

"Of course I'm not," I said, and then excused myself when the phone rang. "This is Savannah."

"Miss Martin."

"Detective." No problems recognizing *this* voice.

"Are you busy? Something's come up that I'd like your help with."

Uh-oh. The last time I heard that statement, she had wanted me to come to the morgue to identify Lila Vaughn. "Is... um... nobody's dead, I hope?"

Tim gasped theatrically.

"Not this time," Detective Grimaldi said. I thought for a second.

"Does this have anything to do with... um... Rafe?"

This may seem like a major leap of deduction, or maybe it seems like everything in my life revolves around Rafael Collier, but in actuality, nothing could be further from the truth. Most of the time, I go through life without thinking much about him at all. In fact, during the twelve years between the end of my freshman year of high school and when I saw him again two months ago, I don't think he crossed my mind once. In this case, however, it seemed like a logical question. Tamara Grimaldi was a cop. Rafe was a criminal. It made sense that she'd be calling to talk about him.

"In a way," Detective Grimaldi said.

"Has something happened to him?"

Tim squeaked again, clasping his hands in front of his chest, his baby-blue eyes round. I turned away, not needing that kind of distraction at the moment. My own heart was thudding hard and loud enough.

"Not as far as I know," Tamara Grimaldi said. "Look, Miss Martin, could we cut this short? I have a situation I have to take care of. When can you be here?"

"Where's here?"

She made an impatient noise. "My office. Downtown."

"No offense," I said, "but the last time you called me like this, you wanted me to come to the medical examiner's office to look at crime scene photos. Fifteen minutes."

"I'll see you then." She hung up before I had the chance to say anything else.

I arched my brows, but didn't waste time standing on ceremony. Instead I got up from the desk, grabbed my purse from the floor, and brushed past Tim. "Duty calls."

"But what's wrong?" Tim called after me. I glanced at him over my shoulder. He looked worried.

"I don't know. All she said was that she had a situation. I guess I'll find out when I get there."

I swung through the door out onto the sidewalk and headed for the parking lot across the street.

Three

"Spicer and Truman found her walking down the street in her housecoat and slippers," Detective Grimaldi said twenty minutes later.

I had driven hell for leather into downtown, found a parking space a block and a half from Police Plaza, and hoofed it up to her office with five seconds to spare, only to find her entertaining Tondalia Jenkins, who was drinking Diet Pepsi and eating peanut butter crackers from a vending machine, in front of a TV in the lounge. Her fuzzy slippers were dirty and worn through on the bottom—clearly not meant for walking long distances outside—and her hair stood out at weird angles to her head, the way it had back when she was living in an old folks' home where nobody cared for her.

"They drove her back to the house, but no one was there. Since they didn't feel good about leaving her by herself, to wander off again, they brought her to me."

"And you called me," I said. She shrugged unapologetically.

"I figured you'd be the most likely person to know how to get in touch with her grandson."

We were standing in the doorway to the lounge, keeping an eye on Mrs. Jenkins, but far enough away that she couldn't hear our conversation. Or so I thought.

"You figured wrong. I have no idea how to get in touch with Rafe. I haven't heard from him since he left. For all I know, he's been dead for the past five weeks."

Mrs. Jenkins glanced up at that, her beady eyes concerned. I mustered a smile. "Sorry, Mrs. Jenkins. I'm sure he's not. I just haven't heard from him, is all."

I lowered my voice again, and added, for Detective Grimaldi's benefit, "And I have absolutely no idea how to get in touch with him."

"He didn't tell you where he was going? Give you a phone number to use in case of emergencies? Call or write?" Tamara Grimaldi's voice was disbelieving. I shook my head.

"He mentioned Memphis, in a throwaway sort of way, but he didn't actually say he was going there. And the only phone number I've ever had for him, is the one I gave you back in August, after Perry Fortunato's... um... death. You said it had been disconnected."

"And you have no other way of getting in touch with him?"

"None at all," I said firmly. "Have you tried asking Julio Melendez? You've still got him locked up, right? Or what about Ishmael Jackson? Doesn't one of them know how to find him? What would Julio do if he had another job for Rafe?"

"According to Julio," Detective Grimaldi said, with a wolfish snap of strong, white teeth, "Mr. Collier was the one who approached him, not vice versa."

I opened my eyes wide. "You don't believe that, do you?"

"It doesn't matter what I believe. It doesn't matter what he says, either, because he can't prove it. We can't even prove that Mr. Collier was involved. He left town before I had the chance to ask him about it, but all he'd have to do, would be to say that he knew Julio and Ishmael and the others socially, but that he wasn't involved in anything criminal. There's no law against playing pool, even with known felons."

I hid a smile. "Sorry to hear that."

"No, you're not. But that's neither here nor there. Right at the moment, I need to get in touch with him because his grandmother is all alone and wandering around. If we can't find him and get him to make alternative arrangements, we'll have to put her back into the Milton House for the time being."

Mrs. Jenkins's hearing must have been acute when it came to things that mattered to her, because she looked up at the name of the nursing home where she had spent a few miserable weeks. Brenda Puckett had arranged for her to live there, after she had swindled Mrs. Jenkins out of her house, and as soon as Brenda's murder was solved, the first thing Rafe did was get his grandmother out of the Milton House and back into her old home.

"You can't do that!" I protested, turning away so Mrs. Jenkins couldn't read my lips. "It's a horrible place. They never combed her hair or washed her clothes or did anything nice for her."

"Well, what do you suggest?"

"The best thing would be to find Marquita Johnson. Any idea where she is?"

"None at all," Tamara Grimaldi said. "From what I understand, she got a phone call on Saturday afternoon, and left. Mrs. Jenkins thought she went to Sweetwater to see her children."

I nodded. "That's what she told me too, when I was there on Saturday. I was a little worried about leaving her by herself, but she assured me that Marquita would be home by evening. She said Marquita goes to Sweetwater to visit her children regularly."

"From what we can gather, she didn't come back. I've contacted the sheriff down there…"

"Bob Satterfield," I said. She nodded.

"He talked to her ex-husband, apparently he's a deputy sheriff..."

I nodded. "Cletus Johnson. They've been separated for a while."

"He claimed not to have spoken to her since last week sometime, and he certainly didn't call her on Saturday to tell her to come down to Sweetwater. They're fighting over custody and visitation rights, and he's not about to give her any more time with those children than he has to."

"What a guy," I said. Detective Grimaldi snorted.

"Though he told us that if anything had happened to her, he knew who was to blame."

"Let me guess. Rafe Collier."

The detective nodded. "Some history there, I take it."

"Marquita had a crush on Rafe in high school. Cletus liked her, but she wouldn't give him the time of day when Rafe was around. Then Rafe went to jail and Cletus and Marquita got married. I don't think Rafe had anything to do with their splitting up, but I guess Cletus felt he needed someone to blame."

"I'm sure," Detective Grimaldi agreed. "We'll keep looking for her, of course, but aside from talking to her friends and acquaintances down there, there's not a lot we can do. Sheriff Satterfield said he'd tell his officers to keep an extra eye out as they go about their business, just in case someone has seen her. In the meantime, I have to decide what to do about Mrs. Jenkins."

I nodded gloomily. She continued, "I don't really have a desire to put her back into the Milton House—I was there with you, remember, and I know what it's like—but Mrs. Puckett did pay for her care there, so they wouldn't be able to turn her away, and sad as it is to admit, it's a nicer place than some I've seen."

"That's a scary thought."

"She can't stay in her house alone. That's a disaster waiting to happen, and I won't allow it."

"So what do you suggest?" I asked, as if I didn't already know.

She grinned. "Didn't you tell me that Mr. Collier asked you to keep an eye on her while he was away? Maybe you can move in with her until we either find Miss Johnson or until Mr. Collier comes back."

I had known what was coming, but that didn't mean I liked hearing it. "What am I going to do with her when I have to go show a house? Or write a contract? I have a committee meeting for the Eye Ball tonight, although I suppose I can cancel that. But I also have a date with Todd tomorrow. And believe me, he's not going to be happy about me bringing Rafe's grandmother along. Anyone's grandmother, really, but especially Rafe's."

Tamara Grimaldi smirked. "I met Todd Satterfield once, did I tell you that?"

"He told me. He said he gave you those pictures of Rafe and Ishmael Jackson and the others, that he got from his tame P.I. back in September. Isn't there a law against civilians hiring private investigators to follow other civilians around?"

"You'd think," Detective Grimaldi said, "but you'd be wrong. Anyway, I formed the impression that Mr. Satterfield doesn't care for Mr. Collier, or for anyone associated with him. I'd cancel that date, if I were you."

"On the other hand, it would almost be worth bringing her, just to see his face." I grinned unbecomingly for a moment, and then got myself under control again. "I guess I don't have much of a choice. I mean, I promised Rafe I'd look after her. She can move in with me. I'd rather do that, than spend days or weeks in that house on Potsdam Street. I'm sure it's not haunted, but I still avoid looking into the library whenever I'm there, just in case. And it's where Walker tried to kill me, too. I have bad memories of the place. I'd rather stay in my apartment. I've only got one bedroom, but she can have that, and I'll sleep on the sofa. And if I have to go show houses, she can come with me. I'll just have to cancel Todd and the Eye Ball."

The Eye Ball is a charitable event benefiting the optometry department at Vanderbilt Hospital. I was doing some volunteer work for them, preparing for the gala.

"Sounds like you've got a lot to figure out," Detective Grimaldi said pleasantly. "Don't let me keep you."

Right. "I suppose you have work to do?"

"Two dead in a house fire, both with bullets through their brains, and a fatality during a domestic brawl. A woman stabbed her husband four times with a carving knife. Thanks for asking."

I was sorry I had.

"If you think of any way to get in touch with Mr. Collier, let me know. I'll let the Memphis PD and the TBI know we're looking for him, just in case he shows up on their radar. And I'll let you know if I find out anything about Marquita Johnson."

"Please do. Believe me, the sooner you find either her or Rafe, the happier I'll be."

Detective Grimaldi didn't answer, but she smiled.

Ten minutes later, Mrs. Jenkins and I were on our way back across the river into East Nashville, and I was asking her again if she was sure, absolutely positive, she hadn't heard from Rafe in the past five weeks. She shook her head.

"How about a contact number? A forwarding address? The name of a friend to contact in case of emergencies? Did he at least tell you where he was going?"

"He didn't, baby. All he said was he had some business to take care of, and he'd be back."

"Figures," I muttered. That was the way he treated me—there one minute, gone the next, and I never knew when or where he might turn up again, if at all—but I had hoped he'd be more communicative with his nearest and dearest. Apparently not.

"He told us you'd be comin' by now and again," Mrs. Jenkins added blithely, "just to see how things were goin'."

"Marquita must have loved that."

Mrs. Jenkins giggled. "Very offended, she was. Said he made it sound like he didn't trust her."

"I can imagine."

"Course, she likes him."

"I've noticed," I said. Mrs. Jenkins smirked.

"You like him, too."

"I imagine most women like him." I moved into the middle lane going across the Cumberland Bridge.

"Maybe so," Mrs. Jenkins conceded. "Another ladyfriend of his called last week."

"Really?" I glanced at her out of the corner of my eye. A ladyfriend, huh? "Did she give her name?" Maybe this woman, whoever she was, knew where to find Rafe. If I could find him, I could get out of this mess.

Mrs. Jenkins thought for a moment, then shook her head. "Don't know, baby. Marquita talked to her. She didn't mention no name."

"Figures. Well, if—when—Marquita comes back, we can ask her then."

I looked left and right before I crossed the intersection of Main Street and Interstate Drive. We were almost in sight of my apartment building when Mrs. Jenkins added, pensively, "Guy called, too. Few times. Every week or so."

"A man? Did he give a name?"

"Can't rightly say, baby. Marquita talked to him, too. She said he just wanted to know how everything was goin'."

"Interesting." I calculated rapidly for a moment, then made an abrupt right turn on 5th, causing Mrs. Jenkins to fall against my shoulder. "I just thought of something. Do you mind if we go for a drive?"

"Sure don't, baby. Don't get out much these days. It'll be fun." She settled herself back in the passenger seat and folded her hands in her lap. They were tiny and wrinkled and specked with age-spots. I hoped she'd enjoy this particular outing, although I rather doubted it.

The trip didn't take long. Only ten minutes later, we were where I wanted to be.

On 8th Avenue South, right in the middle of the antiques district, there's a small, brightly-painted bungalow with pretty flowers outside. The name on the door is Sally's. From the street, it looks as if Sally ought to sell, if not seashells at the seashore, at least colorful lawn ornaments or vintage clothes or something else quaint and pretty. Sally doesn't. Sally is a middle-aged, beefy woman with a tattoo and a rooster-red Mohawk haircut, and she peddles security. More specifically, weapons and self-defense type stuff. Detective Grimaldi had recommended her to me a month or two previously, for the purpose of arming myself. She didn't say it, but I thought that Tamara Grimaldi may have wanted me to have some protection in case Rafe got out of hand—this was back when she suspected him of having cut Brenda Puckett's throat.

I pulled the Volvo into the parking lot and helped Mrs. Jenkins out of the passenger seat. She looked around curiously. "What kinda place is this?"

"Police issue security gear," I said, looking around. There were no other cars in the lot at the moment, which boded well for my visit. Sally was likely to talk more freely if no one was around to hear. The Harley-Davidson parked by the side of the house caused my pulse to quicken, but only for a moment. Rafe's Harley is midnight-black, and if he had plans of replacing it, he wouldn't choose something bright red. This Harley belonged to someone else; most likely Sally herself. The color matched her hair, and she looked like she'd feel perfectly at ease riding it. "Detective Grimaldi recommended it to me. She was worried about me and wanted me to have some protection."

"Nice lady, that detective."

I nodded. "She is. Sally is a friend of hers, I think. Are you ready to go in?"

"Sure, baby." She grabbed my arm and shuffled along beside me. Even in three-inch heels I walked faster than she did in her fuzzy slippers, so I moderated my steps to hers and gave her a boost up the steps to the front door.

Inside, everything was as I remembered it. Displays of various lethal and non-lethal but nonetheless scary implements stood along the walls. Tasers, handcuffs, cans of mace and pepper spray. Under the counter, guns and Chinese stars rubbed elbows with trays of miniature knives masquerading as deceptively innocent-looking tubes of lipstick. Behind the counter, Sally herself stood, muscular forearms braced on the glass counter.

"Morning, princess," she boomed when she saw me.

"Hello, Sally," I answered, as Mrs. Jenkins and I made our slow way toward the counter. The trip wasn't made any easier by the fact that Mrs. J was slowing down to gawk at everything we passed.

"You use up all your pepper spray already?"

I smiled. "Not really. In fact, I haven't had occasion to use it at all. The one time I needed it, I couldn't get my hands on it, so it did me no good."

"Sounds like maybe you could use some self-defense training, princess. How to break a man's arm in three easy steps. Tamara told me what happened last month."

I nodded. "It was pretty scary. But I got out of it all right, so I guess I can't complain."

"Never a good idea to complain when you walk away in one piece," Sally agreed. "So what can I do for you today, missy? You need a bigger knife? Pistol? Handcuffs?"

"Information," I said, and watched as her face closed.

"Can't help you with that, I'm afraid."

"You don't even know what I'm going to ask," I said.

"Know the look on your face, though, princess. But I guess I could hear you out. Least I can do."

"Thank you." I indicated my companion. "This is Tondalia Jenkins. Mrs. Jenkins, this is Sally. I'm sorry, I don't know your last name, Sally."

"Harmon," Sally said. She extended a beefy hand across the counter and very gently shook Mrs. Jenkins's much smaller one. "Nice to meet you, ma'am."

"Pleasure's all mine, baby," Mrs. Jenkins replied. She calls everyone baby: Rafe, me, Marquita, Detective Grimaldi, even Walker Lamont, up until the moment he tried to shoot her. "Nice place you got here."

Sally grinned. "Look around all you want. Maybe you'll find something to buy. Like one of them lipsticks princess here bought last month." She winked. I watched as Mrs. Jenkins shuffled off, peering around nearsightedly, before I turned back to Sally.

"Her grandson left town five weeks ago. If Tamara Grimaldi talks to you about her cases, you've probably heard of him. His name is Rafe Collier."

"Happens I have heard of him," Sally agreed. "Saved your life last month, didn't he?"

"He did. And then he left town the next day. He asked me to keep an eye on his grandmother while he was gone. She has a live-in nurse, but as he put it, she's paid to care and it isn't the same."

Sally nodded. "Can't fault that."

"Especially as the nurse is now nowhere to be found. She left a few days ago, supposedly for a half day off, and never came back. No one seems to have seen her since. Nobody knows where she is. She isn't where she's supposed to be, which is with Mrs. Jenkins."

"Tricky," Sally said.

"Tamara Grimaldi has all her squad-cars keeping an eye out, and in the meantime, she wants me to try to track down Rafe."

"Wish I could help," Sally said, "but I don't know him. From what Tamara says, sounds like I'm missing out." She winked.

"You two would probably get on like a house on fire," I agreed. Aside from the fact that Rafe seems to be able to wrap any female around his finger, regardless of age, marital status, and sexual orientation, he and Sally had a lot in common. "Is that your Harley outside? He rides one, too."

"My kinda guy." Sally grinned. "If you find him, you bring him by to see me, princess."

"I'd love to," I said, "if I could find him. And that's why we're here. I think you might know an associate of his."

"Yeah?" Her eyes turned watchful. "Who's that?"

"His name is Wendell. At least that's what I was told. Older man, mid-fifties, maybe. Black. Military haircut. I've met him once or twice, and spoken to him on the phone a few times more. Not a big talker, at least not with me. The last time I saw him was here, last month. He came in while I was going out, and he held the door for me."

I paused, expectantly. Sally contemplated me, and I could see options ticking over in her brain. "Happens I might know who you're talking about," she admitted at last, reluctantly. I beamed. "Can't give you his name or number, though, princess. Though if you've spoken to him on the phone, sounds like you've got it already."

"I did," I said. "Then I gave it to Tamara Grimaldi last month, when she was trying to track down Rafe, and next thing I knew… poof! It was disconnected."

Sally hid a smile. "Can't say I'm surprised. Some of these guys can be kinda secretive. The ones that are involved with the criminal element, especially. If you want, I can try to get a message to him. That work for you?"

"That would be great," I said, relieved. "If you could just tell him that Savannah is trying to track down Rafe, I'd appreciate it. If he asks, you can tell him what I told you about Mrs. Jenkins and the nurse, although I doubt he will. He never asks me any questions."

"I'll see what I can do, princess," Sally promised, and looked up as the door opened. A young cop in full uniform came through the door, hat in his hand. Sally grinned at the stunned look on his face as he looked around, and I smiled.

"Hi, Officer Truman."

He looked at me, somewhat wild-eyed, for a second before my face seemed to register. "Oh. Hi, Miz Martin. How are you?"

"Just leaving. This is Sally. She'll take care of you."

Officer Truman, peach-fuzzed and as bright and shiny as a new penny, looked at Sally and swallowed.

Four

We stopped at 101 Potsdam Street on the way home, in the hope that Marquita had returned, and to pack an overnight bag for Mrs. Jenkins if she hadn't. The house looked just as it had when I was there a couple of days ago, only more dirty and messy, and there was no sign of Marquita. The nurse's disappearance was worrying me. Between Detective Grimaldi and Sheriff Satterfield, they probably had things well in hand, though; or so I had to trust.

Mrs. J didn't own an overnight bag or suitcase, but she told me Rafe might, and dispatched me to his room to look for it. I had misgivings, but she was ancient and her feet were sore from wandering the neighborhood in fuzzy slippers, and I couldn't in good conscience refuse.

I'd never been in Rafe's room before. That is, I had, but it hadn't been Rafe's room then. This was two months ago, when the house was on the market. He'd had me show him all around, before we discovered Brenda's body in the library. Mrs. Jenkins's bedroom, which was now a lovely lavender with gleaming white trim and a nice reproduction four-poster bed with lilac-printed sheets, had been home to an old mattress and a colony of mice. (Rafe said they were rats, but I prefer to hold on to my illusions.) And what had ended up being Rafe's room, in the front of the house, overlooking the overgrown yard and circular driveway, had been sporting peeling wallpaper with a faded pattern of twining roses, along with several broken windows, a waterlogged ceiling and crumbling windowsills.

I'd been back to the house many times since then, especially in the five weeks since he left, but I'd endeavored not to go into his room. I didn't think Marquita would let me, for one thing, and for another, I was feeling ambivalent enough towards him already; I didn't need any more temptations thrown in my path.

I stopped outside the door and took a deep breath, steeling myself before I turned the knob and pushed the door open.

I don't know what I had expected, but whatever it was, I wasn't disappointed.

The first thing to strike me was the smell. Spicy and citrusy, just like Rafe himself. Aftershave, shower gel, shampoo, laundry detergent... I had no idea what it was—maybe a mixture of a lot of things—but it was distinctly his, and heady. If I closed my eyes and breathed deeply, I could imagine that he was standing right next to me.

The second thing I noticed (after I opened my eyes again) was the bed, and before you think too badly of me, I should mention that it did rather dominate the room. King size, with crisp white sheets and a black duvet-cover. Satin. Horribly clichéd, but it packed a punch nonetheless. It didn't take much effort to picture him there: all hard muscle and golden skin warm against those cool sheets, with hot dark eyes under long, smudgy lashes, and that melting grin...

Giving myself a hard mental kick, I turned toward the closet. Nothing good would come of having erotic daydreams about Rafael Collier, especially since I couldn't act on any of them.

There was a black duffel in the closet, and I grabbed it and carried it back down the hall to Mrs. J's lavender and white bedroom. There, we layered flowered housecoats with several more pairs of fuzzy slippers and old-lady underwear. I zippered the bag and hoisted it over my shoulder, and away we went. Leaving a note for Marquita on the kitchen table, pinned down by a salt shaker, to the effect that I had removed Mrs. Jenkins from the premises, and if Marquita was ready to take up her duties again, she could call my cell phone and let me know. If Rafe happened to come home—and there was a little flutter under my breast bone at the thought—he'd know where to find us, as well.

My apartment is only a couple of miles from Potsdam Street as the crow flies, but it's a whole other world. East Nashville is one of those transitional areas of historic homes that have done a whole lot of changing over the past twenty years, but which still has a ways to go. And it's comprised of several different neighborhoods, that are not all at the same level of gentrification. In the area where I live, on the corner of Fifth and East Main, renovating has been going on for years and years. It started with the bachelors, back when no one else dared move into the ghetto, and these days, you'd be lucky to touch a house for less than a half million dollars. The Potsdam area, on the other hand, is still lagging behind. There are a few big and impressive houses—like Mrs. Jenkins's Italianate Victorian—but mostly the neighborhood is made up of small mid-century cottages. And where renovators are always happy to get their hands on big, potentially beautiful Victorians and Craftsman Bungalows with tiled fireplaces, pocket doors and built-in china cabinets, they're not so excited about rows of cracker box houses built in the 1950s, with no particularly fine features and not a lot of room. So gentrification is slower in coming to Potsdam. In my neighborhood, nice-looking young people jog and push strollers and walk their well-groomed dogs on the spic-and-span sidewalks. On Potsdam Street, unshaven homeless men and kids with pants falling down around their ankles scowl at you as you drive by, and the only dogs are mongrels, scavenging for food.

"Nice place," Mrs. Jenkins said when we pulled up outside my condo complex on the corner of Fifth and East Main. I looked around, too.

"Thank you."

Her grandson was well aware of where I lived, having a habit of knocking on my door at inopportune moments—like, when I was getting ready to go on a date with Todd—but this was the first time Mrs. J had visited.

"That's my apartment, up there." I pointed to the balcony and the sliding glass doors on the second floor. "It's just a one-bedroom, but you can take the bed and I'll sleep on the sofa in the living room."

"OK, baby." I'm not sure whether my words actually registered or not; she was already on the move toward the gate. I snagged the duffel from the back seat, grabbed my purse, and followed.

It took some time climbing the stairs to the second floor, and I had to keep my hand under Mrs. J's elbow the whole way, and boost her from step to step the last few times. Upstairs, I pointed down the hallway. "Just down there. Third door on the right."

Mrs. Jenkins nodded and made a beeline for it, her speed better now that she was on level ground. She tilted to one side, though, and I hurried after her, hands outstretched to catch her in case she over-balanced.

"Door's open, baby," Mrs. Jenkins said.

I stopped and lowered my arms. "Pardon?"

She nodded to it. I looked.

Yes, it was. Open, that is. The heavy metal slab was pulled to, but not latched: a small corner of the welcome mat had gotten caught in the crack and kept the door from shutting all the way.

My first reaction was telling. A stab of excitement jabbed me in the pit of my stomach, and I caught my breath quickly.

A moment later I was chastising myself for my response: in order for Rafe to get here this quickly, he'd have to be in Nashville already, and if he were in Nashville, I'd already know about it. Or Mrs. Jenkins would. Still, there was that shiver of anticipation when I pushed the door open. Or maybe it wasn't anticipation so much as apprehension. Or fear.

"Hello?"

No one answered.

"Don't think nobody's here, baby," Mrs. Jenkins said from behind me.

Maybe not, but it didn't hurt to be careful. I dug Sally Harmon's little bottle of pepper spray out of my purse and thumbed the lid off before I ventured into the apartment. Slowly.

It isn't a big place. A tiny foyer with a coat closet and a postage stamp-sized powder room leads directly into the living room/dining room combination. The kitchen is on the way, opposite from the coat closet and half bath, and the single bedroom is to the left of the living room, with the master bath behind the kitchen. It's less than 1,000 square feet all told, and it was empty.

Though someone had clearly been by. It wasn't just the open door: the stack of mail on the kitchen counter had been riffled. An electric bill had pride of place on top of the stack, where I last remembered looking at a circular from the Opry Mills Outlet Mall. Ditto for the stack of magazines and paperwork on the coffee table; the corners were squared, where I'm not usually that neat. And hadn't I left "Desire under the Desert Moon" on the sofa, pages splayed and spine up, last night when I went to bed? Now it was sitting on top of the stack of magazines, closed, with a piece of scrap paper—a coupon from Starbucks—in lieu of a bookmark.

It was something my mother would do, but she didn't have a key to my apartment, and even if she did, I couldn't for the life of me imagine Margaret Anne Martin driving all the way from Sweetwater to Nashville, just to straighten my living room.

So if not my mother, then who? And why?

Nothing seemed to be missing. My little laptop was still sitting on the dining room table, open but intact, and the TV and other electronics were in their respective places, as well. I don't own much of value; anything joint stayed with Bradley after the divorce, including the expensive furniture, and my apartment was furnished mostly with reupholstered second-hand furniture and things I'd bought at Target. It was bright and cheerful, but not valuable.

So if not a thief, then who? Someone looking for something? But what?

While I'd been contemplating the living room, Mrs. Jenkins had shuffled to the bedroom door, and now she turned to me.

"You're prob'ly gonna wanna see this, baby. And then you're gonna wanna call that nice detective."

"Why? What's going on?"

I went to join her in the doorway, and staggered at the level of destruction in my bedroom.

The rest of the apartment was pretty much pristine, or as pristine as I keep my living quarters. If the front door hadn't been open, I might not have noticed that anyone had been here. I could have left the electric bill on top of the stack of mail myself, and just didn't remember; and I could have bookmarked and closed "Desire under the Desert Moon" instead of leaving it tented, as is my usual habit. It was possible.

This was another matter. Whatever had been going on in the other part of the apartment—whatever my uninvited guest had been looking for, and had or hadn't found—he or she had made up for in here.

My bedroom looked like a chicken coop. There were feathers everywhere, where someone, using something sharp—like a knife; and my stomach clenched at the idea—had slashed my pillows to ribbons and scattered the contents throughout the room. The padding was protruding from my washed silk comforter, which was a total loss. My shimmery nightgown lay crumpled on the floor, it too sporting long gashes, and on the wall above the headboard was written a single word in red, the letters spiky and angry. *Trollop.*

It wasn't blood. Just lipstick. Which was bad enough, since I'd probably have to repaint the wall to get rid of it. Blood washes off, or so I've heard. L'Oreal Endless Kissable 16 hour No Fade, No Smudge Ruby-Ruby lipstick, not so much.

The rest of the stick was ground into the tan carpet. I might have to replace it, too. Or maybe I should just let the landlord keep my $500 security deposit and call it even.

"Don't touch nothing, baby," Mrs. Jenkins admonished me. I shook my head. No, I wasn't about to touch anything. Except for my cell phone. I fished it out of my purse and dialed Tamara Grimaldi's number.

"Detective? This is Savannah Martin. I have a problem."

"What kind of problem?" the detective wanted to know. I explained what had happened, and she said, "Get out of there. Now."

"We were going to stay here..." I said inanely, looking around at the destruction.

"Are you listening to me? Get out of there. Go to a hotel. Stay at the house on Potsdam Street. Or drive to Sweetwater and ask your family to put you up for a few days."

I snorted. My mother might be willing to help me, but accommodating Mrs. Jenkins—the notorious Rafe Collier's grandmother—was not the same thing at all.

"Spicer and Truman are on their way," Tamara Grimaldi said in my ear. "Leave the apartment and wait for them outside. Don't touch anything."

"Can I pack a bag? I'm going to need something to wear for the next couple of days."

She hesitated. "Has this maniac been in your closet? Will packing clothes disturb the crime scene?"

I opened the louvered closet doors and peered in. "Doesn't look that way." Everything was neat, hanging on hangers. My underwear was another story; the drawers in the bureau were open and a tangle of silk and lacy scraps were falling out. Blushing, I pushed them back in and closed the drawer with my hip. Crime scene or no crime scene; I wouldn't have Officers Spicer and Truman pawing through my lingerie.

"OK," Tamara Grimaldi said. "Gather some things, but be sure not to touch anything important. Clothes and toiletries only. And then get out of there. Fast."

I promised I would, and—heart beating—started yanking clothes off hangers and dropping them into a suitcase. We were back in the courtyard within five minutes.

Spicer and Truman showed up shortly thereafter, and I left Mrs. Jenkins outside by the fountain while I walked the officers upstairs to the apartment, and showed them the crumpled welcome mat that had held the door open, the electric bill, and the book. "I can't swear I didn't close it myself, but I usually just leave it tented."

"Nice, glossy cover," Spicer remarked appreciatively, eyeing the picture of the half-dressed Bedouin with the headcloth clasping the swooning Lady Serena to his manly—and supremely well-muscled—chest. When I looked at him, incredulously, Spicer added, "It'd take fingerprints well. If whoever was here touched it, and wasn't wearing gloves, we might get lucky."

"Oh." Of course. "I guess I'd better leave it here, then." I'd rather looked forward to losing myself in the adventures of Lady Serena—and the imaginary arms of Sheik Hasan—but if leaving the book here would help the police figure out who had broken into my place, then they were welcome to it.

"That'd be best," Spicer agreed.

"Just lock up when you're done, please. We'll be at the house on Potsdam Street."

Spicer nodded. "The boy and I'll wait for someone from CSI to get here. The detective'll let you know when you can move back in."

"Thank you." I shivered.

"You want I should send the boy for a new lock?" Spicer asked. "No telling how this yahoo got in, but a new lock, and some chains and bolts, ain't gonna hurt none."

"That would be great. Thank you."

He nodded. "We got it covered. Just take care of Mrs. J. I don't wanna go back to driving around looking for her couple times a day."

I promised I would. And then I left the two of them there, to wait for CSI and to replace my lock, and I headed back down to the courtyard and Mrs. Jenkins, who was still sitting there in the sun, looking around with beady little black bird eyes.

"Ready?"

She got to her feet. "Where we going now, baby?"

"I figure we'll just go back to your house. We can stay there just as easily as we can stay here." If a little more uncomfortably, at least on my part.

"OK, baby." Mrs. Jenkins didn't seem to care one way or the other. She shuffled toward the blue Volvo. I followed, clutching my suitcase and toiletries bag, and with Rafe's duffel over my shoulder. Life was just getting worse and worse.

I spent the rest of the day setting up house at 101 Potsdam Street. We had to go back out, to the grocery store to restock the kitchen. Apparently, Marquita hadn't done any shopping in a while, and Mrs. J had eaten her way through most of the groceries in the days since Marquita left. After that, I had to make dinner, to feed the poor old dear, and clean up the kitchen and wash the dirty dishes. By hand, since Rafe hadn't gotten around to installing a dishwasher before he had to flee. Although there was a hole between the cabinets, where one was supposed to go.

This kitchen was where I'd first set eyes on Mrs. Jenkins, back in August. She'd scared the bejeezes out of me. It was also where Rafe had first seen his grandmother, on that same occasion. And it was where Mrs. J and I had come face to face with a murderer, and damned near hadn't gotten away with our lives.

That thought brought me back to my apartment, and the destruction of my bedroom, something I'd tried really hard not to think about for the past few hours. Detective Grimaldi hadn't called, so presumably the CSI-team was still doing its thing. Seeing as I was someone who'd gotten herself mixed up in two different homicides in the past two months, the police were probably taking my break-in a little more seriously than they would have otherwise.

Whoever had been in my apartment didn't seem to have chosen it at random. If so, surely the TV and laptop would be missing, along with the few pieces of semi-valuable jewelry I own.

I really ought to tell the detective about that phone call I'd gotten the other day. The one where the caller had wanted me to go out on the balcony. I had complied, thinking he or she wanted me to see something outside. But what if *they'd* wanted to see me instead? If the burglar was someone who knew that I lived in the complex, but not which unit was mine, it was a reasonably safe way to discover where my apartment was located. My cell phone number is easily accessible; as a Realtor I broadcast it far and wide. My home address is harder to come by. I'm not listed in the White Pages, and since I don't own the place, I don't show up in Metro Nashville's courthouse records, either.

My burglar was not someone I knew well, then. Unfortunately, that left most of Nashville. Maybe I needed to come at it from another angle instead.

It seemed I'd been singled out, but why? It wasn't to steal anything, since nothing seemed to be missing. That left someone looking for something, or someone who just plain wanted to scare me. Maybe a little of both. Riffling the mail and digging through my lingerie drawers seemed to imply someone looking for something. But shredding my pillows and lipsticking my wall... that was either someone holding onto sanity by a shred, or someone very calculatedly trying to scare the living daylights out of me. And succeeding.

My hands stilled in the sudsy water as I went down the list of people I had upset lately.

First there was Walker, of course. I'm sure he didn't appreciate the fact that I proved he'd committed two murders. But he was in jail—Tamara Grimaldi would have told me if he'd escaped or been released—and besides, we'd parted on reasonably good terms last time I saw him. Plus, he wasn't stupid; he had to know that doing, or ordering, something like this would only make things worse for him.

Maybelle Driscoll and I hadn't ended up as best friends during that whole fiasco, either. Maybelle was Brenda Puckett's neighbor, and Brenda hadn't even been in the ground a week when Maybelle managed to get herself engaged to the grieving widower. The fact that Alexandra, Steven and Brenda's daughter, liked me and didn't like her, didn't help. The obscenely devoted Maybelle was loony enough to do something like this. But I hadn't seen any of the Pucketts for a month at least, and Maybelle herself for even longer.

Maybe there was a clue in the writing. A trollop is a loose woman, a prostitute or adulteress. The last time I'd come across the word, was in a Barbara Botticelli novel. Historical, of course; it isn't an expression that's much in use these days. Anymore, a promiscuous woman is more likely to be called a slut. Or, if you're my mother, maybe a hussy.

Barbara had used it to describe a character who was sleeping with someone else's betrothed. I wasn't. I wasn't sleeping with anyone at all, and the men in my life were—by their own assertion—single. I'd never had even the mildest of flirtations with Steven Puckett, who was at least fifteen years older than me, and not my type. Todd had been married for a couple of years, but he and Jolynn separated just after Bradley and I did. By now, they were probably legally divorced, as well. Bradley was married to Shelby now, and I hadn't seen him since the divorce, so Shelby had no reason at all to suspect me of anything. If he was cheating—and I wouldn't put it past him—it was with someone else. I wouldn't touch him with the proverbial ten foot pole. And Rafe had told me he'd never been married. On most subjects, I wouldn't trust Rafe any farther than I could throw him, but in this case, I was inclined to take his word for it. His lifestyle over the past ten years hadn't been conducive to steady relationships, and his personality doesn't seem to be, either.

Perry Fortunato had had something of an obsession with loose women. He had killed Lila Vaughn because she, as he put it, always flaunted her body and then refused to put out. He'd had some of those same issues with me, in spite of my never, ever being anything but perfectly businesslike with him. If you ask me, it was all in his head. Besides, Perry was dead. And not by my hand. If anyone had decided to avenge his death—and I couldn't imagine who—they'd come after Rafe, not me. I'd been tied to a bed when Perry died. Rafe was the one who had wielded the knife.

Funny how everything that had happened in my life over the past couple of months seemed to come back to him. To Rafe. I shook that particular thought off, and went back to soaping and rinsing dishes, no closer to figuring out what was going on than I had been when I started.

Detective Grimaldi called some twenty or thirty minutes later, and caught me in the middle of contemplating sleeping arrangements.

"Miss Martin." She sounded tired.

"Detective." It was after eight; I couldn't blame her. She'd probably put in at least twelve hours today. And not in a nice, relaxing, comfortable desk-job, either.

"The CSI-team is finished at your apartment. With your permission, I'd like to stake it out for a couple of days, just in case whoever broke in comes back for another look."

"Sure," I said. "What do you think they were looking for?"

"No idea. It's possible they were looking for you."

That idea gave me a shiver down my spine, as an image of my slashed nightgown came back to me. Someone who would do that to my clothes, might equally well do it to me. "Surely not?"

"No way to know. That's why I'm going to station a decoy in your place for a couple of nights."

"Whatever you need to do. Please. Did the CSI-team find anything of interest?"

"Fingerprints," Tamara Grimaldi said. "Yours. Mr. Satterfield's— they're on record with the state, seeing as he's a D.A.. Mr. Collier's; they're on record with the state—"

"Because he's a felon. I know." No one ever passes up an opportunity to remind me. "Anyone else's?" I don't entertain much, and very few people have ever been to my apartment.

"The late Lila Vaughn's. We took them after her death, while we were investigating her murder."

"And that's it?"

Detective Grimaldi sighed. "There are several others, including a lovely set on the glossy cover of that masterpiece you were reading. But they're not in the system, so until we have a suspect, there's no one to compare them to."

"At least it isn't a professional criminal, then." To look on the bright side...

"Unfortunately not," Tamara Grimaldi said. "Believe me, Miss Martin, in these situations, the devil you know is almost always preferable to finding the needle in the haystack. Any ideas who this could have been? Somewhere for us to start?"

"I'm afraid not. I've been wracking my brain, but I can't imagine who would want to scare me this way. Or what they could have been looking for."

The detective didn't answer. The silence lengthened. A sort of pregnant, very eloquent silence, that kind that said, loudly, that I should know what she was thinking.

"What?" I said.

"You said your mail had been riffled, is that correct? You may not have realized it, but your email was accessed, too. New messages as well as sent, deleted, and your address book. And someone looked through your Rolodex."

I blinked. "That's weird."

"Very," the detective said dryly. "Would you consider that this might have something to do with Mr. Collier?"

"Why would it?"

Her voice was patient. "Because he's been gone for... what is it, almost six weeks now? If someone were looking for him, your apartment might be a good place to start. The two of you spent some time together before he left, and from what I understood, you'd become..." She hesitated delicately, "close."

"Where did you hear that?" Rafe and I weren't close. Not in that tone of voice, anyway.

"Officers Spicer and Truman told me they'd found the two of you steaming up the windows of your car not too long ago."

"I told you," I said, my cheeks pink, "we were just looking for Julio Melendez." Body temperatures might have ratcheted up a little—mine, at least—but it was from the conversation. Nothing else had been going on.

"And then there was that evening when Mr. Collier left town, on the sidewalk outside your apartment. Officer Spicer said he was considering running you in for indecent behavior...?"

"Officer Spicer was joking," I said. "It wasn't indecent. Rafe kissed me. Because he was leaving. But that was all it was. And I haven't heard from him since he left. By snail mail, e-mail, or telephone. Or carrier pigeon or anything else. I swear."

"Of course," the detective said blandly. "But to someone who doesn't know that, it might seem reasonable to think that you would know where he is."

"I don't!"

"I believe you. However, if your unknown visitor was looking for an address or a location for Mr. Collier, and didn't find it, and can't find Mr. Collier, he or she may be back to try again. Just on the off-chance that you might know, but haven't written the information down anywhere."

"Hence the decoy in my apartment," I nodded. "I get it. I'll be staying here for the next couple of days anyway. You know where to find me if anything happens."

"I do, indeed. And if Mr. Collier should happen to get in touch..."

"I'll let you know," I said.

"Of course you will," Tamara Grimaldi answered. And hung up, without waiting for my answer. I made a face and went back to contemplating sleeping arrangements.

Five

I ended up sleeping in Rafe's bed. Like Goldilocks, I considered and discarded Mrs. Jenkins's bed—she needed it herself—Marquita's bed—what if the nurse came back in the middle of the night?—and the love seat in the parlor—too hard and at least six inches too short. But Rafe's bed was just right: unoccupied, big enough—a little too big for just one person; two would have been better—and already made, with crisp sheets and a soft comforter. There was no chance that he'd come home and find me there—or at least only a very slim chance—and the benefits seemed to outweigh the minimal risk. I changed into another lacy nightgown, similar to the one that had been hacked to pieces back in the apartment, and crawled under the satin comforter. And did my best to go to sleep.

It wasn't easy. There was some kind of ruckus outside in the middle of the night that woke me, and the strangeness of being in someone else's house and the knowledge that I was sleeping in Rafe's bed, surrounded by the smell of him, made it hard to sleep. Then there were the nightmares and the—pardon me—pornographic dreams, and between all of it, I woke up bleary-eyed and exhausted, with a lingering sense of having spent the whole night breathless. Someone was after me, some nameless, faceless someone with a sharp knife, and no matter where I went or how fast I got going, they were always there, just out of sight. Waking up didn't do much to dispel that feeling either, unfortunately.

The appraisal for my clients Gary Lee and Charlene's new home was today, so after making Mrs. Jenkins pancakes and coffee, I got her washed and dressed and medicated, and myself washed and dressed, and both of us out the door and into the Volvo. Pulling out of the circular driveway, I glanced over at Mrs. J, perched in the seat next to me, her small, wrinkled hands folded in her lap and her black bird eyes alert.

"Did you sleep all right, Mrs. Jenkins?"

She nodded. "Oh, yes, baby. Well, other than the hollerin'."

She must have been the same ruckus that had woken me up in the middle of the night.

"Poor lady," Mrs. Jenkins said, "carryin' on something awful out in the street in the middle of the night."

"I think I heard her. Some woman screaming obscenities."

"Prob'ly drunk," Mrs. J said sadly. "Happens sometimes around here."

We pulled to a stop at the corner, and I signaled a left onto Dresden. Directly in front of us was the Milton House Home for the Aged, where Mrs. Jenkins had lived when I first met her. At the time I had thought that if it came down to a choice between putting one of my loved ones into the Milton House, or shooting them, I'd go with the latter option. Bless Rafe; whatever his other faults, he'd at least gotten her out of there.

Behind us, a sleek, black SUV turned the corner. It had been parked halfway down Potsdam Street, and had been in the process of pulling out when we approached. The driver, invisible behind the tinted glass, had waited to let us pass and had fallen in behind. Now it went in the same direction we did.

In a movie, that would have meant something, and I admit I kept an eye on the car in the rearview mirror as we made our way into the 'better' part of East Nashville and over to the townhouse that Gary Lee and Charlene wanted to buy. The SUV stayed with us almost the whole way there, only peeled off at the last minute, into the parking lot of the Walden Development on Eastland Avenue. The driver was probably on his way to the Ugly Mugs coffee house for a caffeine jolt. I put it out of my mind and concentrated on the task at hand.

The appraiser was waiting outside the townhouse up the street, clipboard at the ready, tapping his cowboy-booted toe. I left Mrs. J relaxing in the Volvo with the radio and AC going, and got out to meet him.

"Mr. Cobb? I'm Savannah Martin. Agent for the buyers. Sorry I'm late."

I wasn't actually late, or if I was, it was by less than a minute, but I've been brought up to take responsibility for things like that. Keep the menfolk happy. Mr. Cobb looked impatient, so I apologized for keeping him waiting.

He grunted something and took a tighter grip on his clipboard. He was a small, spare man with lots of white hair pulled straight back from his forehead, falling past his collar in the back. The snake-skin cowboy boots were paired with loose jeans and a tan sort of safari jacket with about a hundred pockets. Many of them were weighted down with heavy objects.

"Let me just unlock the door for you," I said, suiting action to words, "and you can get started. Let me know if you have any questions."

Mr. Cobb grunted noncommittally. He brushed past me and into the house. I followed, after a glance over my shoulder to make sure Mrs. J was still comfortably ensconced in the Volvo.

Mr. Cobb didn't turn out to have many questions, and the appraisal was a pretty short process. He walked through the townhouse, muttering and making notations on his clipboard. He measured the height of the walls in a few places upstairs, where the ceiling slanted down—height has to be a minimum of seven feet to be considered proper living space—and he made note of any upgrades, like hardwood floors vs. carpets, brushed nicked faucets vs. plain nickel-plated ditto, granite counters, stainless steel appliances, and that sort of thing. And that seemed to be it.

"So how did we do?" I asked brightly when he came toward the front door again. "Will it appraise for the purchase price?" Or would the deal fall through because the bank wouldn't want to lend more money than the house was worth?

"Dunno," Mr. Cobb said.

"When will you know? My clients are eager, as I'm sure you understand."

"Gotta get back to the office," Mr. Cobb explained, his voice gravelly. "Gotta put the info into the computer. Coupla days."

"A couple of days?"

My disappointment must have been obvious, because he looked maliciously amused. "Can't rush this stuff. Bank wanna be sure they ain't lending too much."

"Right." I could understand that. Still, a couple of days? To input the results of this ten-minute surface-inspection into the computer? "Just get it done as quickly as you can, would you? My clients are—"

He nodded. "Eager. Yeah. I got that."

"Right." OK, then. There was nothing I could do but smile graciously, the way mother taught me. "Thank you for your time, Mr. Cobb. Here's my card, in case you have any questions after you leave here."

Mr. Cobb grunted and stuck the business card into one of the many pockets of his jacket. The others had contained items like a hundred foot tape measure, a screwdriver, a ball of string, and a digital camera, all of which he had used.

He wandered toward his truck, a green behemoth parked in the lot beside the condo. The engine started up with a roar and a gush of exhaust, and I turned toward the curb and the pale blue Volvo. Only to stop after a few steps when I saw that Mrs. Jenkins wasn't alone.

For just a second—less; half a second, maybe—my heart stuttered in my chest at the sight of the man leaning on the car. Tall, dark, muscular... One arm braced above the passenger side window and dark head inclined toward Mrs. J, he was dressed in faded jeans that molded long legs and a nice posterior, while a plain white T-shirt stretched across broad shoulders and well-developed arms.

My breath caught in my throat, my stomach swooped... and then I realized that it wasn't Rafe after all. Just another tall, dark, muscular guy in faded jeans and a T-shirt. One who was bugging Mrs. Jenkins.

"Excuse me!" I raised my voice and sped up, my heels clicking against the pavement. "Sir!"

The man straightened and turned. Up close and from the front, he looked less like Rafe. The coloring was the same—dark hair and eyes, golden skin—but this guy's hair was longer than Rafe's, straight and shiny, slicked back. Rafe keeps his hair cropped short. The man had a trim goatee, while Rafe stays clean-shaven, and he had an earring, a small silver cross, that Rafe doesn't have. He also had some sort of tattoo—a dragon or demon, maybe; something green and scaly—that extended a claw above the neck of the T-shirt in the back, and around the side of his throat. And though the eyes were the same—brown bordering on black, deep and dark, fringed with long, sooty lashes any woman would sell her soul for—the expression in them was different. Where Rafe rarely looks at me without some form of amusement, even when he's about to kiss me and his gaze is hot enough to scorch, this guy's eyes were flat and expressionless.

"Can I help you?" I came to a stop in front of him. He was a little shorter than Rafe, too. Just an inch or so over six feet tall.

He looked me over. From head to toe and back. If it had been Rafe, the inspection would have been slow, insolent, appreciative, and ending in a killer grin. It would have made my cheeks flush and my stomach quiver. This appraisal made a chill go down my spine. There was no feeling there. No appreciation, no curiosity, no anger—nothing but cold assessment.

I forced myself not to show a reaction. "Sir?"

"I'm looking for Rafe." His voice was low, harsh, with a hint of an accent. Not Southern. That was different, too. Rafe's voice is husky and warm. Only when he's angry do his voice and eyes go dead and flat, like this man's.

"That's quite a coincidence," I said. "So am I. I'm sure Mrs. Jenkins told you we haven't seen him for more than a month?"

I leaned sideways, to try to get a bead on Mrs. J, in the front seat of the Volvo. Just to make sure she was OK and still breathing. The way this guy was looking at me, I wouldn't put it past him to have slit Mrs. Jenkins's throat if he didn't get the answers he wanted.

She was still alive. Staring straight ahead, her wrinkled face blank. I recognized the expression, or rather, the lack thereof. Clearly, whatever the guy had said or done to her, had scared her practically witless. She'd retreated into this place she goes, where she isn't living in the same world as the rest of us anymore. She gets a vacant look in her eyes, and she babbles. About old Jim Collier shooting her son Tyrell, about Walker Lamont cutting Brenda Puckett's throat, about Walker coming after the two of us with a gun... The poor dear has had some tough breaks in her life, and obviously, being related to Rafe isn't destined to make anything easier for her.

I added, pulling my attention back to the man in front of me, "He left almost six weeks ago. He mentioned Memphis, although that could have been just a ruse. No one's heard from him since. For all I know, he's dead."

The man parted his lips, just far enough to squeeze out a few words. "He ain't dead." The unspoken last word of that sentence, I thought, was *yet*.

It took another superhuman effort to keep my voice from shaking. "I'm sorry. As I told you, we haven't heard from him. Not since he left. I'm sure he'll be back sooner or later, but I have no idea when. And I doubt I'll get advance warning. He usually just shows up. One day I'll turn around, and there he'll be." *Please, God...*

The man didn't answer. Just kept looking at me with those dead eyes.

"I'll be happy to give him a message," I offered, a little desperately. Maybe that would make him leave. "Whenever he comes home. Or in case he calls."

The man looked at me again. Up and down. The regard was still impersonal, but his eyes lingered for a second longer than necessary on my legs and on the top button of my blouse. And on my throat. I paled. It was only too easy to guess what he was thinking, and I hadn't meant that I wanted to *be* the message.

He must have seen the realization on my face, because he smiled. Chillingly. By which I mean that the corners of his mouth stretched, but his eyes stayed the same. "Tell him to watch his back."

I nodded. Fervently. "I can do that. When I see him. Or talk to him. Whenever that will be."

He nodded. And turned on his heel and walked away. I watched him cross the street, and then I turned to Mrs. J. "Are you OK?"

She turned and blinked at me. "Hi, baby. What're *you* doing here?"

"Letting the appraiser into this house." I pointed to it.

"You and my boy plannin' to move in here when the baby comes?" She squinted through the windshield and her face fell. So did her voice. "Oh, baby, it's gotta be real expensive. I don't know..."

"Don't worry," I said. "Your boy—" I knew she was talking about Tyrell, not Rafe, "won't be living here."

She clutched at my hand, her wrinkled face worried. "You ain't plannin' on leavin' him, are you, baby? He loves you!"

"I know he does."

If Old Jim Collier hadn't come along with his shotgun, LaDonna and Tyrell would probably have gotten married and maybe even lived happily ever after. LaDonna certainly was never the same again after Tyrell was killed. Then again, raising Rafe on her own would have been enough to drive any mother to drink.

"And no, I'm not leaving him. This is for someone else." I'd been through this conversation enough times by now, that I knew it didn't do any good to try to explain. I just had to go with the flow, and sooner or later she'd come back on her own.

"Oh." Mrs. J looked relieved for a moment until her face puckered again. She lowered her voice, her hand tightening on mine. "That man... he's gonna try to hurt my boy!"

"I'm sorry," I said, patting her small, wrinkled claw. Mrs. Jenkins had actually seen Old Jim shoot Tyrell, outside the house on Potsdam Street one night when Tyrell was coming home from work, and whenever she got upset, she tended to relive it. "What did he tell you?"

She shook her head. "Didn't tell me nothin', baby. Just asked me where Rafe was." She looked confused for a moment, before reality realigned itself and she remembered that Tyrell had been dead for thirty years and Rafe was her grandson. And that I wasn't LaDonna at all, but Savannah; not her son's pregnant girlfriend, but her grandson's... something or other.

"Did he tell you his name? How he knows Rafe? What he wants him for?"

But Mrs. Jenkins shook her head again. "Didn't say nothin', baby. Just asked me where Rafe was. I said I didn't know, that I hadn't heard from him since he left."

I nodded. Unfortunately, the man with the cold eyes probably wouldn't be satisfied with that. "I think we need to call Detective Grimaldi."

"The cops?" Mrs. Jenkins made a face. She doesn't trust the police. They used to return her to the Milton House every time she wandered away, which didn't exactly endear them to her, although it started much longer ago than that, back when the police didn't believe Mrs. J when she said her son had been killed by a middle-aged white man.

"Remember Detective Grimaldi? You like her. And this may be the guy who broke into my apartment yesterday. I think he probably followed us from the house this morning..."

Mrs. Jenkins blinked. Her face started to pucker, and I stopped talking before my words could throw her into another tailspin. Instead, I made my voice deliberately perky as I walked around the car and got into the passenger seat. "Let's go do something fun. Would you like some ice cream?"

Mrs. J's face cleared. "Sure, baby."

"Great." I put the Volvo in gear and pulled out of the parking lot.

WE DROVE TO BOBBIE'S DAIRY DIP across town, and while Mrs. Jenkins was spooning up her chocolate soft serve with chocolate sprinkles at one of the tables under the awning, I stepped aside to call Tamara Grimaldi and tell her about the latest development.

"Ms. Martin." She sounded tired again.

"Long night?" I asked sympathetically.

"No longer than usual. Is everything all right? Any word from Mr. Collier?"

"I'm afraid not. Although you're not the first person to ask me that today." I told her about my conversation with the man outside the townhouse.

"Interesting," the detective said politely. Not quite the reception I'd been hoping for. When I said as much, she added, "You said he didn't actually threaten you, right?"

I had to admit that he hadn't. "Not per se. It was more his demeanor than the words he used."

"I'm afraid I can't arrest someone for demeanor, Ms. Martin."

"You wouldn't be able to arrest him anyway. He's gone."

"Right." Tamara Grimaldi hesitated. "But if he didn't actually threaten you..."

"He didn't. Not in so many words. It was just the way he looked at me. And the way he said what he said. The look in his eyes."

"You don't think you could have imagined it?"

I shook my head, then—because she couldn't see me—added an emphatic, "No. I've come face to face with two coldblooded killers in the past couple of months; I think I can recognize what one looks like."

Detective Grimaldi sighed. "What do you want me to do about it?"

"I don't know what I want you to do," I said. "But I wanted you to know. There's a good chance this was the guy who broke into my apartment, and that makes me nervous. And what if he got hold of Marquita Johnson and had a 'talk' with her, and that's why she's not coming home? What if she's lying in a ditch somewhere with her throat cut?"

"We have no evidence to support that," Grimaldi said. "No reason at all to suppose that Mrs. Johnson didn't go off voluntarily, and is staying gone for reasons of her own."

"What sort of reasons?"

"Well..." She hesitated. "Perhaps Mr. Collier contacted her? And asked her to meet him somewhere? She'd go, wouldn't she?"

"Of course she would." Marquita worships Rafe. Has ever since they were in high school together. If he crooked his little finger in her direction, she'd set a world record to get to him, knocking down anyone who stood in her way. "Why isn't she coming back, though? Surely you're not suggesting that *he* did something to her?"

Grimaldi didn't answer, but her silence was eloquent. The lightbulb went off over my head. I shook it. "Oh, no. Absolutely not. He's told me more than once that there's nothing between them. They're not shacked up in some motel somewhere going at it like rabbits. Absolutely not."

"Fine," Detective Grimaldi said. "So they're not together. That doesn't mean she isn't alive and well somewhere."

"Have you heard from Sweetwater?"

She had. Bob Satterfield had called with an update just a few minutes ago. "Still no sign of her down there. Her family and friends haven't seen her."

"Do you know if they've checked the Bog? The trailer park? That's where she grew up." And Rafe, too. "It's empty these days; someone bought the land and kicked everyone out a couple of months ago. I don't think anyone's lived there since July or August, at least."

"What would she be doing there?" Tamara Grimaldi wanted to know.

"I have no idea. But it's where she's from. It seems worth checking."

"I'll call Sheriff Satterfield back. If they haven't already been there, I'll ask him to have someone swing by."

"And let me know if they find anything?"

Grimaldi promised, a little reluctantly, that she would. "And if you see the man you saw earlier again, let *me* know. And this time, try to get a name. Or a license plate number. Or something I can use."

"Would you like me to come look at mug shots?"

I could practically hear her eyes roll. "You can if you want. But let me warn you, it'll take you the rest of the day, if not longer. Nashville is full of men with black hair and brown eyes. Plenty of them are close to six feet tall. And that's assuming he has a record. And is from Nashville."

"Right." Probably not worth the trouble, then. If it hadn't been for Mrs. Jenkins, I might have been tempted—now that Gary Lee and Charlene's appraisal was done, I didn't have anything else to do for the rest of the day, and I'd rather be doing something than nothing—but I was damned if I was going to make Mrs. J sit in a room in Police Plaza watching mug shots scroll by on the computer for eight hours. "We'll just keep an eye out."

"You do that," Detective Grimaldi said, and hung up.

Six

Mrs. J and I spent the rest of the day running around. We went to the office, where I responded to a couple of emails and endured Tim's snarky attempts at humor. We went to the mall, where I replaced my kiss-proof lipstick and my copy of Barbara Botticelli's "Desire Under the Desert Moon." We went to the movies, and watched an animated Disney film about woolly mammoths and dinosaurs that was a big hit with all the kids in the audience and with Mrs. J. We went to dinner at Burger King, since that was what Mrs. Jenkins wanted. She walked away with a plastic woolly mammoth that came in her chicken nugget kid's meal, and she was delighted. Though I usually avoid fast food places, I didn't object, since the meal only set me back ten bucks, versus the twenty I would have spent elsewhere, and since it so obviously made her happy.

We drove across town in every direction at least twice, coming and going, and I kept an eye peeled for black SUVs with tinted windows. It did me no good. There are just too many. I hadn't really noticed what kind of black SUV we had seen this morning, and as it turns out, there are lots of varieties. Jeeps and Hummers, Nissans, Hondas, Lexus, Mercedes... And frankly, I didn't even know that the black SUV from this morning had anything to do with anything. Or that the white Toyota I'd seen a few times over the past couple of days did. If that had been the same white Toyota every time, and not several. If it had been a Toyota at all, and not a Honda. Or a Nissan. There are plenty of all of them out there. We didn't see the Hispanic man again, anyway, or anyone else I recognized either.

We got back home—back to the house on Potsdam Street—after dark, and I must admit my heart was beating faster when I unlocked the front door and reached around the jamb to flip the light switch. Once upon a time, just after Brenda Puckett's murder, I'd had a bad experience here, doing that same thing: walking up to what I thought would be an empty house, only to find someone inside. It had only been Mrs. Jenkins, escaped from the Milton House yet again, but at the time, it had scared me out of my mind. I had left the door wide open and had turned on my heel and hightailed it out of there with a spurt of gravel. If I could have done the same thing now, I would have.

I couldn't, though. I had to go inside and make sure we were safe. And I'll frankly admit that my heart was pounding as I checked the place from top to bottom once I'd locked and bolted the door behind us.

No one was there. No one seemed to have been there, either. Everything was in its place, nothing was out of order, there was no sign that anyone had been inside the house during the time we'd been gone.

It was not even eight o'clock, but poor Mrs. Jenkins was worn out from the busy day we'd had; much busier than the poor dear was used to. She went to bed. After checking and rechecking that the front and back doors were locked and that all the windows were securely fastened, I went upstairs, too. Changed into my lacy nightie and crawled into Rafe's bed, where I tried to get lost in the adventures of beautiful, blonde Serena and handsome, swarthy Sheik Hasan.

No sooner had I found my place in the book, than the phone rang. My cell phone, plugged in and charging on the floor next to the bed.

Rafe didn't have a bedside table. I had stopped myself before I tried to figure out where he kept his condoms, although I can't deny that the thought had crossed my mind. For a tenth of a second or so before I banished it. Maybe he just didn't entertain here, I'd told myself. The idea that he might have been with someone, in the same bed I was sleeping in, was more disturbing than I wanted to admit, even to myself.

Anyway, I rolled over onto my stomach and flipped the phone open, squinting at the display down there on the floor. And I thank God I did, because if I had answered without checking first, all hell would have broken loose.

"Oh, no."

It was Todd.

And suddenly I remembered what I'd forgotten in the whirlwind of the last two days: that I was supposed to have had dinner with him tonight. A date I hadn't remembered to call and cancel. Todd must have driven up to Nashville from Sweetwater, to pick me up. Only to find a decoy, maybe an undercover police officer, in my apartment.

"Oh, no!"

Did the undercover cop know where I was, I wondered? Had she told him? Was Todd even now on his way over here? I tried not to imagine the look on his face when he saw me in a lacy nightgown snuggled up in Rafe's bed. Even without Rafe around. Maybe I should get dressed again, just in case Todd knocked on the door.

But no, surely my lookalike didn't know where I was; surely Tamara Grimaldi would have kept that information to herself. Wouldn't she...?

In any case, I really ought to answer the phone, to set Todd's mind at ease. Even if he didn't know that I was here, specifically, he'd be worried that I wasn't at home. Chances were that the undercover cop had told him what had happened, even if she hadn't been able to tell him where to find me. I mean, Todd Satterfield wasn't just anybody: he was the assistant district attorney in Columbia, and he wouldn't have scrupled to put pressure on if he had to. I couldn't bring myself to pick up the phone, though. If I talked to Todd, he'd ask me where I was staying, and then I'd either have to tell him the truth, which would send the manure winging its way toward the fan, or I'd have to lie. Something I do very poorly. So instead of answering, I watched the display until the call went to voicemail, and then I started breathing again.

He didn't call back. After a minute, the phone sounded the new voicemail ding, and I steeled myself to listen to Todd's message.

It wasn't as bad as I'd feared. "Savannah? This is Todd. I'm standing outside your apartment, but you're not here. Someone else is. Her name is Megan, and she says she'll be staying for a few days, while you're away. You didn't tell me you were going away, Savannah. You didn't call to cancel our date, either. I'm worried about you. Where are you? Please call me."

And that was it. I gnawed on my bottom lip for a second while I debated what to do. If I didn't do something, he'd be talking to mother and Dix in no time flat. It didn't seem as if Megan the undercover cop had told him what had happened—it sounded like she had pretended to be a friend house sitting for me while I was elsewhere—but still, that was enough to make Todd, Dix, and mother worried. Just the fact that they didn't know where I was.

I didn't want to call Todd, and I couldn't call my mother, who'd have an aneurism if she discovered where I was. But maybe I could call Dix. I've had him run interference for me before, and he knows a little more about my practically non-existent relationship with Rafe than the rest of the family. Of everyone, Dix is least likely to judge me. Or if he judges me, at least he's fairly nice about it.

"Where are you?" were the first words out of his mouth when he picked up the phone.

I sighed. "Obviously you've already heard from Todd."

"He called two minutes ago, to say you weren't at home when he came to pick you up for dinner. Where are you?"

"Staying with a friend. My apartment was broken into yesterday."

"Damn," Dix said after taking a second to process the news. "Todd didn't mention that."

"He probably didn't know. Megan wouldn't have told him."

"Who's Megan?"

"She's a police officer who's staying in my apartment for a few days. Supposedly she looks like me."

"Todd didn't mention that, either," Dix said. "How did you swing an undercover officer after a simple break-in?"

"Detective Grimaldi thought that with everything that's been going on in my life this fall, it was better to be safe. Just in case this has something to do with Walker Lamont or Perry Fortunato."

"Right." Dix hesitated. "Are you all right, sis?"

"I'm fine. I wasn't home when it happened."

"So where are you now?"

"I told you. I'm staying at a friend's house. And I'd appreciate it if you'd call Todd back and tell him that I'm sorry for standing him up. Cancelling slipped my mind in all the excitement."

"Why can't you call him yourself?" Dix wanted to know.

"Because then I'll have to tell him what happened and where..." I bit my tongue, but not soon enough.

"Let me guess," my brother said, his voice resigned, "you're staying with Collier."

"I'm staying with Mrs. Jenkins. Rafe is still in Memphis. Or wherever he went. So no, I'm not staying with him. If he was here, I wouldn't have to be. I'd come home to Sweetwater until things blow over. But since Marquita's missing, Mrs. Jenkins needs someone to stay with her. And since she can't stay with me, I'm here."

"Marquita Johnson's missing?"

"Apparently so. She left on Saturday afternoon for a half day off and never came back. Sheriff Satterfield is looking for her."

"Huh," Dix said.

"Right. Anyway, can you please talk to Todd for me? And tell him I'm fine and I'm sorry, but without telling him exactly where I am? You know he'll have a fit if he finds out, and then he'll tell mother, and she'll have a heart attack."

"So I should do it to protect our mother's health?"

"That, and because you love me. You know the kind of trouble I'll get into if mother and Todd find out about this."

"You should have thought of that," Dix said and hung up. I grimaced and did the same.

OK, so that hadn't gone as well as I would have liked. Still, I thought I could trust Dix not to tell mother and Todd where I was. He'd call them and assure them I was fine, but he'd keep my whereabouts to himself. I hoped.

The phone didn't ring again, so whatever he'd told them must have done the trick. Tomorrow, I'd have to call Todd myself, to reassure him—he wouldn't be satisfied until he heard my voice, and my personal apology—but for now at least, I could rest easy.

That proved to be more difficult than anticipated. Between the worry over Todd's and mom's reactions and the encounter with Mr. Threatening earlier in the day, it took reading "Desire Under the Desert Moon" through to the end before I was ready to turn out the light. And even then I found sleep elusive. My mind spun, going over the events of the day. When I closed my eyes, the Hispanic man was looking at me with that lack of expression that had sent my stomach plummeting. The way he'd sounded when he told me that Rafe was alive, like it was just a matter of time before he wasn't anymore, sounded in my ears. I re-experienced Mrs. Jenkins's fear, palpable enough to touch. I saw the sinister tinted windows of that black SUV that might have been following us. Again, we drove across town, watching for it in the rearview mirror...

It all translated into another uneasy night haunted by nightmares. I was running again, this time from the Hispanic man, who was coming after me with the sharp knife that had been used to slash my nightgown the other day. The sharp knife he was planning to use to slash the nightgown I was wearing, and me along with it. And I was running from mom and Todd as well; they were looking for me, to drag me back to Sweetwater and the Martin plantation, where they'd wrap me in cotton wool and put me on a shelf, up and away from harm. Under the circumstances, the idea should have held more appeal than it did.

Through the middle of these dreams wove the plot of the book I had just read: I was the virginal Lady Serena, running from the lecherous Sayid Pasha and from the conventions of my proper British family. I was looking for someone to save me, not only from the harem but from a life of propriety and boredom as the wife of some chinless sprig of British nobility.

Enter the dashing and dangerous Sheik Hasan, who, when he showed up in my subconscious, bore an uncanny resemblance to Rafe.

After that, the dreams changed. The need to hurry, to run away, became a different sort of need; no less frantic and even less controlled, but not so terrifying. Or perhaps just as terrifying, but in a different way.

So vivid were the dreams that the next morning, in that state between sleep and full wakefulness, with the sun shining on my closed eyelids, I could still feel the warmth of his body at my back and smell the citrusy, spicy scent I had come to associate with him. One of his hands was skimming lazily over my shoulder and arm, warm and hard, and I stretched luxuriously, lips curving with remembered pleasure. I'd feel guilty when I came back to my senses—a lady doesn't entertain dreams like those, and if she does, she certainly doesn't enjoy reliving them in the morning—but for the time being, I reveled in the warmth and smell and the drowsy heaviness. Until reality intruded, in the form of an insistent melody from my cell phone. My eyes popped open, the drowsiness gone. The hand, however, remained.

For a second, I went as stiff as a board, in total shock and denial. There couldn't really be a man in my bed, touching me. There hadn't been a man in my bed for two years, and I'd certainly remember if I'd had one there when I went to sleep. The only logical explanation was that I was still asleep and I just *thought* I'd woken up.

A soft chuckle gave the lie to that explanation. I knew that chuckle, and the voice that accompanied it. Sex-appeal incarnate, that voice. Dark and husky and full of things a woman shouldn't be faced with at daybreak. "Morning, Goldilocks."

The ringing phone fell silent when I didn't pick it up. I was afraid to turn around. "Rafe?"

"Who else?"

I glanced over my shoulder, cautiously. Just in case I was losing my mind and it was the man from yesterday, here to rape and kill me, to send a message to Rafe. Or just in case the past two years hadn't happened, and I was still married to Bradley.

I felt all the air go out of my lungs when I met a pair of brown eyes, long-lashed and dark as those on a Jersey cow, smudgy with fatigue.

"Oh, my God. It *is* you." I scrambled all the way around, not sure whether I wanted to throw myself around his neck in relief, or disappear under the covers in abject embarrassment. I compromised by pulling the sheet up to my nose and peering at him over it. "What are you doing here?"

He quirked a brow, glancing around. "Don't you think that oughta be my question, darlin'? You're in my house, my room, my bed… Guess you musta missed me, huh?"

I flushed. "Maybe just a little."

He grinned. "Looks like maybe more than a little."

I avoided his eyes. "Actually, I'm only here because of Marquita. Spicer and Truman found your grandmother wandering the streets two days ago, and she says Marquita never came home the day before that. They were going to take Mrs. Jenkins back to that awful place she was living when we met her, and I couldn't let them do it. So I said I'd take care of her until Marquita came back or until I could get in touch with you and you could make other arrangements. But then someone broke into my apartment so we couldn't stay there, and I didn't want to sleep in Marquita's bed, just in case she came back, and of course your grandmother's in her own bed, but yours was just sitting here, empty..."

Rafe's grin had been getting wider and wider as I babbled on, trying to justify my actions. My reasoning had made perfect sense two days ago, but now, with him sitting on the edge of the bed looking like he wanted to crawl in beside me, I was wondering what the hell I'd been thinking. If this ever got back to my mother, she'd drop into a dead faint on the spot.

"Did you sleep well?" The end of that sentence hung in the air, unspoken. *In my bed...*

I flushed. "Reasonably well."

"Dream of me?" He winked.

"Not at all," I said robustly.

"Uh-huh. I've told you before, darlin', you're a lousy liar."

"Fine. So maybe you turned up in my dreams once or twice." More like two or three dozen times, really, over the past few weeks, but telling him that would make him insufferable. More insufferable than he was already.

His voice was smooth. "You know, darlin', it's OK to admit that you like me. Most women do."

"I've noticed," I said. "Just out of curiosity, how many women threw themselves at you during the time you were gone? A dozen? Two?"

"I wasn't counting. Any chance you'll be throwing yourself at me anytime soon?"

"None at all."

"Pity." His eyes slid over me, from my disheveled bed-hair over my naked shoulders down to the not very demure neckline of my nightgown, on display now that I'd forgotten to hold the sheet up to my chin. I blushed again, asking myself why on earth I hadn't made sure to wear something that covered me a little better than this frothy confection of satin, ribbons and lace. Just in the unlikely event that he'd come home and catch me red-handed, so to speak.

Or had I, in my heart of hearts, secretly wished that he'd arrive to find me sleeping in his bed? Wearing this nightgown that was as good as an invitation?

I don't know what showed on my face, but something did. His eyes turned darker and his lips softened in a way I'd seen before, usually as a precursor to his kissing me. And with me in my nightgown—and in his bed—that seemed like a very dangerous proposition. Before he could act on what I knew he was thinking, I put out a hand to stop him. The cotton of his T-shirt was soft against my palm, and I could feel the heat of his skin and the steady beat of his heart through the fabric. He glanced down, then up again. "No welcome home kiss?"

"Not here." If he kissed me here, I wasn't sure I'd make it out of bed today.

His lips curved. "Who are you afraid of, darlin'? You or me?"

"Both," I answered honestly. "I know how... persuasive you can be. And I'm at something of a disadvantage at the moment." In his bed, in my nightgown. And because I was really, really happy to see him. So happy that I couldn't be trusted to remember all the reasons why getting involved with him was a bad idea.

"You're gonna be the death of me one of these days, darlin'." He took the hand I had planted against his chest and lifted it to skim a chaste kiss over my knuckles. I smiled, but then caught my breath sharply as he turned the hand over and pressed another kiss against my palm. And there was nothing chaste about this one. His eyes caught mine, and the rest of the world receded until there was just him.

I was in his arms before I had any recollection of having moved. Mouth to mouth, chest to chest, my arms tight around his neck. I could taste coffee on his breath, and surprise, before desire knocked them both out of the way in a headlong rush. And then it was like being back in my dream from last night, all blistering need and desperation: a frantic rush to kiss, to touch, to caress.

I was vaguely aware of my back hitting the bed, of him following me down, the weight of him heavy on top of me. He had both hands fisted in my hair, the slight sting keeping me in the present instead of letting me step back, emotionally check out, the way I usually do when I'm this close to him. I've always thought it was from terror, but maybe it's just simple self-preservation. Now that I wasn't guarding myself, determined not to feel anything or remember this later, the sensations were overwhelming. I was drowning in need. His lips slanting over mine, his tongue licking into my mouth, his body, hard against mine, even through the padding of the comforter. Smooth skin, like hot silk under my hands. A thunderbolt of pure lust hit me low in the stomach, making me shiver, and I could feel his lips curve against mine. If I'd had any sense of decorum, of self-preservation left, I would have been upset by the fact that I'd given myself away, that he knew I wanted him when, as a properly brought-up Southern Belle, I should be above such base desires, but I couldn't muster the proper outrage at my own weakness. Not even the knowledge that I'd given him ammunition he could use against me if he chose, was enough to make me feel ashamed of my need for him.

The phone rang.

"Let it go," Rafe murmured against my mouth.

I turned my head to the side, which only served to allow him access to my neck instead. I didn't recognize my own voice. "What if it's important?"

"They'll call back." He ran the tip of his tongue down my throat as the phone continued its rendition of the Alleluia-chorus. I didn't want to think about how embarrassingly appropriate the ringtone was, under the circumstances.

"They've already... oh, God..." He was moving south, pushing the comforter away, his hands bunching fistfuls of my nightgown, pulling it up and out of his way. If I were going to do something, it had to be now. Another minute of this, and there'd be no return. "They're already calling back."

The phone had rung earlier, and I'd ignored it in my shock and surprise that he was here. But if whoever it was, was calling again, it might actually be something important.

I made a superhuman effort to get my hands up to his chest. I didn't push hard enough to budge him—with his hands on me, and his lips on mine, I had no strength left to speak of—but I managed to show him that I wanted him to move. He rolled over onto his back as I scrambled out of bed and snatched up the phone, adjusting the nightgown with my other hand. My fingers were shaking when I pushed the buttons, my eyes still on Rafe, unable to look away.

He lay back against the pillows, breathing hard. Pushing a hand through his hair, he scooped it back and off his forehead. He must not have had it cut in the past six weeks, because it was longer than I'd ever seen it, at least since high school. And it was a shade lighter than I remembered, too: not black but brown, like espresso. The same color as his eyes, which were hot and liquid. "Come back to bed." His voice was rough, husky with heat and promise.

I swallowed, scared by how much I wanted to ignore the phone and do as he said. "Hello?"

He was bare-chested, with a pair of faded jeans low on his hips. I had a vague recollection of running my hands over naked skin, smooth and hot, but I couldn't remember helping him off with the T-shirt. It was on the floor, several feet away, and I crossed to it on unsteady legs.

"Ms. Martin?" the phone said.

"Detective?"

Just the other day, I'd imagined Rafe in this bed, his skin warm against the white sheets, his eyes simmering with desire when he looked at me. Now I was looking at my vision, and I realized just how woefully inadequate my imagination had been.

"Did I wake you?" the voice in my ear asked.

I grabbed the T-shirt off the floor and tossed it toward the bed. It landed on the comforter, a white blotch against the black satin, but Rafe made no move to put it on. His eyes didn't leave mine. "Come here." He crooked a finger. His low voice had the roughness of velvet, trickling over my skin, raising goose bumps.

"No," I said, my voice a little too loud. He smiled, damn him. "No, you didn't wake me. I was... um... up."

The smile turned to a grin, and I had no problem reading his thoughts. Yeah, he was up, too.

I turned my back on him, deliberately. How was I supposed to think when he looked like that? When he looked at *me* like that? "What can I do for you, Detective?"

"I wanted to give you an update."

At—I pulled the phone away from my ear and squinted at the display—seven twenty-eight in the morning? "Has something happened?"

"You might say that," Detective Grimaldi said.

"What? Did someone try to break into my apartment again? Have you figured out who did it? Arrested someone?"

"No, no, and no. This is about something else."

Uh-oh. "What?"

"Remember yesterday, when you suggested I ask Sheriff Satterfield in Sweetwater to send someone to check out that trailer park where you told me Mrs. Johnson had grown up? Where Mr. Collier grew up as well?"

"Of course I remember." I snuck a glance at Rafe. He still hadn't put his shirt on, and all those muscles against the black satin were distracting, but the heat was gone from his eyes. His face was serious.

"Deputy Johnson drove out there first thing this morning."

Oh, God. "Did he find anything?"

"I'm afraid so," Tamara Grimaldi said. "He found his wife's body. Still in her car. Which was parked out of the way, behind one of the trailers."

Mobile homes, in my new professional lingo. I didn't bother correcting the detective's phraseology. "Which trailer?"

Grimaldi's voice was carefully neutral. "I'm not sure it matters, but it was Mr. Collier's old place. Deputy Johnson remembered."

Of course he did. And why I had expected anything different, I didn't know.

I swallowed. "How...?"

"She was shot," Detective Grimaldi said. "Once, through the head. Entry wound at the right temple. Close range, most likely by someone sitting in the passenger seat."

"Someone she knew, then?"

"If not, it was someone she trusted enough to let him or her into the car with her. As far as we can tell, it must have happened a few days ago. Most likely the same day she left Nashville, or perhaps the following day. We'll know more when the M.E. is finished."

"God." I closed my eyes against the picture her words painted. Over on the bed, Rafe grabbed the T-shirt and pulled it over his head. "Did she... um...?

"Do it herself?" Grimaldi suggested. "It's possible, but too soon to tell. We'll have her brought up to Nashville for examination, along with the car. My team will be cooperating with Sheriff Satterfield's staff in Sweetwater. We'll investigate on our end, they'll investigate on theirs, but because our facilities are better for crime scene and forensic investigations, we'll be handling that end of it."

"Plus, she lived here." I watched Rafe uncoil from the bed, smoothly as a panther. I had to force myself to stay where I was and not to step back when he moved into my personal space, and didn't stop until our bodies brushed. Then he grabbed my wrist and adjusted the phone so he could hear the detective, too. I wondered if he could feel my pulse tripping under his fingers.

"That, too," Detective Grimaldi agreed. "I'm going to need you and Mrs. Jenkins to come in this morning and make a formal statement about the last time you saw Mrs. Johnson."

"Of course." Gracious, how would this affect poor Mrs. J? Yet another person she cared about, another presence in her life, gone. Yet more violence heaped on violence for the old lady.

"You haven't heard from Mr. Collier, have you?"

My eyes shot up to Rafe's. His lips thinned, and he shook his head.

"No," I said into the phone, "I haven't heard a word."

Grimaldi didn't answer.

I added, "Surely you're not thinking that *he*...?"

"I'm not thinking anything. But I do need to talk to him. So when you see him, please tell him to get in touch."

I promised I would, looking up at him the whole time. His face was grim, and those eyes that had been filled with simmering heat just a few minutes ago were cold and hard.

"I'll expect you around nine." The detective hung up the phone, over my babbled assurances that yes, I'd be there, with Mrs. Jenkins in tow.

Seven

Rafe's face might have been carved in stone for all the expression it showed.

His voice was equally neutral. "She's dead."

It wasn't a question. I nodded anyway. "I'm sorry."

He shrugged, a jerk of his shoulders. The lack of grace told me more about how he was feeling than any words of his ever would.

Or maybe not. He looked at me. "Is this on me?"

I bit back an automatic, *Of course not!* "You mean, is it your fault?" I asked instead. "How could it be? You didn't shoot her. You weren't even here. Were you?"

He shook his head. "But she worked for me. Lived under my roof. Someone mighta..." He didn't finish the sentence. He didn't have to. Someone might have killed Marquita to send Rafe a message. Someone like the man from yesterday.

"What have you gotten yourself into now?" I said.

He hesitated for a moment before he answered. "Nothing you need worry about."

"What do you mean? If someone killed Marquita because of you, what's to stop them from..."

I managed to bite my tongue before I blurted out something I'd regret. But if someone had killed Marquita just because she worked for him, how much more satisfying would it be to kill me, who had been one phone call away from getting naked with him just now?

He looked at me in silence for a moment. "You should get outta here." He turned away.

"Rafe..."

But I didn't know what more to say.

I'm sorry we didn't get to finish what we started?

I'm sorry we started anything in the first place?

Now that I was away from him, out of the magnetic pull of his body, it was almost unbelievable that just a few minutes ago, I'd been tangled in bed with this man. What had I been thinking? If word of this got back to Todd—or God forbid, to my mother...!

Moving blindly, I grabbed a set of clean underwear from the suitcase in the corner, and a skirt and blouse from the closet. Rafe didn't watch me, just walked to the rumpled bed and laid down, folding his hands across his stomach like an effigy on a tombstone, looking up at the ceiling. It was the most awkward morning-after atmosphere ever, especially considering that nothing had happened earlier. Nothing I couldn't get over. And it wasn't like I knew much about mornings-after, anyway, but I could imagine that they must feel like this. He acted like he couldn't wait for me to get out of his space. So maybe what had happened hadn't meant anything to him. Maybe he was glad we'd been interrupted before anything more had happened. Something we couldn't come back from.

Feeling horrible inside, I went across the hall into the bathroom to change and brush my teeth, and then came back into the bedroom to put my nightgown in the suitcase. May as well pack, since I wouldn't be spending another night here.

Rafe still hadn't moved. If it weren't for the fact that his eyes were open, I'd have thought he'd fallen asleep. Frankly, he looked like he could use some rest. His face was drawn and the circles under his eyes almost black.

I hesitated next to the bed. To talk, or not to talk? Leave without a word, or break the silence?

Before I could make up my mind, he turned his head to look at me. Took in the change from rumpled nightgown and tangled hair to primly buttoned blouse and tight chignon without comment. His eyes lingered on my tidy hair for a second, though, and I could see the shadow of memory in his eyes: how he had driven his hands into my hair earlier, holding me in place so he could kiss me. My cheeks heated as I remembered his mouth on mine, the feeling of his hands in my hair, angling my head for the perfect fit...

So much for my attempt to take control of the situation by taming my hair.

I cleared my throat. "We have to talk. Someone broke into my apartment two days ago. Searched my bedroom, went through my stack of mail and my laptop, and slashed my nightgown with a knife. We think whoever it was, was looking for you. And there was this man yesterday..."

His eyes returned to mine. "Who?"

"He was Hispanic. About thirty five. Six feet one, muscular. Scary. Also looking for you."

Rafe shook his head. "Doesn't ring any bells."

"I know. It could be anyone. Detective Grimaldi said the same thing."

He nodded. "You really oughta get going, darlin'. You don't wanna keep Tammy waiting."

"You do know that she doesn't like it when you call her that, right?"

He smiled. I sighed. "I'll be back later to drop off Mrs. Jenkins and pick up my things. Are you planning to be around for a while?"

"Figured I'd have to be."

Great. "If you've got your grandmother taken care of, I'll move out. Maybe go to Sweetwater for a few days, until the police are finished with my apartment."

His lips curved. "You're more than welcome to stay here, darlin'."

"I don't think that would be a good idea," I said primly. "For either of us."

The smile widened. "You afraid you won't be able to keep your hands off me if you stick around?"

Something like that. "I'll be back in a couple of hours," I said, deliberately ignoring the question.

"I'll be here." He closed his eyes. I watched his lashes, long and thick and dark, make shadows against his cheeks in the sunlight streaking through the slats in the blinds, and then I walked to the door and out.

GIVING TAMARA GRIMALDI MY STATEMENT didn't take much time at all. I hadn't seen Marquita the day she left for Sweetwater, and the last time I did see her, a day or two earlier, she hadn't said anything about leaving, and hadn't been acting any different than she always did.

"She didn't like me," I explained. "The first time I met her—since high school, I mean—was in the Bog in August, and she thought Rafe had brought me there. So she took against me from the start."

And some of it, admittedly, had been my own fault. Instead of being gracious to someone who was clearly less fortunate than I, I had chosen to take offense at her behavior, and had retaliated by being condescending and snarky. As well as by patronizing Rafe, and essentially dissing Marquita to him. Yes, I knew why she hadn't liked me. Of course, she hadn't liked me before I'd done any of those things. And she had certainly let me know it, before and since.

"So she wouldn't have told you about anything that was going on in her life."

I shook my head. "Our conversations pretty much always went the same way. I knocked on the door and she told me Rafe wasn't there. I said I was there to see Mrs. Jenkins. Marquita told me I couldn't. I insisted, and pushed my way inside. She grumbled until I left."

"And that's it?"

"That's it. I don't know anything about her personal life. Other than that she used to be married to Cletus Johnson, and they separated a while back. There are a couple of kids." Who were now motherless. "She had a crush on Rafe. He swears there has never been anything between them, that they needed a nurse and she needed a job, and that's it. She was pretty good at what she did. For as long as she was taking care of Mrs. Jenkins, Mrs. J has been clean and well-fed and taking her medication regularly."

Detective Grimaldi nodded. "You can't think of any reason why she'd want to kill herself?"

"Is that what happened?"

The detective didn't confirm nor deny, just kept looking at me across the desk, and I said, "No, I can't. But I wouldn't. As far as I knew, everything was fine."

"You don't think the pressure might have gotten to her? Being alone with Mrs. Jenkins for all those weeks while Mr. Collier was gone?"

I thought about it. "I suppose it might have. Although if she couldn't handle being alone with her patient, why would she have taken the job?"

I knew the answer before I'd finished asking the question. Because it brought her closer to Rafe, during those times when he was around.

I'd spent the past two days with Mrs. J, so I had a pretty good idea what daily life with her was like, and now I tried to imagine what it would be like to spend weeks like that. I had known that my tenure was limited, that sooner or later Rafe would be back to relieve me. But if I'd been looking at an eternity of reminding Mrs. Jenkins to take her medication, of making her coffee and laying out her clothes and combing her hair, with no end in sight, I might have started to feel a little claustrophobic, too.

Not claustrophobic enough to kill myself, though. I might have been tempted to run away, to get in my car and go back to Sweetwater to hide in the bosom of my family, but I wouldn't have put a gun to my head and pulled the trigger. There are easier modes of getting away from it all, like buying a bottle of Jack Daniels or a ticket to Aruba. So where I might see Marquita being fed up with her job and her charge, and leaving Mrs. Jenkins high and dry to head to Sweetwater for a change of pace, I couldn't see her killing herself over it.

Detective Grimaldi nodded. "Those are my thoughts, as well. But I have to keep an open mind."

She leaned back in the desk chair, dark eyes steady on my face. "Now that that's out of the way, would you care to tell me what my call interrupted this morning?"

"What do you mean?" My voice sounded stiff and fake, even in my own ears.

The detective rolled her eyes. "Don't bother trying to lie to me, Ms. Martin. I have a well-honed bullshit detector, and you're a terrible liar."

I sighed. "So I've been told."

"I've gotta figure you were either asleep—and there's no reason why you would lie about that—or you were with someone."

Ugh.

"You weren't in your apartment—I know because Officer Slater was there. There was no activity overnight, by the way, other than that Mr. Satterfield showed up last night a few minutes before seven."

I nodded. "He called. We were supposed to have dinner, but I forgot. And then I forgot to call and cancel."

The detective nodded. "So what did you do with Mrs. Jenkins while you went on your date with Mr. Satterfield?"

The implication that I'd gone out gallivanting and left the old lady alone at home made me bristle. "I didn't do anything with her. I didn't see Todd. She and I stayed out all day, and had an early dinner at Burger King, and by the time we got home she was tuckered out and went to bed to watch TV. I spent the evening reading."

"So you didn't see Mr. Satterfield."

I shook my head. And realized too late where this line of inquiry was going.

She didn't bother spelling it out, just shot it at me, point-blank. "When did Mr. Collier show up?"

"What makes you think..." I bit off the rest of the sentence. What was the point of trying to deny it? She was right: if all she had done was wake me, I would have said so. And if I hadn't been with Todd, then the only logical explanation was that she had interrupted me with Rafe. I'm not the type of woman to pick up a man I don't know for an overnight quickie, and the detective knows it.

"He was there when I woke up. Sitting on the edge of the bed. So I guess he arrived sometime in the early morning." And if the exhaustion I'd seen on his face was any indication, he hadn't taken the time to sleep in the past 36 hours or so.

She leaned forward, pulling a yellow notepad closer. "You don't know when?"

"I have no idea. I woke up, and he was there."

"And then what happened?"

"None of your business," I said, my cheeks flaming.

She looked at me for a moment in silence before she asked, "Did he say where he'd been? What he'd been doing?"

I shook my head.

"Did he mention anything about being questioned by the TBI in connection with a cargo heist in Memphis last week? Half a million dollars worth of electronics and furs and brand-name clothes going missing?"

"Not a word."

"Did he mention that he wasn't supposed to leave Memphis? That he'd been specifically told to stick around?"

I shook my head. "We didn't really talk." And then I realized my error and tried to backpedal. "I mean..."

"Right," the detective said, her voice dry as sawdust.

I opened my mouth and closed it again. We'd been doing exactly what she thought we'd been doing, and she and I both knew it.

Tamara Grimaldi capped her pen and leaned back in the chair. "A little unsolicited advice, Ms. Martin."

"Call me Savannah," I said, "please. If you're going to give me advice on my love life, we should be on a first name basis, don't you think?"

She didn't answer. Didn't answer that, I should say. "I don't know you well," she continued, "and it's none of my business anyway, but I would strongly recommend that you not get too involved with Mr. Collier."

"Define 'too involved.'"

She arched her brows. "I suppose it's too late to tell you not to sleep with him. But don't make a habit of it. Don't get into a relationship with him."

I shook my head. "God, no. I wouldn't. I can't. My family would have a collective fit."

"Maybe you should consider that they have a point."

"And maybe they're just being overprotective. I'm not stupid, you know. And I haven't slept with him. You called before we got that far."

She actually looked relieved. "You might want to consider keeping it that way."

Right. "Are you sure you don't just want him for yourself? Back in August, you did seem somewhat interested in him. And not only in a professional way."

Tamara Grimaldi actually flushed. "No, Ms. Martin. Savannah. I admit the man's attractive, but I know his type too well to want to get involved with him."

The detective was discombobulated, and that was a rare occurrence. "His type," I said. "Which type is that?"

"Would you consider that he's dangerous?"

"To me?" I shook my head. "No, I wouldn't. He won't hurt me." I was absolutely sure of that. And I didn't care what Todd or even Tamara Grimaldi said.

"*He* might not. But some of the people he associates with may not be as particular. I'd hate for you to get caught in the crossfire." Her eyes were serious.

I sat up, any amusement I might have felt gone. "Have you found out anything about the man from yesterday?"

She shook her head. "I told you, the description is too vague. He could be anyone. But I'm talking about people like him. People who aren't particular what they have to do or who they have to go through to get to Mr. Collier."

Danger by association.

"I see your point," I admitted. I wasn't sure, though, whether it wasn't already too late to worry about this. After this morning... heck, after yesterday morning, the Hispanic man knew who I was, and that I'd been staying with Mrs. Jenkins. He had already considered using me to send a message to Rafe. I could perhaps cut off all contact with him—with both of them, Mrs. J and Rafe—and make sure I didn't see either of them again. That might work. Maybe then I wouldn't end up dead.

"Is there any reason why you'd need me to stay in Nashville for the next few days?"

She looked surprised. "I don't think so."

"How long will Megan be staying in my apartment?"

Tamara Grimaldi thought about it. "Now that Mr. Collier is back, chances are that whoever went through your place will leave you alone and concentrate on him. Even so, I'd like to keep Officer Slater there another day, just to make sure."

"That's fine with me. I think I'll run down to Sweetwater for the night. Stay with my mother, have that date with Todd Satterfield. Let them both see that I'm fine."

Grimaldi nodded. "Sounds like a good idea."

It did. It would get me out of Nashville, get me away from Rafe, give me time to process what had happened between us this morning and what, if anything, it meant. Plus, it would allow me to mend fences with Todd, who was probably worried about me. And who, although he couldn't turn me to goo with a look, was a good, solid marriage prospect.

I stood. "If you're done with Mrs. Jenkins, I'll take her home, grab my stuff, and hit the road."

The detective got up, too. "Drive carefully, Ms. Martin. Try not to get in Sheriff Satterfield's way while you're down there."

"Bob Satterfield likes me," I said. "He wants me to marry his son."

"Does his son know?"

"Oh, yes. Todd wants me to marry him, too. As does my mother. In fact, everyone wants me to marry Todd."

"Everyone except Mr. Collier." Tamara Grimaldi opened the door.

"Only until he talks me into bed. After that he doesn't care who I marry." I stepped into the hallway. "You'll let me know what you find out, right? And when I can move back into my place?"

She promised she would. I collected Mrs. Jenkins, who had given her statement before I did, and who was sitting in the lounge eating crackers and watching TV, and set out for the house on Potsdam Street.

When we got there, Rafe's motorcycle was gone from the circular drive, and for a few minutes I worried that he'd up and left again, and that I'd have stay on with Mrs. J. Truth be told, the idea wasn't only worrisome, either; if I stuck around, at least I knew I'd get to see him again whenever he resurfaced. But then while I was upstairs, packing the rest of my things into my suitcase (and trying hard, and unsuccessfully, to keep my eyes and my thoughts away from the rumpled bed), I heard the sound of an engine out front. I went to the window and peered out, onto the roof of a black car.

After a second, the driver's side door opened, and Rafe got out. He stood for a second, scanning the front yard, before slamming the car door, and I allowed myself to look at him, staring in a very unladylike manner.

After only two long-term relationships it may be premature to talk about types, but if I have a type of man that I always get involved with, that would be the blond, blue-eyed, well-dressed, and well-educated WASG. Wealthy Attractive Southern Gentleman. Like Todd, and Bradley, and for that matter my brother Dix. Or perhaps not Bradley, since he had turned out to be lying, cheating scum and no gentleman at all. Just tall and blond, wealthy, attractive, well-educated, and Southern.

Rafe is Southern, and God knows he's attractive, but as far as the rest of it goes, he's batting zero. Any money he has, is ill-gotten gains. He doesn't have a job, at least not a legitimate one, and he barely squeaked through high school before he went to prison. Physically, he's dark—eyes, hair, golden skin—and a few inches taller than Todd and Bradley, who both come in at around six feet. Rafe's at least six three, and he looks dangerous, with that tattoo of a viper curled around his left arm—a very muscular left arm—and with the build and reflexes of a predatory animal, a panther or mountain lion. Fluid, graceful, and deadly; tightly controlled power and strength. He doesn't look like someone you'd want to tangle with, in any sense of the word. And I couldn't quite believe that I'd done just that this morning.

I also couldn't quite admit that as I was standing here watching him, I wanted to do it again.

As if the thought had somehow communicated itself through the window and down, he turned and looked up. I stepped back, quickly, my cheeks hot. I wasn't sure whether he'd seen me or not, and I didn't hang around to find out. I turned my back on the window and went about the business of packing up the rest of my things.

Eight

arrived in Sweetwater in the middle of the afternoon. After lunch, but well before dinner.

Saying goodbye to Rafe and Mrs. Jenkins hadn't taken long. Mrs. J was thrilled to have her 'boy' back, and couldn't have cared less whether I was staying or going. And Rafe didn't look like he cared much, either. If he'd seen me gazing at him earlier, he didn't mention it. "Everything go OK with Tammy?" he asked when I came downstairs, carrying my suitcase.

I nodded. "Fine. She doesn't know much yet. It's too soon."

"D'you tell her I'm back?"

I kept my expression neutral. "She knew already."

"How?"

"She realized she interrupted something this morning. She knew that my date with Todd hadn't happened, and by process of elimination, she decided you had to be back in town."

His lips quirked. "No kidding?"

"No. That's how she knew."

"You were supposed to get together with Satterfield yesterday?" He sounded pleased. Rafe doesn't like Todd any better than Todd likes him.

I smiled sweetly. "I'll make it up to him tonight."

If I'd hoped for some kind of reaction, I didn't get one. "You headed to Sweetwater from here?" His voice was perfectly level and perfectly pleasant.

"Detective Grimaldi wants to keep Officer Slater in my apartment for one more night. She thinks that now that you're home, whoever broke in will leave me alone and concentrate on you instead, but she wants to make sure of it."

He nodded. "I'll keep an eye out."

"I'll be back in a day or two. As soon as the detective tells me I can move back into my place."

"I'll be here." He turned away. I took it for what it was, a dismissal. Carrying my suitcase, I walked out the door, got into the car, and drove away. Without a kiss, without a goodbye, without anything. Almost like nothing had happened.

It was two o'clock in the afternoon by the time I got to Sweetwater, which is located about an hour south of Nashville. I would have been there earlier, but I stopped at the office on my way out of town, to make sure nothing was going on that I needed to deal with—Tim commented on the blush in my cheeks—and then I stopped again, at Beulah's Meat'n Three outside Sweetwater, for lunch.

It was just a month and a half since I'd been at Beulah's, and had realized that an old schoolmate worked there. Yvonne McCoy was two years older than me, the same age as Dix—whom she'd always had a soft spot for—and she was one of Rafe's old conquests. Or vice versa. The way she'd explained it to me—and he hadn't contradicted her version—was that they'd been bored and curious one day, and had decided to have sex for something to do. Yvonne had enjoyed the experience and would have been happy to do it again, but Rafe hadn't offered, so that had been it.

Anyway, she wasn't 'our' sort of people, so Yvonne wasn't someone I'd known well growing up. She wasn't from Sweetwater originally—Columbia High is huge, and had students from several different small towns in Maury County—and because she was two years older and hung out with a much rougher crowd than I and my best friend Charlotte, I'd never really spoken to her until that time a month and a half ago when we'd bonded in our mutual dislike of Elspeth Caulfield.

I was annoyed with Elspeth because she wouldn't tell me what had happened between her and Rafe back in high school. Yvonne was annoyed with her on general grounds, because Elspeth, who was a fundamentalist preacher's daughter and the kind of girl who talked about being 'ruined,' disapproved of Yvonne's loosy-goosy lifestyle. She's been married and divorced a couple of times, and she's still a year shy of thirty.

She's nice, though, in her brash way. I was happy to see that she was working when I walked through the door to Beulah's.

She greeted me with a big smile. "Hiya, Savannah! Whatcha doing down this way? Slumming?"

"Coming down to spend the night with my mother and hopefully have dinner with Todd Satterfield." I slid into a booth by the back wall, under a picture of a mule in a flowered bonnet. Columbia is the self-acclaimed Mule Capital of the world. We have had Mule Days every year since 1840, a huge festival that brings more than two hundred thousand people into the area.

"Oh-ho!" Yvonne grinned. "Anything I should know about? Wedding bells?"

She gyrated her eyebrows, kind of like Groucho Marx. Apparently everyone in Sweetwater knew what was going on. It's one of the curses of growing up in a small town: everyone knows your business, and everyone's watching your every move. Especially when you're Margaret Anne Martin's perfect younger daughter. There was probably a bet going on when Todd would pop the question. I wondered whether there was one going on what my answer would be, or whether everyone just assumed I'd say yes.

I shook my head. "Not yet. He's hinted, but he hasn't come right out and proposed."

"Think he will? Tonight?" She pushed a hank of obscenely red hair behind her ear. It had been a natural copper in high school; now it was more like merlot, the texture of straw.

God, I hope not. The words trembled on the tip of my tongue. I knew the proposal was coming, but I hoped Todd would put it off a little longer. I didn't want to disappoint him, but I wasn't ready to say yes, either.

My marriage to Bradley had been a confidence-shattering experience, both while I was living through it and while it dissolved, and I was afraid to try again. If I hadn't been able to satisfy one husband, what made me think I could satisfy another? And especially someone like Todd, who already had his own failed marriage to look back on? He may have married Jolynn because she reminded him of me, but obviously she hadn't measured up. I wasn't sure I'd measure up either. I was pretty sure the Savannah in Todd's mind had only a nodding acquaintance with the Savannah who had looked at me from the bathroom mirror in Mrs. Jenkins's house this morning, and living up to someone else's expectations is a tough job.

"What're you having?" Yvonne asked when I didn't answer. I yanked my mind back to the present.

"Oh. Sweet tea and a Cobb salad. Thank you."

"You bet." Yvonne sashayed off to put in my order. Two minutes later she was back, carrying a tall glass of iced tea. "Did you get that thing figured out last month?" Lila Vaughn's murder. I'd been looking into it last time I was in Beulah's. "They didn't arrest Rafe, did they?"

I shook my head. "It turned out to be someone else. Not that I ever really thought it was him."

"Course not. How is he?"

"Fine." I couldn't help the blush that crept up into my cheeks. I'd probably blush every time someone said Rafe's name for the next week at least.

"Oh-ho!" Yvonne said again, and nudged me with her hip. "What's going on, hon? Something I should know about?"

"No. Nothing." Definitely not. I didn't want anyone in Sweetwater to know what had happened this morning. Or almost happened. If one person knew, it was just a matter of time before word got around, and then I'd be unable to show my face in Sweetwater ever again. "I saw him for a minute this morning. When I had to bring his grandmother to the police station to talk about Marquita Johnson. I suppose you've heard?"

Yvonne nodded, snapping her bubblegum. "Bless her heart."

"Did you know Marquita?"

"Oh, sure." She leaned against the edge of the table. "We went to school together. Hung out some. Not lately, though. She married Cletus and left Cletus and then she moved to Nashville to work for Rafe. I ain't seen her in a while."

"She didn't come in while she was in town?"

Yvonne shook her head. "I didn't know she was here till this morning. Suddenly everyone's talking about the other body in the Bog."

The first body in the Bog had been Rafe's mother. LaDonna Collier had died from a drug overdose sometime in July. No one was exactly sure when, since it had taken a week or more before anyone found her, and by then it was more difficult to determine time of death. Sheriff Satterfield had investigated the situation as a homicide for a while, mostly because Todd wanted Rafe to be guilty. But there had been no evidence of anything criminal—and certainly no evidence that Rafe was involved—so eventually the sheriff had had to close the case.

Now I started wondering, though, as Yvonne took in my distracted expression and wandered away to check on my salad.

Two dead bodies found in the Bog within three months of each other? That was quite a coincidence. Was it possible that the sheriff's suspicions were right, and LaDonna's death hadn't been accidental? Or self-administered? Had someone killed her, and gotten away with it, and now that same person had killed Marquita?

Not Rafe, I told myself. Rafe had been in Memphis when LaDonna died, and he'd been in Memphis again now. Five hours away. Of course, I had no way of knowing that positively, but I knew he hadn't killed his mother. I'd seen his face when I blurted out what Sheriff Satterfield was thinking. That icy menace in his eyes, on top of my knowledge that he'd spent two years in prison for almost killing the man who had beaten LaDonna black and blue twelve years ago, had removed any lingering doubts I may have had. And he *had* been in Memphis last week. Detective Grimaldi had said so.

My Cobb salad came, and Yvonne left me alone to eat it and to think. She didn't talk to me again. Not until it was time for me to go. "Say hi to Rafe," she told me then, as I was taking my credit card back at the cash register. I glanced around, guiltily, worried that someone I knew was nearby and had heard. She grinned, enjoying my discomfiture, and added, "Tell him if he's ever down this way to look me up. I'm between husbands."

"I'll do that," I said. When hell froze over.

"Here. Take my phone number." She scribbled it on the back of my receipt for lunch. "Tell him..."

"To call you. I will." I tucked the receipt into my pocket. Where, hopefully, I'd forget about it by the time I sent the skirt to the cleaners, and by the time I got it back, the ink would have run and the number would be illegible.

"Hey." She shrugged, grinning. "If you don't want him, there's no reason why I shouldn't throw my hat in. You don't want him, right?"

"Of course not."

"So, no problem."

I smiled back. "None at all. I'll make sure he gets it." When pigs fly. Yes, I was in fact aware of the total incongruity of my feelings.

As I got into the Volvo and drove out of Beulah's parking lot toward the Martin mansion, I tried to justify the discrepancy to myself, but without much success.

The thing is, for as long as Rafe had been gone, I had been able to tell myself that I didn't really miss him, that I wasn't worried about him, that I just didn't want anything to happen to him because I'm a nice person and I don't want bad things to happen to people I know. That it wasn't him, specifically, I was worried about.

All of which went out the window when I saw him.

My reaction had, frankly, scared me a little. That overwhelming relief that he was back, that he was safe, that nothing had happened to him.

The sight of him, sitting there on the edge of the bed, had been like a punch to the stomach, leaving me breathless and shaking.

And then that kiss...

I had kissed him. Granted, it hadn't taken him long to get with the program, but in that first instance, *I* had kissed *him*. And surprised him. As well as myself. I'd never kissed him before. He had kissed me a few times; once when I'd responded, once when I hadn't. But this was the first time I had initiated the kiss.

The Savannah who had launched herself at him this morning was a far cry from the prim and proper Southern Belle who had been afraid of standing too close to him just two months ago.

And I did want him. For as long as he was the one initiating the contact, the one kissing me, I could tell myself that I didn't, that I didn't enjoy his kisses, or enjoy being close to him, but after this morning, I hadn't a leg to stand on. If the phone hadn't interrupted us, I wouldn't have lifted a finger to stop things from going much, much farther.

But the thing is, I didn't want to want him. Wanting him was scary. And would surely end in misery. He wasn't someone I could have a relationship with. I couldn't marry him. Couldn't have his children. Couldn't even bring him to Christmas dinner at my mother's house, unless I wanted to make my entire family—and him—uncomfortable.

And I didn't.

Besides, he wasn't the settling-down kind, anyway. So even if I were willing to go out on a limb and get involved with him—and this morning, that had definitely been part of what I wanted—he wouldn't stick around. He might give me a few weeks, or even a few months, but marriage and children weren't options for him either. Not judging by his lifestyle so far. He might like me, but he didn't like me enough for that.

So I should just do everyone a favor and leave him alone. No matter how difficult it would be, or how much I just wanted to grab him and hold on. I should give him Yvonne's phone number and tell him to call her, and then I should sit back and wait for Todd's proposal.

Or precipitate it. There are things a woman can say to make a man want to propose. I'd gotten a thorough grounding in all the tricks during that year in finishing school. Maybe if I was engaged to Todd, my thoughts wouldn't constantly turn back to Rafe, to the feel of his mouth on mine, and his hands in my hair, and his body...

When I pulled the car to a stop at the bottom of the steps outside my childhood home, I had to keep the engine—and the air conditioning—running for a few minutes while I waited for the color in my cheeks to calm down and my breathing to return to normal. If I walked in looking like I'd been having pornographic daydreams while driving, mother would be sure to notice. I forced my mind onto innocuous subjects and waited until I could get out of the Volvo and climb the steps without setting off any alarms.

The Martin mansion is a large antebellum structure built in 1839, back in the days when the Martins grew tobacco and cotton and owned slaves. Rafe once compared it to a mausoleum, and I guess there is a sort of resemblance. It's big and red, with two-story white pillars out front.

I didn't bother knocking, just pushed the door open and walked in. This was, after all, my childhood home. "Hello? Mother?"

There was a scuffling sound from the direction of the kitchen, and then my mother's face appeared in the doorway, topped by her usual halo of perfectly tinted champagne-colored hair. "Savannah? Darling!"

The rest of her looked just as pulled together and amazing as she came down the hallway toward me, her high heels clicking a rapid rhythm against the hundred and seventy year old wood floors. As usual, she was dressed in her version of hang-out-at-home casual wear: elegant slacks and a loose silk shirt. They were covered with an old-fashioned 1950s style apron, green and white check with a bib.

The apron was covered with flour, so I leaned in from the side to peck her cheek. "What are you doing?"

She made a moue. "Didn't you hear, darling? Poor Deputy Johnson's wife died. I'm making a casserole."

Of course. When someone dies, you have to drop off a casserole. Even if the deceased has been murdered, and was separated from the spouse receiving the food. And who might even be a suspect. Usually, the police take a close look at the husband or wife when someone is killed. I wondered if Cletus would be exempt, by virtue of being a deputy, or whether Sheriff Satterfield would investigate him.

And then I wondered if he might be involved. They were separated, so obviously there had been some kind of animosity there. He had custody of the children, I knew, since he had the steady job and the income. Detective Grimaldi had told me they were fighting over visitation rights. But what if Marquita had filed some kind of motion to take them back? She had a steady job now, and God knew there was plenty of room in Mrs. Jenkins's house for couple kids. If something like that was going on, it might have given Cletus reason to want to get rid of her.

It was pure speculation, of course, but it might be worth looking into. I made a mental note to mention it to Bob Satterfield the next time I saw him. Or maybe Tamara Grimaldi would be a better recipient for this particular brainstorm.

"What are you doing here, darling?" Mother had grabbed me by the arm and was towing me toward the kitchen. Now both our sets of heels were clicking on the hardwoods.

"Didn't Dix tell you? My apartment was broken into. I've spent a few nights at a friend's house, but this morning her grandson came to stay with her, and I decided to leave."

Mother nodded. "Dix called last night. As did Todd. He was terribly worried, poor boy."

"I'm sorry. We were supposed to have dinner, and I forgot."

"Oh, dear." Mother clicked her tongue disapprovingly. I'm not supposed to forget my manners, and obviously she didn't think having my apartment broken into was reason enough for the lapse.

"I know," I said humbly. "I was hoping to make it up to him today."

She shook her head. "Oh, I don't think that'll work, darling. He left for Chattanooga this morning. Business trip. A seminar. As far as I understand it, he won't be back until sometime tomorrow."

"Really?" That was too bad. And a bit of a relief at the same time. I'd have a little more time to prepare myself.

"I'm afraid so," mother said. "He'll be sorry he missed you, I'm sure."

"Well, I was planning to spend the night. Assuming that's OK with you. Maybe I can make it up to him tomorrow instead. If he's home by then."

"Maybe so," mother agreed. "Bob and I were planning to have dinner together tonight, since he would be spending the evening alone anyway, but if you'd prefer that I stay here with you..." She trailed off.

I shook my head. "That's not necessary. I can fend for myself. Or maybe I'll see if anyone else wants to have dinner with me. I still have a few friends in Sweetwater."

"Of course, darling," mother said.

So that was that. I spent the rest of the afternoon helping mother make chicken and dumplings, and then we got in the car and drove the casserole over to Cletus Johnson's house, in a subdivision on the east side of town.

In the old days, and even while I was growing up, Sweetwater was a very segregated sort of place. There were white churches and black churches, and white restaurants and black restaurants. Obviously there were white neighborhoods and black neighborhoods. The north side, along with the historic areas around the town square, was white; the south side, with its small tract houses and sad, overgrown lots, was black. Except for the Bog, the trailer park, which didn't discriminate. As long as you were poor and common, you were welcome in the Bog.

Over the past ten or fifteen years, that had changed, at least somewhat. The Bog was empty now, and was on its way to being leveled; someone had bought the land and was planning to put up a subdivision of 'affordable' housing. I made a mental note to figure out who was in charge of that, to see if maybe I could inveigle my way into selling a few of those affordable houses once they were built. Maybe I'd have the opportunity to ask a few questions at the same time.

Cletus's subdivision was also new within the past few years, and was on the east side of town. It was called Mulberry Downs, and the streets had names like Primrose and Azalea and Goldenrod. On our way to Hollyhock, where Cletus's home was, we saw street after street of cookie-cutter houses, built of partial brick and vinyl siding, on postage-stamp sized lots. They all had big garages in the front, and the driveways held everything from BMWs and Audis to pickup trucks and minivans. Lots of minivans. Also many bicycles, trampolines, and skateboards. What realtors call a family friendly neighborhood. Mixed. It looked like Sweetwater was finally moving into the twenty first century.

Mother looked uncomfortable, though, when she pulled the car to a stop outside 541 Hollyhock. While she opened the back door for the casserole, I gave the house a quick once-over.

I'd certainly seen worse. The grass was cut, the windows were clean, and the driveway was free of toys. A black SUV was parked there, next to a white Saturn. There were curtains in all the windows and a black ribbon on the door.

Mother looked around as if she expected ninjas to appear and drag her off. "Perhaps you should stay in the car, Savannah."

I resisted the urge to roll my eyes. She can't help being the way she is, and it really isn't her fault. Entirely. "That's not necessary. This looks like a nice place."

Mom looked around again, the casserole dish clutched in her hands.

"Cletus is a policeman," I added. "I'm sure he wouldn't live somewhere unsafe. Especially with his children."

"I'm sure that's true." She didn't look convinced, though, and she kept looking over her shoulder as she picked her way up the driveway and along the flagstones to the front porch. "We won't stay long, Savannah. We'll just drop this off and go home."

"Really, I'm not uncomfortable at all. Believe me, I go to worse neighborhoods every day."

I didn't say anything else, because now the door opened. I turned to it and smiled. "Hello."

The person in the opening wasn't Cletus, although I might have been excused for thinking so, for a moment. She was in fact female, and about twenty five years older than me. Mid-fifties, at a guess, with short hair and no makeup. And she looked uncannily like her son, or at least like I remembered him from the last time I'd seen him, some years ago. Shorter by a few inches, but dark-skinned, dark-eyed, with a broad face and steady eyes. "Yes?"

"I'm Savannah Martin," I explained. "This is my mother, Margaret Anne. We wanted to drop off a casserole and give Cletus our condolences on the loss of his wife."

Mrs. Johnson blinked. After a second, she took the dish my mother mutely held out. Both of them seemed too overcome with emotion to speak when they made the transfer.

"How is Cletus holding up?" I inquired. "And the children? This must be difficult for them."

"They ain't seen Marquita much lately." Mrs. Johnson finally got it together to look from mom to me. "Ever since she went to Nashville to work, she ain't been coming by but once every couple weeks."

"Still, she was their mother..."

"A fine mother," Mrs. Johnson opined, meaning the opposite. "Running off to Nashville to shack up with LaDonna Collier's good-for-nothing troublemaker...!"

I bit back the first retort that came to mind. And the second. "I believe she worked for him," I said at last, mildly.

Mrs. Johnson snorted. "Likely that's just what she told you."

"No, actually, I—" ...*happen to know for a fact that there was nothing going on between them.* I swallowed that, too.

We stood in silence for a few seconds, until Mrs. Johnson remembered her manners. She stepped back. "Would y'all like to come in?"

"Oh, I don't think..." mother said, at the same time as I smiled brightly.

"Just for a second. To give Cletus our personal condolences." I scooted past her and into the house. Mother didn't have any choice but to follow.

Cletus's house looked just like a million others. The walls were painted in neutral colors, the floors were fake hardwood and tan carpet, the decor was typical of houses with small children: big screen TV with game attachments, a pile of toys over in a corner, small jackets on hooks in the front hall, small shoes lined up underneath. Kindergarten art on the refrigerator.

Cletus was standing in the kitchen, staring blankly at the array of casseroles ranged across the kitchen island. His mother put ours down next to the others and laid a hand on his arm. "Son."

He looked up at her, blankly. Then noticed that she wasn't alone. "Oh. I'm sorry. Mrs. Martin. Savannah."

Mother murmured something. "Hi, Cletus," I said. He and I had gone to school together, and although—again—we hadn't had much to do with one another, we were on a first-name basis. "I'm so sorry about Marquita."

He nodded.

"Does Sheriff Satterfield have any idea what happened?"

Cletus shook his head.

"I'm sure he'll figure it out. Especially now that the Metro Nashville PD is involved."

I looked around, but could see no obvious clues. No letter from the divorce lawyer pinned to the fridge, no smoking gun. "We just wanted to tell you in person," I added. "We'll leave you alone now."

"Thanks for coming," Mrs. Johnson said, as she herded us back toward the front door. Mother was in the lead, walking fast; her heels clicking against Cletus's fake hardwoods. I straggled, peering left and right.

Two minutes later we found ourselves in the car, on our way back to Sweetwater proper and the Martin mansion. Mother looked like someone who had just survived a walk through the Valley of Death, and I don't think it was the recent demise of Marquita that had so flustered her. It was probably the first time in her life my mother had been inside a black person's home, and I guess she had been surprised to see it looked quite a lot like her own.

"Are you all right?" I said.

She glanced over, with a polished, professional smile. "Of course, darling. Why wouldn't I be?"

"Can't imagine," I said, and concentrated on driving.

Nine

Sheriff Satterfield came to the house and picked mother up in his truck just before seven. Looking quite handsome, too, in his sports coat and open collar.

Todd takes after his mother Pauline, who was a cool blonde. The sheriff's brown hair is shot through with gray now that he's pushing sixty, but like his son he's tall and lean, with clear, gray-blue eyes. He and Pauline and mother and dad used to hang out together when we were small, and now that Pauline and dad are gone—Pauline from cancer, dad from a heart attack—mother and Bob Satterfield have continued their friendship. They have dinner together regularly, and always seem to enjoy one another's company. The sheriff did look a little surprised to see me, though.

"Savannah." He glanced at mother. "What're you doin' here, darlin'?"

"I drove down this afternoon," I explained. "My apartment was broken into the other day, and there's a policewoman staying there right now."

He nodded. "The boy mentioned that. What happened?"

"Nothing happened. Other than that I came home and discovered that someone had broken into my place and gone through my things. Detective Grimaldi with the Metro Nashville PD thought it might be a good idea for me to get out of there for a few nights."

"I've been talkin' to Detective Grimaldi," Bob Satterfield nodded. "Seems like a capable woman."

"She is. Very. That's right, she called you about Marquita Johnson, didn't she?"

"Sure did, darlin'. Seems Marquita left her job and never come back, and the detective thought we mighta seen her."

"And had you?"

He shook his head. "Didn't see hide or hair of her until this mornin'. And then it was only 'cause someone had the idea of checkin' the Bog."

I'd had the idea of checking the Bog, although I didn't mention that, because the sheriff continued, "If I'd known she'd be there, I wouldna sent Cletus, though. Damfool woman was givin' him enough trouble without him findin' her like that."

"What kind of trouble?"

Sheriff Satterfield had turned to look at mother, and now he turned back to me. "Pardon me, darlin'?"

"What kind of trouble was she giving him?"

He shrugged. "The usual. Movin' out. Leavin'. Goin' to Nashville to live with young Collier."

"She was working for him."

"You sure they weren't just tellin' you that?"

"Positive," I said.

The sheriff shrugged. "Todd'll be sorry he wasn't here to see you."

"He's coming home tomorrow, though, right? Mother told me he was." I glanced at her.

"Supposed to, yeah. You want I should call him, tell him you're here?"

"I wouldn't mind," I said, blushing prettily. "Mother always told me not to run after boys."

Of course, that wasn't the reason I didn't want to call Todd, but what the sheriff didn't know, wouldn't hurt him. And if he could set up a date with Todd for tomorrow night, I wouldn't have to call and do it myself. And that meant I could postpone the inevitable conversation until then.

The sheriff chuckled. "Leave it to me, darlin'. I'll call him later. Right now..." He turned to my mother, "are you ready, Margaret Anne?"

Mother simpered. "Ready, Bob."

He crooked his elbow. She latched on, and they walked out the door, leaving me alone in the house.

No sooner had the car pulled away, than I was on the phone with Tamara Grimaldi. "Detective? Savannah Martin. Any news?" I tucked the phone between cheek and shoulder and opened the refrigerator.

"Yes and no," the detective answered. "Where are you? Sweetwater?"

"My mother's house. She and Sheriff Satterfield just went to dinner." At the Wayside Inn. While I was reduced to pilfering my mother's leftovers.

Grimaldi sounded politely intrigued. "Your mother is dating the sheriff?"

"Not really. At least not to my knowledge. They just have dinner a lot."

Probably discussing me. Plotting how they could get me and Todd together. When I dated him in high school, it was mostly because I wanted to make our parents and Dix happy, not because I had any romantic feelings for him. I had always thought he felt the same way; it was only recently I'd discovered that he'd actually liked me.

"I see," Detective Grimaldi said, although it was clear that she didn't. "To answer your question, yes, we have made a little headway."

"Great." I pulled out a package of sliced roast beef and a loaf of bread, and went back to hunt for the fancy remoulade.

"I'm not so sure about that. Did you realize that there's a knife missing from your kitchen?"

"Knife?" There it was, behind the milk. I reached for it.

"From your knife block. Medium sized chopping knife. Sharp."

"No," I said, "can't say as I did. How...?"

"Megan Slater realized it wasn't with the others and had a look around for it. It's not in the apartment."

"It was there a few days ago. I used it to chop a tomato on Sunday night." I felt a chill go down my spine as I closed the refrigerator door. "That must be the knife that was used to slash my pillows and my nightgown. And whoever was in my apartment took it?"

"So it seems," Grimaldi confirmed.

"I'm not sure I like that." The idea that someone was coming after me with my own kitchen knife. Like the tattooed man from the other day. Although I'd have expected him to have his own knife, and not to have to borrow mine.

"Me, either. So be careful."

I promised I would be, while I layered roast beef on whole wheat bread with one hand. "Anything else?"

Her voice got studiedly bland. "I had a chat with Mr. Collier this morning."

"And?" I was bound and determined to allow no emotion to creep into my voice, in spite of the fact that my heart started beating faster.

"He can't prove where he was three days ago."

So much for that resolution. "Surely you're not thinking that he killed Marquita? Why would he?"

"I don't know that yet," Tamara Grimaldi said, "but he would know where to get his hands on a gun."

No arguing with that. It wasn't that long ago that he'd offered to get me one. Still...

I slapped my sandwich together. "You know, Detective, I think maybe you need to consider that you have a slight hang-up where he's concerned. In August you thought he'd killed Brenda Puckett. In September you thought he'd killed Lila Vaughn. Now you think he's killed Marquita Johnson. If he didn't kill Brenda or Lila, would you consider that maybe he didn't kill Marquita, either?"

"You know, Ms. Martin," Tamara Grimaldi shot back, "I think maybe you need to consider that *you're* the one with the hang-up where Mr. Collier is concerned."

She waited for me to respond, and when I didn't, she added, "He's a criminal. And although he's been lucky so far, sooner or later his luck is going to run out. And then he'll go back to prison. For a lot longer than two years."

"Maybe, but he won't be going to prison for murder. He's not a murderer."

"He killed Mr. Fortunato."

My mind flashed back in time for a second: to Perry's face, to the knife, the blood. To Perry curled up on the floor, clutching his stomach. His gasping breaths. My question. "*Is he dead?*" Rafe's unemotional response. "*Not yet.*"

"Self defense." My voice was perfectly steady. "And defense of me. And you know it. You didn't arrest him."

"He left!"

"He stuck around long enough for you to arrest him if you wanted to."

It was Tamara Grimaldi's turn not to answer, because she knew I was right.

"He's not a killer," I insisted. "He wouldn't kill someone in cold blood. I may not know him well, but I know that much."

"We'll see." She changed the subject. "So what's going on where you are? Obviously Sheriff Satterfield is confident, if he's taking the time out to go to dinner with a ladyfriend."

"How could he not be confident, with the cream of the Metro Nashville PD on the case?" I didn't wait for an answer. "You took the body and car to Nashville, so I'm not sure what he's supposed to be doing. But I stopped by Cletus Johnson's house today."

She sighed. "Ms. Martin…"

"Savannah. My mother and I dropped off a casserole. It's what you do when someone dies."

Now she sounded vaguely amused. "I see. And what did you discover?"

"Not much. He drives a black SUV with tinted windows. Or maybe his mother does. She was there, too, and the SUV was parked in the driveway. There was a small white Saturn, too."

"So now you think Deputy Johnson was following you the other day?"

"Probably not." Much as I wished it would be that easy. "I'm sure Sheriff Satterfield would have noticed if Cletus wasn't on duty. Unless it was his day off, of course." I put the sandwich on a plate and carried it to the dining room.

"I'll find out," Tamara Grimaldi promised. "Anything else?"

"Mrs. Johnson—Cletus's mother—thinks Marquita was living with Rafe."

"She was, wasn't she? Until he left?"

"Living with as in sleeping with. And she wasn't doing that. But if Cletus thought she was—and he probably did—maybe he got mad enough to kill her."

"Far fetched," Grimaldi said.

"How about this, then? Cletus and Marquita were separated. The kids lived with him. He was the one with the house and the steady job. But what if she was trying to get them back? She'd been working for Mrs. Jenkins for a while now, and had a place for the kids to live. That house is big enough for a whole truckload of kids, and now that Rafe has done some work to it, it's looking pretty good, too."

"So you think Deputy Johnson might have killed her because she was trying to take her kids back from him?"

"It's worth looking into, don't you think?" I pulled out one of the dining room chairs, circa 1877, property of great-great-a few more greats-aunt Marie, and sat. "I was going to mention it to Sheriff Satterfield, but it's probably better if you do it. He might feel uncomfortable investigating his own deputy."

"He might," the detective agreed blandly. "All right. I'll make some inquiries. I don't think Deputy Johnson did anything to his wife, but you're right, it bears looking into. If nothing else, we can put the idea to rest."

"Thank you."

"You don't have to thank me. I'm just doing my job."

"Right." I looked at the sandwich. It didn't look as appetizing as it had earlier. "I'll probably be down here another day, at least. It turns out that Todd went to Chattanooga for the night. I'll have to wait until tomorrow night to make him propose."

"Pardon me?"

"Nothing." I thought about knocking my head against the mahogany tabletop.

Her tone fell somewhere between incredulous amusement and amused horror. "You're trying to make D.A. Satterfield propose?"

"It occurred to me that if I'm engaged to be married, I won't be tempted to sleep with Rafe." And I couldn't believe I'd said that. Out loud.

"I see," Detective Grimaldi said. "That's drastic, don't you think? Couldn't you just practice saying no?"

"It's hard to say no." Especially to a man who has his tongue in your mouth. And when you don't want to. And God, just the thought of it had me blushing again. "Sorry. I don't know why I'm telling you this."

"I imagine because you can't tell anyone else. You need a friend, Ms. Martin."

"I have friends, Detective. They're just not friends I can talk to about this. And I kind of thought we *were* friends. Sort of. Except friends generally call one another by their first names."

She sighed. "All right. Savannah."

I smiled. "Thank you, Tammy."

"I told you, not even my mother calls me that."

"Rafe does."

"Not to my face," Tamara said grimly. "OK, Ms.... Savannah. You want some advice?"

"I'd love some advice."

"Then I think you should run as far and as fast as you can from Rafe Collier." She hung up.

So that was it. I gnawed on my sandwich and thought dark thoughts until bedtime.

I DIDN'T HEAR MOTHER COME HOME. I fell asleep pretty early, trying to recover from two very restless nights and a couple of rough days. She was there when I came downstairs the next morning, though, so Bob Satterfield must have brought her home at some point.

And of course she was bright-eyed and polished when I stumbled into the kitchen at seven thirty: her hair perfectly coiffed, her make-up perfectly applied, her clothes perfectly matched and accessorized. While I looked like a troll, with my tangle of hair, my heavy eyes, and my worse-for-wear lacy nightie.

Mother looked me over. "Oh, dear. Sleepless night?"

"Kept waking up," I mumbled, crawling onto one of the stools at the breakfast bar and resting my chin on my hand, struggling to keep my eyes open.

Mother clucked sympathetically while she stirred grits on the stove. "Bad dreams, darling?"

"Not exactly." Although she'd probably think so. A glimpse into her perfect younger daughter's subconscious would likely turn her pale with fright. Picturing me naked in bed with Rafe Collier would be pretty close to my mother's worst nightmare.

Once upon a time I would have agreed with her. It was amazing to realize that it was only a couple of months ago. Whereas now...

It would be fair to say that the idea didn't fill me with the same horror as before.

Still, it would be nice if these dreams would leave me alone. I had hoped that after I saw Rafe again, and knew that he was safe, and after I got some of the frustration out of my system, maybe I wouldn't dream about him anymore. So much for that comforting fantasy. Not only was I still dreaming about him, but the dreams had gotten quite a boost in verisimilitude since yesterday morning. Which didn't exactly make them easier to ignore.

"So what are you planning to do today, darling?" mother inquired, pulling my thoughts away from things I ought not to be thinking about anyway.

I yawned. "I didn't really have any plans. Specifically, I mean. I need to scrounge up a dress for tonight—" since the right dress is imperative for soliciting proposals, and since I hadn't realized I'd need a cocktail dress three days ago, when I packed my bag for the move to Mrs. Jenkins's house, "and I also thought I might stop by the Bog to see if I could find the contact information for the construction company that's going to build the houses there. I want to introduce myself and give them my card, and see if I can't get some business from it. Someone has to market and sell those houses, and it may as well be me."

Mother smiled. "How is the real estate going, darling?"

"It's going well. I have a house under contract in Nashville. A nice young couple I started working with a couple of months ago found a house they want to buy. They're supposed to close by the end of month." And then—fingers crossed—I'd finally make a few thousand dollars to offset some of what I'd been spending over the past three or four months of having no income.

"That's wonderful," mother said warmly. "So where are you going for your dress, darling?"

Dress...? And then I realized we were back on the subject of Todd again.

"I wasn't planning to buy one. Surely someone has a dress I can borrow. Sheila, maybe. Or Catherine."

"You can't go to dinner with Todd in one of Catherine's old dresses," mother said. "Why didn't you bring a dress, darling?"

"I didn't think about it. Didn't realize I'd need one. And I can't afford a new dress. Plus, I have lots of dresses at home already." Old dresses, from two years ago, when I was married to Bradley and had the money and the responsibility to look up-to-date. I hadn't had the money to buy anything new for a while.

"That doesn't help you here and now," mother pointed out.

"I know that."

"Audrey will make you a good deal on a dress." She let go of the wooden spatula and reached for the phone.

"I don't want..." I began, but she had already speed-dialed her best friend.

"Audrey? It's Margaret Anne. Listen, Savannah's in town and needs a new dress for a date with Todd Satterfield tonight. Do you have anything you think might work?"

Audrey is my mother's best friend from childhood, and she owns the closest thing to a designer boutique Sweetwater has to offer: Audrey's on the Square. Mother shops there; that should tell you a little about the kind of place it is. Very choice merchandise, very expensive.

"I can't afford one of Audrey's dresses," I protested when mother had hung up the phone and was back to stirring her grits.

She smiled beatifically. "She'll give you a good price, darling. Or wait... why don't I buy the dress for you? As an early engagement present?"

"We're not engaged yet!"

"But if the dress is all Audrey described, you will be by midnight." She beamed. "We'll have lunch on the square after you try on the dress."

"Wouldn't it be better to try on the dress after lunch?" That way I'd know that I'd be able to eat in it.

"Darling," mother said, shaking her head sadly, "what have I told you about gorging yourself on a date?"

"I wasn't planning to gorge myself. But I should be able to eat and still breathe. Todd will think it's strange if all I do is pick at my food. I won't have dessert, though."

"Of course not, darling!" Mother looked shocked that I'd even thought about it.

I hadn't brought that much with me in the bag from the apartment, and in the couple of days I'd spent at Mrs. Jenkins's house I had dirtied some of what I had, so I stayed around the house for a couple of hours, hanging out with mother and washing clothes. At around eleven we got into the Volvo and headed into Sweetwater proper.

It's a cute little place, if you like late Victorian construction and the typical Southern town square with a town hall on one side and three sides of red brick commercial buildings on the others.

The family business is there, started by my great-grandfather Richard Martin more than a hundred years ago: the law offices of Martin and McCall. The current Martin is Dix; the McCalls are Catherine, who spends most of her time at home with her three children these days, and her husband Jonathan.

Mother insisted on stopping in to see the family, of course. I tried unsuccessfully to demur, but it turned out all right in the end anyway: Dix was closeted with a client, and only Jonathan was available to see us. And since he knew nothing about my relationship with Rafe, that touchy subject didn't come up. I was thrilled.

Audrey's place is across the square from the law office, and she was waiting for us when we pushed the door open. I've only rarely seen a live customer in the store, but Audrey has kept the place running for ten years or more. She doesn't have a husband to support her, but she lives fairly cheaply, in a small house just a few blocks away, that she inherited from her parents and they inherited from theirs.

Other than the trip to the drugstore the other day, to replace my lipstick and romance novel, the last store I'd visited was Sally's House of Security, with Mrs. Jenkins. Stepping into Audrey's with mother was almost surreal, and for a second I was floored by the realization that my life in Nashville was so different from my life here, from the life I'd been brought up to have. The life I'd be going back to if Todd proposed and I accepted. For a second, I wanted nothing more than to turn on my heel and run out of there, as fast as I could, and never see Todd again.

Then my good manners reasserted themselves, and I smiled at Audrey. "Hello."

"Hi, Savannah!" She grinned.

Audrey and my mother are pretty much total opposites, at least physically. Mother is shorter than me, blonde, dainty and tastefully elegant. Audrey is tall, almost five ten, with short, dark hair, cut straight across her forehead and severely wedged in the back, coming forward to two points. She has fabulous cheekbones and always wears glossy, bright red lipstick. And of course she's always dressed to the nines, in dramatic colors and cuts. Today's outfit was an elegant black pantsuit, with an emerald green shirt underneath, and black and white polka-dotted shoes that put her over six feet tall.

She and mother air-kissed, so as not to mess up their respective make-up. I'm pretty adept at the air-kiss myself. I leaned in and smacked my lips in the vicinity of Audrey's cheek too.

Mother clapped her hands. "Show us the dress, Audrey. Where is it?"

"Hold your horses," Audrey said, smiling. "It's this way. I have it in a couple of different colors. Black, white, red, and blue."

"Black," mother said decisively, following Audrey toward the dressing rooms in the back. "It's so slimming."

I'm a respectable size eight, so it's not like I'm a heifer, although I will admit to having to lose ten pounds before I'd be comfortable wearing a bathing suit in public. I already own a half dozen little black dresses, though. I wasn't sure I needed another.

"But white is so simple, don't you think?" Audrey retorted. "Pure and evocative?"

Evocative of wedding dresses, I assumed. Or debutantes.

"Her eyes are blue..." mother mused, looking at me over her shoulder.

I own a few blue dresses, as well. And one or two white ones.

"Red," I said.

Both of them turned to look at me.

"Darling..." mother began.

"I already own black and blue and white dresses. I even have a wedding gown. And a debutante gown." That I didn't fit into anymore. "But I've never owned a red dress. I want one."

"I don't know, Savannah..." Audrey said.

"Can I at least try it on? If it doesn't look good, I promise I won't insist." I looked from one to the other of them. And yes, I do know that at twenty seven, I'm responsible for my own clothes and what I want to look like, and I don't actually need my mother's permission to wear a red dress. Habits are hard to break, though.

They exchanged a look.

"I suppose it can't hurt just to try it on..." Audrey murmured.

Mother agreed, although she didn't look happy.

As soon as I looked in the mirror, I knew I had to have the red dress. Even if I had to scrape the bottom of the savings account to buy it. If mother refused to buy me a red dress, then by gum, I was going to buy it for myself.

It was stunning. Thick, shiny satin, with a tight bodice and a tight skirt, hitting a demure two inches below my knees. And there wasn't anything special about it other than the fabric and the cut. Simple and elegant. No lace insets, no sequins, no beads. The neckline was square, with straps that fastened behind my neck. Half my back was exposed, and the satin clung to every curve. It managed to be demure and sexy all at the same time, with sexy definitely running ahead. My stomach tightened as I imagined someone's hands slipping over the slick satin, pulling down the short zipper in the back, lifting my hair out of the way to unhook the halter straps...

Even as my cheeks heated, I gave myself a mental slap. This dress was supposed to solicit a proposal from Todd, not a knee-jerk sexual reaction from Rafe. He wouldn't even see me wearing it. By the time I got back to Nashville, I'd be engaged to Todd, and I wouldn't be seeing Rafe again. Especially not wearing this. But even so, as I turned to mother and Audrey and announced, "I'll take it!" it was a pair of hot, dark, knowing eyes I saw in my mind.

Ten

By the time I made it out to the Bog, it was late afternoon. I'd had to try on all the other dresses, too—mother liked the slimming black, Audrey the bright blue that brought out my eyes—but I had insisted on the red, and eventually they had given in. It did look good on me, and as mother reluctantly admitted, other than the bright color, it really wasn't common at all. As if Audrey ever carried anything common in her boutique.

After shopping, we had lunch with Audrey at the café on the square, and then I drove mom home with the dress. And set out for the Bog, under the guise of wanting to look for the contact information of the construction company that was developing the land, but really to take a look at the crime scene.

Growing up, I had never visited the Bog. I didn't know anyone who lived there, and honestly, I thought driving down the rutted track from the highway would be like taking my life into my hands. The stories I heard about the Bog made it sound like the Wild West. Shootings, murders, fights... and of course the presence of LaDonna

Collier's son, who was enough in and of himself to scare all us prim and proper future debutantes into a tizzy. Even then, he'd had the kind of sex appeal and charisma that drew women. Or girls.

THE PLACE LOOKED JUST LIKE it had last time I was here, two months ago. Just after I'd found Brenda Puckett's butchered body in Mrs. Jenkins's house. I had come down to Sweetwater for mother's birthday, and when I mentioned running into Rafe in Nashville, she had told me that LaDonna Collier had died. And my mind had put two and two together and gotten five, and I had driven out to the Bog to see if I could discern a connection between Brenda's murder and LaDonna's death. Back then, I would have been perfectly happy to think Rafe guilty of both or either.

He'd been here, cleaning out his mother's mobile home, and we'd been talking—or flirting—when Marquita came driving down the track. That was the first time I'd seen her too, in over twelve years. I'd left shortly after that, with her snapping at my heels like a Rottweiler.

And now she had died. Here.

The place looked the same. The small creek—or crick—was still sluggish and brown, the trees were spindly and stunted, and the homes—ancient singlewide trailers and leaning clapboard shacks—were downtrodden and sad. There was no sign of life. Not even the chirp of a bird.

Of course, there'd been no sign of life last time either, and Rafe had been here then. Probably parked behind his mother's home. Where Marquita's car and body had been found. I looked around for the yellow crime scene tape and spied it, behind one of the decrepit fifty-year-old trailers.

Last time I was here, I had gotten the heel of my shoe stuck in a snake hole and had fallen flat on my butt in front of Rafe, so this time I was careful about where I put my feet. I made it over to the trailer without any trouble, and peeked around the corner.

There was no one there, and although I hadn't expected there to be, I was aware of a sense of disappointment. No, I hadn't really expected him to be here, but I'd been hopeful. Since I couldn't in good conscience seek him out again, it would be nice of him to oblige by finding me.

But there was nothing exciting to see behind the trailer. Just the crime scene tape strung around a sort of carport stuck to the back of the structure. I peered down, but saw nothing of interest. The ground was too dry for tracks, and the only thing I noticed was a big splotch of oil that had sunk into the dirt. Marquita's old Dodge must have had a leak, and over the couple of days it had been sitting there, the drip had made a spot on the ground.

However, the back door to the trailer stood ajar.

No reason why it shouldn't be, of course. No one lived here anymore. LaDonna was dead, and Rafe hadn't lived here since he was eighteen. Chances were the police had walked through yesterday, to make sure there was nothing inside that seemed connected to Marquita's murder, and they had neglected to close the door when they left.

The temptation was too much for me.

Looking over my shoulder first, to make sure there really weren't anyone else around to see me, I ducked under the crime scene tape and detoured around the oil spot, making my way over to the door. I pushed it open. It creaked, of course. In a place like this, it would. The trailer looked like no one had ever cared enough to perform even the most basic maintenance, and the atmosphere and oppressive silence was eerie and made the small hairs at the back of my neck stand up.

I held my breath as I climbed up the two metal steps and ducked inside.

The back door led directly into the kitchen, classic 1970s vintage. Chintzy pressed-wood cabinets with shiny brass handles, faded green laminate countertop, bottom-of-the-line faucet and sink. Almond colored scratch-and-dent refrigerator, chipped vinyl floor. Dead cockroaches with their legs in the air. I shuddered. It never ceases to amaze me how some people live.

The rest of the place was just as bad. Wandering down the narrow hallway, I tried not to feel like filth was crawling up my shoes from the dirty shag carpets. Ugly paneling and uglier wallpaper covered every wall, black mold dotted the baseboards, and the low ceilings felt like they were pushing down on me. Rafe probably had to duck his head to get past the cheap brass and wood ceiling fans.

I found what I assumed would have been his room down at the other end of the long structure. Another low-ceilinged room with thick, green shag rugs on the floor, dirty and spotted, and with a hole in the wall from when someone, sometime, had put a fist or something else through the thin material. The metal window frame was buckled and the window itself was cracked. I pegged it for Rafe's room not because of the fist-sized hole in the wall—that might equally well have been made by his Uncle Bubba, during one of Bubba's periods of parole, or by Old Jim, who wasn't averse to taking fists or his belt or whatever else was handy to both his daughter and his grandson when the mood struck him. No, whoever had cleaned the place out after LaDonna died—Rafe, as far as I knew— had either forgotten, or left on purpose, a centerfold pinned to the wall.

I wasn't sure how I felt about that.

Here's the thing: I may be naive, but I know that most men like to look at naked women. Rafe had never made a secret of the fact that he does, although I'd always gotten the impression that he preferred them living and breathing, in the flesh, to two-dimensional. Dix had hidden dirty magazines in the old slave cabin when we were teenagers, so mother wouldn't find them, and Todd might even have had the odd issue of Playboy stuck under his mattress, too. Bradley certainly had. And it had always made me feel weird when he leafed through a dirty magazine and then wanted to make love to me. And of course I'd come across Perry Fortunato's collection of nastiness a month or so ago, and been appropriately disgusted and appalled.

I knew that Perry's obsession was sick, and that it had contributed to two murders and his own death. But Dix seemed well-adjusted enough, and although Bradley's interest in looking at other women had been disconcerting—how could I possibly measure up to the wasp-waisted over-endowed bottle-blondes in the pictures?—he certainly wasn't a pervert. Rafe had never struck me that way, either.

The picture wasn't disturbing in any way, other than the simple fact that it was there. As soft porn goes, and compared to some of the stuff I'd seen in Perry's house, this was squeaky clean. It wasn't much worse than the covers of Barbara Botticelli's romance novels, if it came to that. Except for the missing hero with the well-developed chest, of course. Although I had no problem picturing him. Especially in this space.

I don't know why I should have been surprised by the fact that the woman in the picture was white. Caucasian. Blonde and blue-eyed, with pink lipstick and a French manicure. Dressed—sort of—in virginal white lace.

In my mind, and the minds of lots of people in Sweetwater, Rafe was defined by the fact that his father had been black. He was LaDonna Collier's colored boy. Different from us, from me. I had teased him about Marquita and thought about introducing him to Lila Vaughn because they were black. Now I realized, with something of a shock, that maybe Rafe didn't consider himself black. And I realized, with even more of a shock, that the two women I knew for a fact that he'd been involved with, Yvonne McCoy and Elspeth Caulfield, were both fair-skinned and blue-eyed: Elspeth a blonde like me, and Yvonne a redhead.

Coming face to face with your own racial prejudices isn't a comfortable feeling. It is, however, more comfortable than coming face to face with someone else in an empty house.

I turned around blindly, my mind spinning along with my body, and stopped with a shocked exhale when I saw someone in the doorway.

After a second, I was able to catch my breath again. I even managed an unsteady laugh. Think of the devil... "Goodness, you startled me. What are you doing here?"

"What are *you* doing here?" Elspeth Caulfield answered.

"I'm visiting my mother. In Sweetwater. And I... um... heard about Marquita Johnson and got curious. And when I got here, I saw that the door was open, so I went in."

I walked toward her. For a second, I wasn't sure she would step out of the way to let me through. If she hadn't, and I'd had to, I could probably have pushed her aside. She was small and slim, no taller than she'd been at sixteen. A mere five feet three inches or so to my five eight, although she wore sensible sneakers instead of my high heeled slingbacks, and jeans instead of my flouncy pink skirt, and if it came to running away from her, I wouldn't have a prayer.

She stepped aside, so it didn't become an issue. I brushed past her and walked down the narrow hall toward the kitchen, the skin between my shoulder blades prickling. I didn't draw a deep breath until I was outside, under the carport.

Elspeth stepped down after me. We looked at one another.

"So how are you?" I ventured.

The fact that she was here at all was freaking me out a little, and those pale blue, unblinking eyes were even more disconcerting. I would have liked nothing better than to just get in my Volvo and drive off, but that would have been rude, so I made an effort to be polite instead.

Her answer had that same dreamy calm I'd noticed last time I spoke to her. Like she wasn't quite living in the same world as the rest of us. "I'm wonderful, thank you. And you?"

"I'm pretty good too, everything considered."

She still hadn't told me what she was doing here, but I didn't think it would do any good to ask again, since she'd proven herself to be quite adept at stonewalling. Plus, I figured I could make a pretty accurate guess. She was still hung up on Rafe, and for all I knew, she might have had a habit of coming over here to gaze at the place he used to live. Twelve years seemed like an extraordinary amount of time to be carrying a torch, but after those brief couple of minutes yesterday morning, I was willing to accept the fact that Rafe might be the type of man to haunt a woman's dreams for years after the fact. He was certainly haunting mine at the moment.

Before I could think too hard about that and start hyperventilating, I thought I'd better speak up again. "Horrible what happened to Marquita, isn't it? I saw Cletus yesterday, when mother and I dropped off a casserole, and he looked absolutely devastated." A slight exaggeration, considering that they'd been separated for a while, but it's the way it's supposed to be, after all. "And those poor kids, having to grow up without their mother."

A shadow crossed Elspeth's smooth face. "Very sad, when children have to grow up without their mothers. Do you have any children, Savannah?"

I shook my head. "Bradley and I didn't have time to have any." That wasn't strictly true—I'd gotten pregnant and had a miscarriage—but it wasn't any of Elspeth's business. "We were married for less than two years."

"Sometimes it takes a lot less than that," Elspeth said. I was tempted to pursue the remark, to try to pin her down again and get her to tell me one way or the other whether she'd gotten pregnant that one time she slept with Rafe twelve and a half years ago, but before I had the opportunity, she continued. "Have you seen Rafael lately?"

"Rafe Collier?" I shook my head, lying without really thinking about it. "He left Nashville five or six weeks ago. I saw him before that, but I haven't seen him or heard from him in the time he's been gone."

OK, so the only real lie was the head-shake. The rest of it was true. He *had* left five or six weeks ago, and I *hadn't* seen or heard from him in the time he was gone. The fact that he was back now, and that I'd seen him since, was something I'd just as soon keep from Elspeth. If she was still stuck on him, she didn't need to hear what he and I had been doing yesterday morning. I hadn't been above poking Marquita, but poor Elspeth seemed so fragile, I couldn't find it in my heart to say anything that might upset her.

"I should get going," I said. For good measure, and just to make sure there were no misunderstandings, I added, "I'm having dinner with Todd Satterfield tonight. You remember Todd, don't you? From high school? You two were in the same year, I think."

"Of course." Elspeth nodded, making that cute, little, blonde ponytail bob. "Have a good time, Savannah. Tell Todd I said hello."

I said I would. Although I'd have to rewrite the story a little before I presented it to Todd. Leave out the fact that Elspeth and I had run into one another in the Bog, while I'd been standing in the middle of Rafe Collier's old bedroom. Todd didn't need to know that. "Well... it was nice to see you again. Take care of yourself."

"You too," Elspeth said, smiling sweetly. She stayed where she was, under the carport on the back of the trailer, while I walked around the corner, got into my car, and drove away. It wasn't until I was off the track and onto the road that it occurred to me that I hadn't noticed her car anywhere.

The Wayside Inn, where Bob Satterfield had taken mother the night before, is the best restaurant in Sweetwater. Naturally, that was where Todd wanted to go as well.

I didn't mind. The food is wonderful, and I'm as fond of excellent food—that someone else is paying for—as the next financially strapped woman. Plus, I wanted a place that would do justice to my new dress.

Although I had to admit, at least to myself, that I was no longer sure I wanted to wear it. At least not for the purpose I'd originally intended. With last night's dreams at a more comfortable distance than when I'd just woken up, and with most of another day between me and that episode with Rafe yesterday morning, marrying Todd solely to avoid sleeping with Rafe did seem, as Tamara Grimaldi had put it, a little drastic. So maybe I didn't need to actually make him propose tonight. Maybe I just needed to go have dinner with him, and enjoy his company, and remind myself what a nice, handsome, well-educated, perfect-for-me man Todd was. Why do anything rash, after all?

But of course there was no way to explain to my mother why I no longer wanted to wear the new subliminally powerful dress, so I didn't have a choice but to put it on. Along with a pair of strappy silver sandals Audrey had had sitting around the shop, that just happened to look fantastic with the dress while they just happened to be my size. The result was that Todd was extremely complimentary when I walked into the Wayside Inn a few minutes after seven, to find him waiting at a table for two.

"Savannah!" He stood up, blue eyes admiring as he looked me over, from loosely piled hair to skimpy dress to shoes and back. "You look beautiful!"

"Thank you, Todd." I went up on my toes to kiss him on the cheek. Normally I try to avoid touching him, since I've been trying to keep him from proposing. But I was thinking that if I got a little closer to Todd, maybe that'd help to make the closeness to Rafe feel a little less momentous. Maybe the problem was, at least partially, that in the two years since Bradley and I got divorced, I hadn't been in any kind of relationship. Todd took me out to dinner and kissed me goodnight; but a kiss outside the door at the end of the evening doesn't make a physical relationship. So maybe I'd just been so overcome by Rafe's nearness because I hadn't, to put it bluntly, gotten any for quite a while.

Todd looked surprised, and actually touched his fingers to his cheek for a second, as if he couldn't quite believe I had kissed it. I felt my heart sink. This wasn't going to end well.

Although things started out well enough. Todd ordered for both of us: white wine for me, red for himself. Grilled chicken for me, steak for himself. Black coffee for me, cheesecake for himself. Todd is partial to cheesecake. So am I, if it comes to that; I just can't eat it while I'm out with him. It's been firmly ingrained in me that a Southern Belle has a sixteen-inch waist and eats like a bird. So when Todd and I go out, I pick at my food and have black coffee for dessert, while I watch him enjoy his cheesecake. Yes, I resent it, but it's life. I'm used to it by now.

While we ate, we talked about the obvious things. Todd's seminar—a proper Southern Belle always turns the conversation first, last, and always back to the man she's with—and the break-in at my apartment and the fact that I hadn't been there when he came to pick me up two nights ago. Todd was quite concerned, he assured me.

"You should have called me, Savannah," he said, for what was at least the third, if not the fourth time. "It's not that I mind driving to Nashville to see you, but to arrive at your apartment and find someone else there... And not just anyone else, but an undercover police officer!"

"I'm sorry," I said, also for the third or fourth time, "it just slipped my mind. I was rattled, and there were arrangements to make, and I didn't even remember that I'd promised to have dinner with you until later. I'm really very sorry, Todd."

"I understand, Savannah," Todd said. And added, "But you really should have called me."

"I know I should. And I'm sorry. It just slipped my mind." I took another sip of coffee for something to do, other than apologize again. Todd is the perfect Southern gentleman, really he is, but he's a lot like a dog with a bone as well, and sometimes I just wish he'd let go of whatever it is he's gotten his teeth into and give me some peace.

The truth was that sitting here with him, I had no desire whatsoever for him to propose. He was still tall, blond and handsome, still healthy, wealthy, and perfect for me, but he was also driving me slowly up the wall. He loved me, I knew that. He wanted to marry me, and take care of me, and support me financially, and protect me from harm, and do all those things that husbands want to do to and for their wives. And I appreciated it. Sadly, though, he felt more like a smothering blanket than the safe haven I'm sure he intended to be. He was wrapping me in warm, supposedly comforting folds of caring, but I found myself clawing to free my face and be able to breathe.

The thing is, I'd gone directly from my parents' house to finishing school to university to Bradley's house, and this was the first time in my life I'd been on my own for any length of time. For the first time ever, I was responsible for myself, for paying my own rent and buying my own groceries and putting gas in my own car, and it was frequently nerve-wracking and I worried almost daily about what would happen when the money from my divorce settlement ran out. But I'd also found that I liked the independence. I could go home and not have to worry about looking perfect, or behaving a certain way, or owing anything to anyone else. I could do what I wanted when I wanted. I could wear ugly sweatpants, eat all the ice cream I wanted, and watch Cheaters on TV if I wanted, without having to worry about what anyone thought. I could read Barbara Botticelli to my heart's content without having anyone complain that my literary tastes were too low-brow. And I could get mixed up in murder investigations and hang out with Tamara Grimaldi and babysit Mrs. Jenkins and kiss Rafe... and there was nobody around to tell me I wasn't behaving properly.

So the fact that Todd made no move to propose was just fine with me.

When the cheesecake was devoured, he returned to one of his favorite subjects of conversation.

No, not the break-in at my apartment. For now, at least, it seemed we had moved past that.

"Any news from Collier?" He asked the same question pretty much every time we got together. The fact that Rafe had left and stayed gone, that every time Todd asked I'd had to tell that him that no, I hadn't heard a word, had made Todd very happy.

But all good things must come to an end. I'm a terrible liar, and Todd knows it; I didn't even try to prevaricate. "He's back."

Todd sat up straight. "He is?"

"He came back yesterday. I saw him for a few minutes."

Todd's eyes narrowed.

"Marquita Johnson died," I said. "She was taking care of Mrs. Jenkins. Now that there's no nurse, Rafe had to come back to make other arrangements."

"What other arrangements?"

"I have no idea," I said. "We didn't talk much."

Todd didn't answer. I could see from his expression that he was thinking dark thoughts. "I was hoping to have more time," he muttered.

"I beg your pardon?"

"I was hoping for more time. That he wouldn't come back so soon. Or ever."

I'm sure. "Why would you care that Rafe Collier is in Nashville? You don't have to see him."

Todd made an impatient sound. "I know I don't. But when he's around, you can't seem to stay away from him. Or he from you."

Here it was again, that awful burden of proper behavior. "I don't mean to be rude," I said, "but I'm not sure that's any of your concern, Todd." I would have put it more strongly, but I held back.

"I would like to make it my concern," Todd said.

As if he hadn't already done that. "That's nice of you, but..."

But please don't say what it sounds like you're going to say!

"I was hoping to have more time," Todd said again, more to himself than to me, "but if he's back..." He shook his head, then looked up. Reached across the table and took my hand. And squeezed it until I looked at him.

"Oh, God," I said faintly.

Todd smiled. "I'm sure you've guessed what I'm going to ask you, Savannah. I've loved you since we were teenagers. Will you do me the honor of becoming my wife?"

Eleven

I'm not sure how I got out of there, although I'm pretty sure I got out without committing myself. I know I didn't say yes. And I don't think I nodded or smiled. I managed to stammer a thank-you and tell him how honored I was, but that I needed to think about it. That's how we were told to handle unwanted proposals in finishing school in Charleston. And Todd probably knew it, because I watched his face congeal when I didn't immediately jump up and throw my arms around his neck.

"Is it Collier?" he asked.

"How could you even think that?"

"I don't know, Savannah," Todd said. "I used to think I knew you, but lately I'm not so sure. You've made some choices that I do not understand and frankly cannot condone."

My voice would have trembled if I'd let it. I refused to. "I'm sorry to hear that. I'm not entirely sure what you're talking about, but it sounds like I've disappointed you, and if that's the case, I'm sorry."

"I'm not disappointed, Savannah," Todd said, looking disappointed,

"I'm just worried. About you. And about the choices you've made. The people you associate with. The fact that you've chosen to stay in Nashville on your own instead of coming home to Sweetwater to your family, where people love you and will protect you and care for you."

"I'm twenty seven years old," I said. "I'm not going to move back in with my mother!"

I remembered, a second too late, that Todd had moved back in with his dad. It was a totally different situation, though. Todd had divorced the unsuitable Jolynn and moved back to his hometown, where he had a great job as an assistant D.A. and no need at all to feel ashamed of himself and his accomplishments. I had failed my husband, who had sought solace elsewhere, and I would have had to crawl back to Sweetwater with my tail between my legs, to live on charity in my mother's house and probably go to work for Audrey, since I'd never finished my education and had nothing to fall back on. It wasn't the same thing at all.

"Move in with me," Todd said.

I smiled, trying to make it a joke. "You, me, and your dad? I don't think so."

"Dad can move in with your mother," Todd said. "They're together half the time anyway. Or maybe she can move in with him, and we can take over the mansion." His eyes turned excited at the idea of owning the Martin mansion.

"Mother is never going to leave the mansion. And what do you mean, she can move in with your dad? How can they..." And then lightning struck and I gaped at him. "My mother and your father are involved?"

"For a while now," Todd confirmed.

"I had no idea." Although it surely did explain a few things. Like that night a couple of months ago when I'd seen them have dinner right here, at the Wayside Inn, and then it had looked like mom's bed was never slept in. I'd explained it to myself as my mother just being obsessively neat and having put it in apple-pie order the next morning, but now that I knew...

"Never mind that," Todd said impatiently. "I want to marry you, Savannah. I want to love you and cherish you and take care of you—"

...and wrap me in cotton wool and put me on a shelf.

"I told you," I said, "I have to think about it. I'm not sure I'm ready to get remarried."

He looked like I'd kicked him, and I reached across the table to put my hand over his for a second. "It isn't you, Todd. If I were going to marry anyone, I'd be marrying you. It's just that I don't know if I'm ready to marry anyone yet. It's only been two years, and being Bradley's wife was..."

"I understand, Savannah," Todd interrupted, without—I thought—understanding much at all. In fairness to him, he couldn't; I hadn't told him any of the details of my marriage. He knew that Bradley had fallen in love with Shelby while he and I were still married, and I'm sure Todd had guessed that Bradley might have been unfaithful, but I'd never told him anything about the other problems we'd had. "A failed marriage is always a difficult thing. I know; I went through my own with Jolynn. But this would be different. I love you."

"Didn't you love Jolynn?"

"I thought I did," Todd said, "but I've never truly loved anyone but you, Savannah."

He gazed at me soulfully across the table, reaching for my hand again. I felt like a giant millstone was being tied around my neck.

He loved me.

Well, of course he did, I told myself. That's why he wanted to marry me. He loved me and wanted to spend the rest of his life with me. Marriage made sense.

It made sense to me too, if it came to that. Like I'd told him, if I wanted to marry anyone, I'd marry Todd. Who else could I marry? The only other man in my life was Rafe, and even if he miraculously did want to get married, which he didn't, it wasn't like I could marry him.

I just wasn't ready to say yes to Todd.

"I need to think about it," I told him again. "It isn't you. I swear. And of course it isn't Rafe. You can't seriously believe that I'd want to marry Rafe Collier. Or that I'd pick him over you."

Todd didn't answer.

"It's me. It's all me. I just need some time to think. To make sure I'm ready."

"Take all the time you need," Todd said. What else could he say, after all? But I could tell he was disappointed. I'm sure he'd expected, or at least hoped, that I'd be overcome with emotion and if not say yes on the spot, at least tell him I loved him too.

I couldn't blame him for the disappointment. I couldn't in good conscience say the words, though, when I wasn't sure I did. I wasn't sure I even knew exactly what it meant.

I wasn't brought up to consider love as a particular requisite of marriage. When Bradley proposed, I'd said yes because he was young, handsome, Southern, able to take care of me, and because it was the first proposal I'd gotten. I was twenty three and not getting any younger. And I wanted an excuse to drop out of law school, because I wasn't enjoying myself. I didn't really have a reason to say no. Marrying Bradley—or someone like him—was what I was supposed to do. It was what mother had done when dad asked her. And I'd never doubted that my mother and father loved one another. She had told me that they did. That love came after marriage, from a lifetime of being together. Of being committed to one another, to building a life together, to the same values and beliefs.

We'd all been brought up the same way, all three of us. Catherine and Jonathan seemed happy enough, I thought, as did Dix and Sheila. Catherine had been quite enamored with Jonathan when they first met, but of course he was a Yankee, so things were a little different for them. Dix and Sheila were more of the traditional Southern couple:

two young, healthy, attractive people from two old families getting married and living happily ever after; without a whole lot of passion, perhaps, but with what seemed like a perfectly nice relationship. They got along well, they didn't argue, they had two beautiful little girls...

And if I married Todd, I would have the same thing. A comfortable, comforting relationship with a man who loved me, and who would provide for me and protect me and love me and cherish me. A man whom I liked in return, and whom, if I didn't feel like I loved him right now, I would grow to love in time.

So was it wrong for me to wish for more than that? A little passion? And maybe some clarity? Because if I couldn't bring myself to tell him that I loved him, surely I had no business thinking about marrying him.

We'd arrived at the Inn in separate cars, Todd directly from Chattanooga, and he walked me to mine. Once there, he took me in his arms and kissed me. His mouth was warm and soft, and his arms tight around my body. His lean body was hard under the tailored gray suit, and I leaned in and kissed him back, doing my best to put some feeling into it.

When he let me go, Todd was breathing faster. "I'll be waiting, Savannah." He gave me one last long look before he turned on his heel. I watched him walk away. And then I got in my car and drove out of the parking lot and onto the Columbia Highway.

I wasn't thinking too clearly, or I would have gone back to mother's house for the night. Or at least to pick up my suitcase and the rest of my things. I didn't. I got in the car and started driving. Once I hit Interstate 65, I turned north and drove some more, through the dark and silence. It wasn't but an hour later that I saw the lighted twin towers of the Batman building above the trees in the distance. Downtown Nashville. Home, sweet home.

The driveway of 101 Potsdam Street was empty, although the porch light was turned on. I tried not to feel like I was standing in a spotlight when I knocked on the door and waited. Feeling like an idiot in my satin dress and strappy silver shoes. Wondering if I didn't look like one, as well.

At first I didn't think anyone would answer. Maybe Rafe had done the smart thing and taken himself and Mrs. Jenkins off somewhere safe, until whatever was going on blew over and Marquita's murder was solved and the Hispanic man had moved on to another victim. I wrapped my arms around myself, shivering with a mixture of cold and nerves, and considered leaving. Considered where I might go, with Officer Slater presumably still in my apartment.

The office? A motel? Back to Sweetwater? It was only ten thirty; I could be back there and in bed by midnight.

I was just about to turn and retrace my steps to the car when the door opened. Soundlessly. Seemingly on its own.

I swallowed. "Rafe?"

No one answered. The door stopped moving, halfway open. I peered into the darkness. "Mrs. Jenkins? Anyone?"

There was still no response. I moved a little closer, my heart thudding in my chest. "Hello?"

And then I lost my breath when an arm shot through the opening, grabbed me, and yanked me inside. The door slammed shut as I tumbled against a hard, male body.

For a second neither of us moved. Then...

"Have you lost your mind?" Rafe asked, his voice rough as he set me upright. "What're you doing here this time of night? Dressed like that?"

I tried to fill my lungs, but couldn't quite manage. Between the surprise and fear—fading now—the tight dress and the nearness of him, I was feeling lightheaded.

"C'mon." He led the way down the hallway toward the kitchen, moving like a cat through the darkness. I stumbled after.

The light was on in the kitchen, and it felt homey and friendly. A small TV was playing on the counter—basketball—and a bottle of beer was open on the kitchen table next to a bag of salted cashews. He glanced at me. "Hungry?"

I shook my head. "I had dinner."

"Course." Those dark eyes moved over me. Snagged here and there on the way. My hair, my mouth, the pulse beating at the base of my throat, the top of the dress, the bottom of the dress, and then lingering in the same places coming back in the other direction. He ended by looking into my eyes, his own flat and black, giving nothing away. "Date with Satterfield?"

I nodded.

"Nice dress." He turned away. Grabbed the bottle of beer and lifted it. When he put it down again, it was empty.

I tore my eyes away from the movement of his throat, the muscles in his upper arm, tight under the sleeve of the blue T-shirt. "I bought it this morning. Thinking it might make him propose."

For a second I wasn't sure he'd answer. Then he did. As usual not by responding to what I'd said, but what I had taken care not to say. "Yesterday morning scare you that much?"

Trust him to hit the nail squarely on the head.

I shrugged. Yes. And no. Considering that while I was trying the dress on, I'd also been thinking about him taking it off me.

And what on earth was wrong with me, that I could be thinking about Todd proposing and Rafe undressing me almost in the same breath?

He went to the fridge, pulled out another beer. Held one up with a question on his face.

I shook my head. "I had wine with dinner."

He nodded. Put one of the bottles back and closed the refrigerator door. Then he opened the other bottle and poured half the contents down his throat before he asked, "So how did it go?"

"What?" I had to refocus my eyes again. "Oh, dinner? Fine."

"He propose?"

"He did. Yes."

"Congratulations."

"I didn't say yes." Of course, I didn't say no, either.

"Why go to all the trouble if you were gonna turn him down?" He gestured to the 'trouble'—my dress and hair—with the bottle.

"I didn't know I was going to turn him down until..." I hesitated, "he asked."

He put the bottle on the table and folded his arms, long legs in snug jeans crossed at the ankles. The pale blue T-shirt had a washed-out Corona logo on the chest, and it had been soft when I fell against him earlier. Almost as soft as the skin underneath. The skin I'd had my hands on just a day and a half ago.

I looked away, but not fast enough, because I could see his lips curve.

He didn't comment, though. "What happened?" he asked instead, his voice almost warm.

His eyes were warm too, and a little amused. "I came to my senses," I said.

"Meaning?"

"Marrying Todd because I'm afraid of you seems rash."

Something moved in his eyes. "Why are you afraid of me?"

"Because you—" ...*do things to me, and make me feel things, that no one else does. You make me question everything I've always known to be true and make me want things I know I can't have.*

I couldn't tell him any of that, though, so I just shook my head. "I'm not. Not the way you think. And it isn't really about you. It's about Todd. I looked at him sitting there, across the table, and I just... couldn't."

Rafe nodded. "I know the feeling."

"I'm sure you do." There must have been dozens of women up through the years who had wanted him to commit, when he didn't want to. "And that reminds me, I've seen a couple of your old girlfriends recently. Elspeth Caulfield today. And Yvonne McCoy yesterday. She said to give her a call sometime. She gave me her number to give to you, but I left it in Sweetwater."

"On purpose?"

"Of course not. Why would I do that?"

He smiled. "Did Elspeth tell me to call her, too?"

"I didn't mention that I'd seen you," I said. "She's weird. I met her in your old bedroom in the trailer in the Bog."

Both brows shot up this time. "My bedroom?"

"The one with the green rug and the naked girl on the wall, right?"

He nodded. "I don't recall her being naked. Totally."

"She might as well have been, considering the size of the... fabric scraps she had on."

"Not too different from the fabric scraps I imagine you might have on under there," Rafe said, with another look at my dress. Before I could react, he'd continued, "What were you doing in my bedroom? Both of you?"

"I don't know about Elspeth, but I was curious. The door was open, so I went in."

He stuck his hands in his pockets. I wondered if he was fighting an impulse to shake me until my teeth rattled. Or some other impulse. "What were you doing in the Bog in the first place? Not your kinda place, is it?"

"Hardly. I wanted to see where Marquita's car was found."

"Playing Nancy Drew again?"

I shrugged.

"Find any clues?"

"None. Unless the naked girl on your wall is a clue. Or Elspeth."

"I wouldn't think so," Rafe said. "The naked girl's been on my wall since I was sixteen. And Elspeth—"

"She's been hanging around since you were sixteen, too. Or close to it."

He smiled. "Can we go back to Satterfield for a minute? I wanna make sure I understand something. He asked you to marry him, and you turned him down?"

"Not exactly. I didn't say no. Although I didn't say yes, either."

"Why?"

"I already told you. Marrying him because I'm..."

"Yeah, we covered that. Except you're not afraid of me. Or so you say."

"I'm not." Not the way he thought.

He shifted his stance. "I just can't wrap my head around this, darlin'. Satterfield's gainfully employed, well-off, polite, pure-bred..." He was ticking items off on his fingers as he listed them, "and he knows what fork to use at dinner. He's just the kind of guy a nice girl like you's supposed to marry, ain't he?"

"Maybe I'm not such a nice girl," I said. Muttered, rather. When he didn't answer, I snuck a peek at him under my lashes. He quirked a brow.

"You trying to tell me something, darlin'?"

I hesitated. "I'm not sure what I'm trying to do," I admitted eventually. "I just know that I looked at him, and I couldn't go through with it. See, I did what I was supposed to do when I married Bradley. I was twenty three, and I thought I knew how life worked. I bought into the whole fairytale, the one about 'gainfully employed, well-off, polite'... I did everything I was supposed to do, and look where it got me. I'm divorced, I'm alone, I'm terrified of trying and failing again. I'm afraid that if I marry Todd, it'll be more of the same."

"Satterfield won't cheat on you," Rafe said. "He worships the ground you walk on."

I nodded. "He says he loves me. And I don't know why that should sound like a prison sentence, but it does."

The words were just pouring out, and I had no idea how to stop them. "I'm afraid he'll use it as an excuse to suffocate me. From the very best of intentions, of course. He wants to keep me safe, so he'll try to keep me from doing anything, just so nothing happens to me."

"It's natural," Rafe said.

"Maybe." Although I didn't have to like it. "I know I should marry him. We have so much in common, and he's my brother's best friend and my mother loves him. But Bradley and I had a lot in common, too, and look how that turned out. Why would this be any different? I mean, what if I don't grow to love him? I'll be stuck in a marriage to a man I don't love. *Another* man I don't love. And not to be vulgar, but I spent two years faking orgasms for Bradley. I don't want to do it for the rest of my life."

For a second, Rafe's expression turned blank, before it melted into amusement again. I blushed, giving myself another of those mental slaps. He was so easy to talk to, and so unconcerned with proper behavior, that I found it only too easy to tell him things I wouldn't dream of telling anyone else. All sorts of confessions fell out of my mouth when I was talking to him.

"Sorry," I muttered, my cheeks hot.

His voice was uneven, as if he were trying not to laugh. "No problem. I already knew you and Bradley had problems in bed."

I'd told him that, in another moment of temporary insanity, soon after we met. Thinking that if he knew I was frigid, if I told him that I hadn't been able to satisfy my husband in bed, it might make him back off. Instead he'd informed me that just because Bradley couldn't get the job done, didn't mean that he couldn't.

"And," he added, "I told you I could help you with that."

"I know you did."

"So is that why you're here?"

"I don't know why..." I said, and then I stopped. Took a breath and faced facts. "Yes. That's why I'm here."

That, and because I couldn't seem to stay away. Because my car had somehow found its way here without conscious thought on my part.

Because this was where I'd gone, where I'd run, instinctively. Just like I'd run to him in my dreams last night.

"You want…" It was his turn to stop, to consider his words. "You wanna finish what we started yesterday."

I nodded. I didn't exactly agree that what was between us had started yesterday, but yes. I wanted to finish it.

"And then what? I can look forward to the future Mrs. Satterfield thinking about me whenever it's time to fake another orgasm?"

His eyes were bright and intent. I opened my mouth to say that I hadn't meant it exactly like that, but then I closed it again when I realized that maybe that was exactly what I'd meant. It was a sobering thought.

"If you don't want to…" I said instead.

"There ain't a chance in hell that I don't want to. I just wanna know what I'm getting into first."

Right. "I'm not going to do an Elspeth and chase you for the rest of your life, if that's what you're afraid of."

"Yeah," Rafe said, "that's what I'm afraid of. You chasing me for the rest of my life."

I took a deep breath. This was not going the way I'd wanted at all. "You know, I can tell that this was a bad idea. I don't know what I was thinking, to come here like this. So I'm just going to pretend that this didn't happen and leave now…" I turned on my heel to do just that. And before I had taken more than a single step, I was spun back around, and then pushed up against the front of the refrigerator, the cool metal against my bare back and the heat of his body against my front.

For a second or two, I couldn't breathe.

He had done this to me once before. Slammed me up against a wall and kept me in place with his body. That had been in public, with people walking by; people who probably thought, from his stance and body language, that something amorous was going on between us.

Nothing had been. Not then. He'd actually been threatening me. Intimidating me, by standing too close, leaning in, with all that tightly coiled strength just a breath away. Using his height, his bulk, the fact that he knew his easy sexuality was frightening to me, to keep me there, like a bug under a microscope.

He was doing it again now. In a totally different way. One hand was braced next to my head and the other slipped across the satin of my dress, sliding the fabric against my skin. I couldn't have moved if I'd wanted to. When he leaned in to nuzzle my ear, to skim his lips down my neck to the pulse beating double-time at the bottom of my throat, I caught my breath in a gasp, and felt his mouth curve. He didn't say anything, though, just moved to slide a jeans-clad thigh between my knees and up, pushing the dress along with it.

My legs turned to water, and I clutched at him, bunching fistfuls of that soft, blue T-shirt as my eyes threatened to roll back in my head.

He chuckled. And turned me around, from the fridge to the kitchen table, boosting me up on the edge. And then his hands were there, sliding the dress up, out of his way, so he could step between my thighs.

"Here?" I managed, more breath than actual sound behind the single word.

His voice was husky. "I bet Bradley never made love to you on the kitchen table."

He'd win that bet. Bradley had been pretty traditional in bed. And we'd always been in bed when we had sex. Honestly, I wasn't sure I could handle sex anywhere else. Sex with Rafe at all was frightening enough. But sex on the kitchen table, with the lights on, and a bag of salted cashews next to my ear...

And what if Mrs. Jenkins got peckish and came downstairs for a snack?

In fact, maybe we shouldn't be doing this at all, with Mrs. J in the house. I couldn't believe I'd forgotten about her in the heat of the moment.

"What about your grandmother? She could walk in on us..."

"I sent her to a safe-house," Rafe said, back to nuzzling my neck. "It's just us."

His fingers were skimming over my back, pushing through fallen tendrils of hair to unhook the back closure of my dress, and I barely managed to get my hands up in time to catch the bodice before it fell. He arched a brow.

"No... um... scraps of fabric." I blushed.

He grinned, a flash of white teeth against golden skin. The big, bad wolf getting ready to devour Little Red Riding Hood. "You going commando?"

"Not completely. I've got... um..." Panties on. Underneath. But the bra was built in. With a backless dress, there's really no other option.

"No wonder Satterfield proposed." He stepped back to look at me. I was clutching the dress to my breasts, my cheeks flushed and my skirt hiked up to my hips, much like a heroine on the cover of one of Barbara Botticelli's romances. By the time they returned to mine, his eyes were simmering with heat, and his voice rasped across my skin, raising goosebumps. "Let go of the dress, Savannah."

"I..."

Can't. I mean, how could I just drop my hands? The top of the dress would fall and I would be practically naked. In front of him. On the kitchen table. With the light on. It would be embarrassing. And unsanitary. Not to mention indecent. I was brought up to be a nice girl, and nice girls don't undress in front of men who look at them with hot, dark eyes and think hot, dark thoughts...

He smiled. "Would you be more comfortable upstairs?"

I nodded.

"C'mon, then. We can do it on the kitchen table next time. Or the time after."

If there was a next time, or a time after that. And there probably wouldn't be. But I didn't say anything, just slid off the edge of the table. My legs were unsteady, so he had to hold me, and the dress still bunched around my hips, although it started settling after the first few steps toward the door. He was hustling me along, down the middle of the hallway, until, halfway down, he turned and pushed me up against the wall and kissed me, and I forgot all about the bodice and my lack of underwear, and suddenly I was half naked and clinging to him, and I thought it was going to happen right then and there—

And that's when there was a loud bang and a tinkling sound, and Rafe yanked me down to the floor and rolled me underneath him, and there was absolutely nothing romantic about it at all.

Twelve

His voice was a tight whisper in my ear. "Stay down."

I nodded, my teeth chattering. I wasn't going anywhere. I recognize a gunshot when I hear one, and this one had come uncomfortably close. I'd also recognized the tinkling of the glass in the window next to the front door where the bullet had pushed through. I swear I'd even heard it zoom by, although that was probably just my imagination.

He added, "Are you hit?"

I shook my head. "You?"

"No." He lifted his head. Personally, I couldn't hear anything but the rushing of blood in my ears and the frantic pounding of my heart, but after a second, he rolled off me and got to his feet.

"Rafe...!" I sat up and reached for him, panicked. What if the shooter—the Hispanic man?—was right outside the window, and tried again?

"He's gone." He glanced down at me. I could barely make out the gleam of his eyes in the dark. He must be able to see better than I could, though, because after a second, I could see the gleam of his teeth, too, as he took in the sight of me sitting there, with my skirt twisted high on my thighs and my dress down to my waist. He could probably even see the flood of color that rose in my cheeks. I hiked the bodice over my breasts and reached up to fasten the straps.

"Shame to do that," Rafe remarked.

"I don't want the police to find me on the floor with my dress half off."

"In this neighborhood, we'll prob'ly have to call 'em ourselves if we want 'em. Although seeing you like that would make Truman's day. It's made mine."

I smiled, a little shakily. Patrol Officer George Truman is no more than twenty two, and he blushes if I look at him for too long. "Someone else will call them, don't you think?"

"We'll see." He moved toward the front door, silently, staying close to the wall. I held my breath, but nothing happened. In the distance, we could hear a car starting up and driving away.

"There he goes," Rafe said, not bothering to lower his voice. "Shit."

"At least he's gone."

He glanced at me as I came up next to him. "Yeah, but I didn't get a look at him. I wanted to see if it was the guy you told me about."

"That's why the porch light was on." I felt like a slow child trailing behind. "You expected this. That's why you sent Mrs. Jenkins away. And that's why you were upset when I showed up."

He shrugged. But he didn't deny it.

"Why didn't you tell me to leave?"

"Before or after you told me you wanted to sleep with me, darlin'?" He shook his head. "I figured you were safer in here than out there. But then I got distracted."

"God, I'm sorry."

"Yeah, I really wish none of that woulda happened, too." The tone was definitely sarcastic. "I should be apologizing to you. You coulda been hit. And it woulda been my fault."

"He wasn't aiming for me. He was aiming for you." And because I'd distracted him, he might have died.

"That's if it was the same guy you met," Rafe reminded me. "And anyway, we were standing kinda close together. Wouldn't be hard to shoot the wrong person."

That was unfortunately true. "What do you mean, if it was the same guy? Who else could it be? How many people do you have gunning for you at one time?"

"By now? Could be a few." He turned to look out the broken window, the glass on the floor crunching under his feet as he shifted his weight. I looked up at him.

"What did you do, Rafe? Detective Grimaldi mentioned a cargo heist in Memphis. Lots of merchandise worth a lot of money missing, and the TBI talked to you about it."

"The TBI talked to a lot of people," Rafe said, without meeting my eyes.

"It isn't the first time they've looked at you for something like that, though. Todd was telling me about the weapons thefts at Fort Campbell military base, and the tractor trailers in Knoxville—or maybe it was Chattanooga or Jackson—and of course there was the open house robberies here in Brentwood in September, and the TBI have talked to you about all of it, and somehow you always manage to slither through their fingers and away..." While everyone else around him seemed to get arrested. "No doubt Satterfield told you it's because I'm some sorta criminal genius." He looked at me, his eyes steady. "What do you think, Savannah?"

He only called me Savannah when he was being serious. The rest of the time he called me darlin'. So my answer right now mattered.

"I'm not sure what to think," I admitted. "I really don't want to believe that you're a criminal, but you know how to do a lot of things that normal people don't." Like opening locked doors with my hairpins and intimidating bad guys. He seemed scarily familiar with knives, and having guns pointed at him and shots coming his way certainly didn't faze him for long. Nor did the sight of dead bodies or even having to stab a man to death. Like the Energizer Bunny, he just kept going. "And if the TBI keeps connecting you to crimes..."

"There's another reason they could be talking to me and letting me go, you know."

If he was innocent. I nodded. "But you're involved. At least you were involved in the open house robberies. And Todd seemed pretty positive you had something to do with the other things, too."

"So...?"

"So if you're not innocent, you're either a criminal mastermind, or..." ...what?

He didn't say anything, just watched me puzzle it out for myself. It didn't take long. I'm not actually stupid, and he had given me some pretty broad hints. I stared at him, my eyes enormous and my mouth open. "You're working for them. Aren't you?"

He didn't answer. But he didn't deny it, either. I closed my mouth, and opened it again. "For how long?"

He answered that, anyway. "Since I got out of prison."

"Todd told me you were recruited by a criminal organization while you were there." The Tennessee Bureau of Investigation is hardly a criminal organization. Not in that sense of the word.

"I was. That's what did it. The TBI figured I was their way in. So they sprung me early."

"And you've spent ten years undercover."

He shook his head. "I've spent ten years doing what I prob'ly woulda been doing anyway. And feeding the TBI some information about it along the way."

And probably making a lot of people suspicious about why he kept skating through while all around him, people were caught and arrested.

A sound outside made us both look out the window. It was a car, turning onto the graveled drive. A black and white patrol car.

"Here they come," Rafe said. I nodded. "You wanna go upstairs? Pretend you're not here? They're not gonna search the place."

I hesitated. My car was parked outside, so even if the cops weren't ones I already knew, who already knew me, they'd make a note of the fact that it was here. "They're going to guess what we were doing, aren't they?"

The corners of his mouth turned up. "Anyone who looks at you is gonna guess what we were doing, darlin'."

"Great." Not.

Still, I didn't go upstairs. Outside, the police car pulled to a stop and the passenger door opened. George Truman stepped out. After a second, Lyle Spicer's graying head emerged from the driver's side door. He adjusted his gun belt under his paunch and looked at the house. When he saw the two of us peering at him out of the broken window, he shook his head in resignation.

"You two again," he said when Rafe had unlocked the door. "What happened this time?"

I let Rafe answer, since I wasn't entirely sure how much the police knew about what was going on with him, and how much he'd want them to know.

"We were in the kitchen, back there..." He pointed, "when there was a gunshot out here. Through the window."

"Uh-huh." Spicer looked down at the shards of glass on the floor. "Then what?"

"We hit the floor. When we heard a car drive away, we came out here to look at the damage."

OK, so it was a little different from the truth, but that's essentially what had happened. With a few minor omissions. And it wasn't like I could complain about what he had left out. I certainly didn't want Spicer and Truman to know that when someone had shot at us, I'd been pretty close to having sex standing up in the hallway.

"Any idea who mighta wanted you dead?" Spicer asked as Truman prowled the hall. He stuck his head through the door to the kitchen, flicking on the ceiling light, and took in the two beer bottles on the table—one empty, one half full—and the bag of nuts, along with the TV, which was still playing, sound muted. "Either one of you?"

"Coulda been anyone," Rafe answered with a shrug.

"Right." Spicer looked from him to me. "Miz Martin?"

"What?... Oh, you want to know if there's anyone who wants me dead? Not that I know of. Although there's whoever broke into my apartment the other day. But they wouldn't have known that I'd be here. *I* didn't know I was going to be here until about thirty minutes ago. I had a conversation a couple of days ago with a man who wanted Rafe dead, though."

Spicer's eyebrows crawled up his forehead as he glanced at Rafe. The latter's face was carefully blank.

"She told me about it," he said. "I have no idea who it mighta been. The description coulda been anybody, pretty much."

Spicer looked back at me. "Didya happen to report it to anyone?"

"I told Tamara Grimaldi," I said. "She said the same thing. It could have been anyone. Hispanic man, mid thirties. Black hair, brown eyes. Some sort of tattoo on his back. Six feet tall, give or take."

"We can do a canvass tomorrow," Officer Truman suggested, over his shoulder. "See if anyone in the neighborhood has seen anyone like that hanging around."

Spicer nodded. "See if anyone saw this car you heard drivin' away, too. Where was it, d'ya think?"

Rafe and I exchanged a look. "That way?" I suggested, pointing vaguely to the left. He nodded.

"Parked a coupla houses down, most likely. He had time to get there after he fired. If he moved fast. Someone mighta seen him. Or the car."

"We'll check it out," Spicer said again. "And I'll give the detective a call, too." 'The detective' is what he calls Tamara Grimaldi. As if she were the only detective at the Metro Nashville PD. "Anything else?"

Rafe and I looked at one another again. "I can't think of anything," I said. He shook his head. I turned back to Spicer. "Thanks for coming out."

Spicer nodded. "Always a pleasure seein' you, Miz Martin. Mr. Collier." He winked at me. "Nice dress."

"I had dinner with D.A. Satterfield earlier tonight."

"Right." Spicer glanced up at Rafe on his way past, perhaps wondering what I was doing here, after having dinner with Todd Satterfield. Or maybe not wondering. Then he looked at the broken window. "You better put something over that. And clean up the glass."

"Soon as you're gone."

Spicer grinned. "We'll be back in the morning to dig out the bullet." He gestured to Truman. "C'mon, kid. Time to go. These folks wanna be alone."

Truman grinned too, but moved through the door without comment, other than a polite nod. "Ma'am."

"Nice to see you," I managed.

I stood at the window and watched them drive away while Rafe went into the kitchen. He came back with a piece of cardboard and a roll of duct tape. And then he proceeded to tape the cardboard to the window, ripping off pieces of tape with his teeth. The window had broken in a sunburst pattern, with a tiny hole in the middle and a bunch of cracks radiating out from it. Some of the shards had broken off, but all in all, the hole was actually quite small, considering how big a bang there had been. I wondered where the bullet had ended up.

"Wall over there," Rafe said when I asked. He nodded toward the back of the hall, past the place where we'd been standing earlier. "By the kitchen door. Didn't miss by much."

When I moved away from him to take a look, he raised his voice. "Leave it. They'll get it tomorrow."

I nodded.

"There's a broom and dustpan in the pantry in the kitchen, if you wanna make yourself useful. Get some of this glass up."

"Of course." I moved down the hall toward the kitchen, glancing at the neat bullet hole on my way past, and marveling at the incongruity of my life. Here I was, wearing the satin dress and silver sandals I'd bought for Todd Satterfield, on my way to fetch a broom and dustpan to sweep up broken glass in Rafe Collier's hallway, after almost getting shot and almost having sex. Talk about situations I hadn't expected to be in when I woke up this morning.

After the window was taped and the glass removed to the trash can in the kitchen, Rafe looked at me. Up and down. Rumpled dress, tangled hair, smeared make-up. He seemed amused. "When I said there'd be fireworks, this wasn't what I meant."

"Me either." I smiled weakly.

"Guess the moment's pretty well shot to hell."

He was watching me. Trying to gauge whether I still wanted him, I suppose, or whether I was off the whole idea now.

"I guess so."

Maybe he was the one who was off the idea. I wouldn't blame him, if so. Someone had just tried to kill him, and that had to be upsetting. No matter how used to it he was.

He folded his arms. "It's a long drive back to Sweetwater."

I nodded. "That policewoman is still in my apartment. At least I think so; I haven't heard that she isn't."

"You're welcome to spend the night here. There's plenty of room. Marquita won't be back, and my grandma's gone for a while, too."

Obviously he remembered what I'd told him yesterday morning, that I was in his bed only because Mrs. Jenkins had been sleeping in her own bed, and I hadn't wanted to spend the night in Marquita's because there was a chance she might come back. But now there were two empty beds to choose from, and no need for me to share his. I managed to suppress a grimace. "Thank you. I appreciate it."

He nodded. "Got a preference?"

"Oh. Um..." He was looking at me. Pretty intently, really. "I guess... I would kind of prefer... yours?"

Right answer.

He smiled. "Plenty of room in my bed too."

"Great." I smiled back, relieved.

"Need anything from down here?" He looked around.

I shook my head. Everything I needed would be upstairs with me.

"C'mon, then." He put a hand at the small of my back, warm and hard through the satin. I started up the stairs.

His room looked just as it had when I left it almost two days ago. The blinds were still down over the windows, and the bed was still rumpled. It still smelled like him. I drew in a deep breath before I turned. "We don't have to do this. Someone just tried to shoot you, and if you're not in the mood—"

He didn't answer, just grabbed me, yanked me up against him, and proceeded to pick up where we'd been earlier. Before the fireworks.

Less than a minute later, my back hit the bed. Rafe did not follow me down, though. Instead he stood in front of me, grabbed the bottom of the blue T-shirt and pulled it up and over his head.

I've never been into male strippers. Frankly, that much nudity is embarrassing. Bradley preferred the lights off when we had sex, and I didn't mind, since I don't precisely look like a swimsuit model. And it wasn't like Rafe was stripping in the entertainment sense of the word. He was just getting undressed. But I won't say that the sight of him peeling that tight T-shirt over his head, of muscles flexing and tightening, didn't have my stomach tightening, as well.

Then he pushed jeans and whatever underwear he had on down together, and I choked.

He looked at me. Looked down, and interpreted—correctly—the reason for my sudden panic. "It'll fit."

"But what if it doesn't?" I scooted backwards, closer to the headboard. "It's been a while, and..."

The corners of his mouth turned up. "I'll make it fit."

I swallowed another hitch of breath. "Somehow that doesn't make me feel better."

"This was your idea, darlin'. If you're not ready, I can wait."

"It's not that I'm not ready. I'm just... nervous. It's been a while. I guess I'm out of practice." I smiled weakly.

He smiled back, but it didn't touch his eyes. "I'm not."

"Yes, and that's another thing. You've had all this experience, while I..."

"Haven't?"

I shrugged. Bradley. That was it. But I didn't want to tell him that. If he knew, he might change his mind.

"You afraid I'm gonna be disappointed, darlin'?"

I avoided his eyes. "I guess."

"No need. You couldn't disappoint me if you tried."

"That's not what Bradley said."

"In case you hadn't noticed, I ain't Bradley."

"I've noticed," I said.

How could I not? Bradley had been pale-skinned and fair-haired, businesslike, competent, and perfectly proper. Sex with him had been by the book: proficient and thorough, but hardly earth-shattering. Whereas Rafe was heat and passion, all warm golden skin and hot dark eyes and bone-melting kisses.

My eyes glazed, and he chuckled. "You're gonna enjoy this, darlin'. I promise. And by the time we're finished, it'll be like Bradley never existed."

"Must be nice to be that confident."

He grinned. "Think I can't do it?"

"I'm sure you can do anything you put your mind to," I said demurely. And added, "Unless we get interrupted again. The phone could ring, or someone else could take a shot at you."

He shook his head. "Not this time. The only fireworks are the ones we're gonna make ourselves. And the dress comes off. Now."

He reached out. Slipped both hands around my neck and unfastened the straps. And pulled the dress down to my waist.

It was mostly just sensations and impressions after that. His hands, his mouth, his body moving against mine. Hot skin and hard muscles, soft touches turning impatient and then urgent.

It was different than it had been with Bradley. *He* was different. He knew just what to do, where to touch, the right words to whisper in my ear; hot, dark words that made my insides melt and my skin tingle and my mind go blank, words that made me forget everything but the longing, the desire, the absolute need to have him inside me.

And then he was there, and he *did* fit, if just barely, and that was all it took for the explosions, and the fireworks, and the colored confetti to rain down... and I clutched at him while I shuddered and laughed and tried to catch my breath.

I would have forgiven him for thinking I had lost my mind, but he didn't seem to find anything strange in my reaction. He smiled, pleasure mixing with the desire in his eyes. "Darlin', you're easy."

I stretched against him, enjoying the feel of his hard muscles sliding against my body, and the heavy bulk of him, still inside me. "Bradley didn't think so." In fact, this had rarely happened with Bradley.

"Fuck Bradley," Rafe said.

"No thanks." I sucked my breath in when he moved. "I'd rather..."

I couldn't get my tongue to wrap around the words, but he knew. His lips curved. "I'm good for a few more times tonight."

"Really?"

Another thrust, another gasp from me. "And a few in the morning."

"Really?"

He smiled. "I told you I'd make you forget Bradley."

"Bradley who?" I managed, and made him laugh.

Thirteen

I woke up with a sense of déjà vu. Same warm bed, same sun slanting through the blinds, same smell, same warm presence behind me. Same muscular arm, this time wrapped around me possessively. And for a second, I thought I'd dreamed it all.

As soon as I tried to move, I knew I hadn't. I was sore in places I didn't know existed. And the places that weren't sore were so lax I had a hard time turning over.

Rafe, who had worked even harder than me last night, still had his eyes closed, and his breathing was slow and even. I settled back down, in the curve of his arm, and looked at him.

The dark hair falling over his forehead made him look younger, and there was a softness to his face in sleep that I hadn't seen since we were both in high school, before life and prison took its toll on him. He had a scar on his temple that I hadn't noticed before; it was old and faded, but from up close, I could see that it was jagged, not clean. From a broken bottle, maybe, rather than a slice from a knife. Maybe from that bar fight when he was eighteen, the one that had sent him to prison for two years.

Although I had heard a list of his injuries from that fight, and this cut hadn't been among them, so maybe it had come later.

There were other scars in other places. One I'd recognized, many I hadn't. The one I did know about, the most recent, had come from a bullet from Perry Fortunato's gun, which had grazed his side just under two months ago. The scar was still pink, not yet faded to white. I'd kissed it at some point during the night, sometime in the middle of one of the three—or was it four?—times we'd made love.

And that wasn't all I'd kissed.

Lord, what had I done?

Last night, all I'd been able to think about was getting here. Getting away from Todd and Sweetwater, getting to Nashville, to Rafe. Finishing what we'd started two days ago, because I hadn't been able to think about anything else since. Hoping that if we just finished it, if I experienced being with him, I'd be able to move on, put it aside. Get past it. Past *him*.

So much for that idea. After making love four times last night, all I wanted was to do it again. I choked back a sound that was just as much a sob as a laugh. "I am *so* screwed!"

Rafe didn't open his eyes, but his lips curved appreciatively. I punched him in the shoulder. If he was awake, I might as well. I wanted to hit someone, and he was available. And it wasn't like I could hurt him, was it? Punching his shoulder was like punching the wall. "Not like that, you idiot. What's my mother going to say when she finds out about this?"

He opened his eyes. They were still sleepy, with heavy lids. "You planning to tell her, darlin'?"

"Of course not," I said.

"Then how's she gonna know?" He let go of me to flop back on the bed, one arm thrown across his face in protection against the sharp morning sun, and that viper tattoo staring at me through slitted eyes and sticking out its little forked tongue.

"I figured anyone who looked at me would know." And not just because of the marks his hands and mouth had made on me, but because I probably glowed. Or something.

Rafe opened his eyes again, and inspected me with interest. "You do have the look of someone who's been..." he paused, "well-loved."

I felt myself blushing. "Gee. Such a way with words."

"I thought you'd prefer it to 'fucked blind.'" He lifted both arms over his head and stretched.

"I do. Thanks." It was getting increasingly difficult to keep my mind on the conversation as muscles rippled and the sheet fell away from more and more of his body.

"My pleasure." He grinned, trailing a teasing fingertip down my cheek, then down my throat, and then further down. Curling around the top of the blanket. "So, seeing as you're a fallen woman anyway..."

"Mmm?"

"I'm all rested up. I promised you I'd be ready to go again this morning." He tugged on the blanket. As it fell away and he moved closer, all I could think was, *Thank God!*

EVENTUALLY, THOUGH, WE HAD TO get out of bed and face reality.

I put it off as long as I could, long enough to have sex—all right, make love—twice more. But eventually, it was necessary to get up. Specifically, when a knock on the door downstairs heralded the arrival of Spicer and Truman, come to dig that bullet out of the wall.

Rafe shrugged on his jeans and a fresh T-shirt from the drawer. I waited until he'd left the room to scurry out of bed and into the bathroom for a three minute shower. If I didn't leave bed now, I'd be there all day, and that'd be bad. Good, but bad. After wrapping a towel around myself, I ran back into the bedroom and contemplated my options. I could put the dress from yesterday back on, with yesterday's strappy sandals, but it was rather worse for wear. That kind of dress isn't supposed to be bunched in someone's hands and tugged and tossed on the floor in a heap. It was wrinkled and looked horrible, and as I thought about walking past Spicer and Truman in it—Spicer and Truman, who had seen me in it last night—I couldn't do it. All right, so they had to know I was still here—my car was still parked out front—but I didn't want to go downstairs wearing the same thing I'd worn last night.

Mrs. Jenkins was barely five feet tall, and she wore nothing but ugly house-dresses, which would hit me at mid-thigh. And Marquita was twice my weight, aside from the fact that borrowing her clothes gave me a bad taste in my mouth. That left Rafe's clothes. I had pulled my panties back on—wincing while I did it, because putting on dirty underwear is just nasty—along with a plain, white T-shirt from his bureau, by the time he came back into the room.

He grinned when he saw me. "Looks good on you."

"Surely not." The T-shirt was several sizes too big, and hung like a sack. Down past my derriere, but not so far past that I could wear it as a dress. I needed something else. And a pair of Rafe's jeans would not only be too big around, but eight inches too long.

"You wearing anything under that?" He reached out. I stepped back. If I let him, he'd talk me right back into bed, and then where would I be?

"Underwear. But I need a pair of pants. Or a skirt or something."

"I'll see what Marquita's got." He turned, but not before I'd seen the shutters slam down in his eyes, leaving them opaque. I bit my lip as I watched him walk out of the room, wanting nothing more than to call him back and let him tumble me onto the bed, but if I did, I knew I'd never get out of here again.

He was back in a minute, carrying a pair of drawstring pants— pink with little hearts on them, the bottom half of a pair of scrubs— that looked like they'd fit an elephant. By the time I'd tucked in the T-shirt and cinched the waist, they worked, though. Well enough to get me home and into more appropriate clothes of my own.

I looked up and met his eyes. He'd been watching me the whole time I fiddled with the pants, perhaps waiting for me to speak. To say something. Anything. About last night, about what would happen now. But I didn't know what to say. So I plastered a bright, polite, social smile on my face, just like mother taught me. (Although I don't think she ever considered I would need it in a situation like this.)

"I really need to go."

He nodded. "Sure."

"Thank you for…" …*the clothes, for giving me a place to stay, for not kicking me out, for last night…* "—everything."

"My pleasure."

He had his hands in his pockets. I would have liked to think it was because he wanted to keep himself from grabbing me and throwing me down on the bed, but it probably wasn't. He must be used to this, this awkward morning after, of women saying goodbye. Most of them probably wanted to stay. Most of the women he slept with, at least the ones I'd met, seemed only too eager to have at him again. And God—I cringed inside when I realized that I was now in the same category as Elspeth Caulfield and Yvonne McCoy; running after him, practically begging for more of his attention.

I wouldn't do that. Not in a million years. And this morning, it felt like it would take at least that long for me to get over what had happened between us. Suddenly Elspeth's carrying a torch for him for twelve years didn't seem absurd at all.

And because thinking about it, about what he'd done to me, what he'd made me feel, made my heart speed up and my breath stutter, I gestured to the door. "I should…"

He nodded. "Don't let me keep you, darlin'."

He stepped aside politely, waiting for me to precede him through the door. I did, holding my head high as I walked out of his bedroom, for the last time.

"Guess I'll see you around," he said when we were downstairs, with the front door open. Spicer and Truman had come and gone, with their bullet, and my Volvo was the only car in the driveway.

"I'm sure you will." I managed another bright, polite smile, even as the thought of it made my stomach churn. How would I be able to see him around, to look at him, to remember what we'd done last night, and act like nothing had happened? Like I didn't want to do it again?

"Take care of yourself, darlin'."

I nodded, avoiding his eyes. "You too. Stay out of the way of stray bullets."

"You do the same."

I managed a smile. "Don't worry. No one's out to get me."

"I wouldn't be too sure," Rafe said and closed the door. Politely, but with a distinct click. I walked down the stairs and over to the car, my silver sandals sinking into the gravel and ruining the heels. I couldn't find it in me to care.

It's a miracle I didn't have an accident on the way to my apartment, because I was not paying attention to where I was going at all. I made it, though, and parked in the lot, before I let myself into the building. I knocked before I fitted the key in the door upstairs, just in case Officer Slater was there. It would be rude to just walk in on her.

As it turned out, she wasn't there, but her things were. I ignored them, just went to change my clothes. Marquita's pants went into the laundry basket along with my panties, and Rafe's shirt was headed in the same direction when I caught myself. If I washed it, it would smell like me. My laundry detergent, my dryer sheets. And although I'd washed the scent of him off my body and out of my hair, I wasn't quite ready to let the shirt go. So I folded it, carefully, and put it into my underwear drawer. And then I took it out again, stuck it in a gallon sized Ziploc freezer bag, closed the zipper, and tucked it away.

I was dressed, in a prim skirt and primmer blouse, with patent leather Mary Janes on my feet—Manolos, of course; I have standards, last night to the contrary—and on my way out the door, when the phone rang. My heart sank. Here it came. Mother was calling to ask why I hadn't accepted Todd's proposal and made her the happiest woman in the world.

The area code was right, but it wasn't mother's number. It wasn't Todd's either, and I breathed a double sigh of relief.

"You OK, sis?" were the first words out of Dix's mouth.

"Of course. Why wouldn't I be?"

"Todd said you left the Wayside Inn by nine last night. And mother said you never came back to the house."

It hadn't even crossed my mind that anyone would worry. "Todd proposed," I said.

"That's what he said," Dix answered.

"I needed some time to think. And I knew if I went back to the house, mother would talk me into it. Or at least try to. So I went home."

"To Nashville? You didn't spend the night with Collier, did you?" He laughed.

"I'm in my apartment," I said. It was the truth.

"I was joking, sis." He paused, probably searching for the right words. "Todd said you didn't accept."

"I didn't decline, either. I just said I needed time to think."

"That's what he said." Dix fell silent again. I stood it for as long as I could before I started babbling.

"I'm not sure I'm ready to get remarried. Life with Bradley was no picnic."

"But this is Todd," Dix pointed out.

"I know that."

"You've known him your whole life."

"I know."

"There won't be any surprises."

"None." And he said it like it was a good thing. Not that I'd enjoyed learning that my husband had been cheating on me and wanted a divorce. That was a surprise I could have done without. Still, surprises can be nice things. Life with someone can be a little stale without the occasional surprise.

"He loves you."

"I know he does. He told me."

"Don't you love him?" Dix asked, point blank. I hesitated.

"I've known him my whole life, so of course I love him. I'm just not sure I love him the way I need to, to spend the rest of my life with him."

Dix didn't answer, and I added, "Do you love Sheila?"

"Of course I love Sheila. I married her, didn't I?"

"I married Bradley."

"And divorced him," Dix said. "Sheila and I aren't getting divorced."

"I didn't think you were. It's just... when mother explained the facts of life to me, she didn't say anything about my having to be in love with my husband. And I just sort of assumed I would be, if he was my husband."

"And you weren't?" Dix said.

"I can't imagine I was. If I had been, I think I would have been devastated when he told me he wanted a divorce. Don't you? Instead of just embarrassed and afraid that anyone would find out that he wasn't happy with me."

Dix was silent for a second. "That makes sense," he admitted.

"It isn't that I don't like Todd. Or that I don't care for him. We get along perfectly well, and we have a lot in common, and I know it would make everyone happy if we got married. I just don't want to be in another relationship where we're polite and perfectly appropriate to one another, but nothing more. Is it so wrong to want—I don't know—passion?"

"No," Dix said, "I don't think it is. But Todd loves you. There'll be passion." He sounded embarrassed to be talking about it.

"I'm sorry," I apologized. "I shouldn't be laying all this on you. He's your best friend."

"And you're my sister. Besides, I was the one who called. I just wanted to make sure you were OK."

"I'm fine. Really."

"You didn't answer the phone earlier," Dix said.

"You called? When?"

"At least four times. Starting at eight thirty, when I got to the office and Todd called me."

"I didn't..." I stopped myself before I told him I hadn't heard the phone. Small wonder, when I'd left it in my purse in Rafe's kitchen, while we'd been upstairs in the bedroom totally consumed with other things. "I turned it off because I wanted to think, and I just turned it on again now. Sorry."

"As long as you're fine," Dix said.

"I am. Really. I'm back home, in my apartment. I was just on my way out the door to go see Tamara Grimaldi."

"Don't let me keep you," Dix said. "I have things to do, too." He paused. "So what do you want me to tell Todd? And mom?"

I took a deep breath. "That I'm fine. That I'll be in touch. And tell mom I'm sorry for leaving all my things there. I just didn't want to go back to the house and have to explain. You know. After..."

"I understand," Dix said. "I'll let them know."

"I'll drive back down to pick up my things. In a day or two. There are things I need there. I just don't want to face anyone right now. Until I've had some time to think."

"I'll cover for you," Dix promised. "Call me if you want to talk, all right, sis? I love you."

"I love you, too," I said, touched. And then, as I closed the cell phone, I wondered if he'd still love me if he knew where—and how—I'd spent the night.

Tamara Grimaldi was at her desk when I arrived at her office at Police Plaza in downtown. The desk staff must be used to seeing me, because they let me walk through the warren of desks and cubicles without an escort.

"There you are," she said when I stopped in the doorway. "I wondered when I'd be seeing you. You all right?"

"I don't know," I answered, sitting down in one of the chairs in front of her desk. Properly, the way they taught us in finishing school. Without looking, back straight, folding one leg over the other and making sure the skirt covered the knee. "I almost got shot last night."

She smirked. "That wasn't all you got, from what I understand."

I tried to keep from blushing, but with no success. "Spicer and Truman blabbed."

"There was a report on my desk this morning. You featured prominently. That must have been quite a dress you were wearing."

Lord.

"And then, of course, they volunteered to go back this morning to dig the bullet out of the wall and question the neighbors. They happened to mention that your car was still there."

"I'm an idiot," I said.

"If you spent the night with Mr. Collier, you'll get no argument from me."

When I didn't answer, she added, "I thought you intended for District Attorney Satterfield to propose."

"I did. He did."

"And you left Sweetwater and went to Mr. Collier's house?"

When she put it like that, it sounded pretty bad.

"I didn't say yes." At least I hadn't accepted Todd's proposal and *then* gone to find Rafe.

"I suppose that's something," Tamara Grimaldi allowed. "Why are you telling me this, Ms.... Savannah?"

"I don't know. Because I can't tell anyone else? Because I feel like I made a really big mistake last night? And it would be nice to have someone to talk to about it?"

"Lucky me." She sighed. "Go ahead."

"No. That's all right, but... no."

"I promise I'll be nice."

"It isn't that." I sniffed. "I didn't come here to talk about Rafe. I wanted to ask whether Spicer and Truman learned anything this morning."

"Other than that you and Mr. Collier spent the night together?" She smirked.

I fought back a blush. "Yes, other than that."

"You're in luck." She leaned forward, opening a folder on top of the stack on her desk. "The bullet is the same caliber as the one that killed Mrs. Johnson, and appears to be from the same gun. We'll confirm that after a more thorough comparison."

"Whoever shot at us yesterday is the same person who shot Marquita?"

"It seems so, yes."

"It has to be the man I saw a few days ago, don't you think?"

"It's possible," Grimaldi said.

"Well, who else could it be? He told me he was looking for Rafe, and it sounded like it would be so he could try to kill him, and he did look at me like he was thinking of using me to send Rafe a message. And there isn't much stronger of a message than to drop a dead body on someone's doorstep. Maybe he didn't know that Rafe is living with Mrs. Jenkins. Maybe that's why Marquita's car with Marquita's body was parked behind the Colliers' old trailer in the Bog. To send Rafe a message."

"That's certainly one explanation."

"What other explanation could there be?"

She looked apologetic. "For one thing, he did know about Mrs. Jenkins. That's how he found you. He followed you from the house in the morning. That's what you said, right? And if so, he must have known that Mr. Collier stays there when he's in Nashville."

"Unless he didn't realize that until Marquita told him. Or maybe he thought that because Rafe wasn't with Mrs. J, he'd be in Sweetwater."

"Sheriff Satterfield told me the trailer park is empty. Unless this man is stupid, he must have realized that no one lives there."

Especially when the trailer itself was sitting wide open and was obviously empty of furniture. "Maybe he just assumed Rafe would be there, and when he realized he wasn't, he lured Marquita down there and forced her to tell him where Mrs. Jenkins lives, and then he shot Marquita and came to Nashville."

"It's possible," the detective allowed. "Although if he didn't know about Mrs. Jenkins, how did he know about Mrs. Johnson?"

I shrugged. I had no explanation for that. "Did Spicer and Truman discover anything else? Did anyone see this guy?"

"I'm afraid not. The lady who heard the shot and called it in, also heard the car going down the street. Or perhaps I should say *a* car. She said it was light colored. White or tan. Perhaps light gray or light blue."

I shook my head. "The car that followed us the other day was a black SUV."

"That's what you said. So perhaps it isn't the same man after all."

"Or perhaps the Hispanic man is driving a white Honda or Toyota. I've seen one of those around, too." In that case, he hadn't been in the black SUV the other morning.

"You and everyone else," Tamara Grimaldi said. "There must be at least fifty thousand white Hondas and Toyotas in Middle Tennessee. It could be a coincidence."

"The car just happened to be driving down the street two minutes after someone tried to shoot us?"

"Stranger things have happened," Detective Grimaldi said. "People do drive around, even at eleven o'clock at night. While someone else is shooting off a gun."

I leaned back. "So what happens now?"

Her voice became official-sounding. "The investigation is ongoing. If you would like to look at mugshots, I'll be happy to let you do that. Now that there's a proven connection between the gun that killed Mrs. Johnson and the gun that shot at you, I'd like to try to identify the man you saw. And since we don't know whether he was aiming at you or at Mr. Collier—"

"He was aiming at Rafe. Of course. Who'd want to kill me?"

I meant it to be rhetorical. She answered. "Someone who wanted to hurt Mr. Collier? By targeting the people close to him? Mrs. Johnson, who worked for him. You, who are obviously a person of importance. His grandmother."

"She's not around. He said he sent her to a safe-house."

"Ah." She made a note on the folder. "Spicer and Truman didn't mention that."

"It probably didn't come up. I asked last night. Before..."

"Of course." Her voice and face were studiedly bland. She wasn't as successful with her eyes. They were maliciously amused.

I blushed. "He must be worried about the same thing you are."

"I daresay he is," Tamara Grimaldi said. "He's seen far too much of what can happen in these situations. I'm surprised he let you through the door at all."

"He said he thought I'd be safer inside." I shivered. "He told me, you know. About the TBI."

For a second she looked surprised, before her face went back to bland.

"I already knew most of it," I added. "I just hadn't put it together yet."

She nodded.

"How long have you known?" *And why didn't you tell me?*

"Since shortly after I met him. While we were investigating Mrs. Puckett's death." She avoided my eyes. "I was looking at him for it, seriously at first. He had everything: motive, means, and opportunity. A history of violence. A criminal record. He even had a connection to you. A tenuous one, for sure, but it was there."

"What happened to change your mind?"

She made a face. "I got a visit from a man named Wendell Craig, who explained why I shouldn't waste my time. He's Mr. Collier's handler. Or contact, or something. I had to keep treating Mr. Collier the way I would have if I didn't know. It's what's kept him safe so far. So when Ms. Vaughn died, and you figured out that he was involved, I had to make it look like I was investigating him."

So just a few days ago, when I'd been worried that she thought Rafe had shot Marquita, Tamara Grimaldi had already known the truth. "You couldn't have told me?"

"It wasn't my secret to tell," Tamara said. "I'm surprised he did. He isn't supposed to tell anyone."

"I guess maybe..." I hesitated. Maybe he hadn't wanted to sleep with me under false pretenses. Or maybe he'd just been worried that if I continued to think he was a criminal, I'd change my mind. Maybe it was all just further insurance that he'd get me into bed. "It doesn't matter."

Grimaldi nodded. "Now you know why he was able to move around Nashville without being arrested after the robberies and Ms. Vaughn's murder. And why I haven't arrested him yet in connection with Mrs. Johnson's death."

I thought of something. "Todd doesn't know this, does he?"

She shook her head. "And you can't tell him. This is something you can't tell anyone. Mr. Collier's safety depends on the fact that no one knows the truth." Her eyes drilled into mine. "If you want him to be safe, you'll keep this to yourself."

As if I'd do anything to put Rafe in danger. "This should make it easier for you to figure out who's after him, though. Shouldn't it?"

"One would hope," Tamara said, pushing her chair back. "And on that note, let me get you set up with a computer and a program of mugshots. Find me the man you saw. As soon as I know who he is, I can find him. And then I can keep your boyfriend safe."

"He's not my boyfriend," I said, but I got up and followed her out of the office.

Fourteen

The man with the dragon tattoo proved to be elusive. I went through a couple of hours of mugshots without seeing him.

There were plenty of other Hispanic men in the files. The Hispanic population of Nashville—of all of the Southeast, really—has exploded over the past few years, as is the case across most of the country. And a fair few of them seem to commit crimes. I didn't see the man I was looking for, though. There were several that looked similar—for that matter, they all looked similar, with the same glossy black hair, golden skin, and dark eyes—but I didn't see anyone I recognized. Not until I'd been sitting there for close to three hours. By then, I'd moved from the local database to the national. Detective Grimaldi had hoped it would be simple, and that the man was from Nashville, but nothing's ever easy, is it?

"Detective?" I leaned my shoulder in her door, watching her pore over some papers on her desk. She looked tired, with shadows under her eyes. The same kinds of shadows I'd seen in my own mirror this morning, that were now hidden under concealer. "I think I've found him."

"Really?" She pushed her chair back. "Let's see."

We walked side by side down the hallway toward the room where I'd been working. I had to hustle to keep up with her long legs and low heels.

"Hmmm," she said when she bent over the computer terminal I'd been using, peering at the picture. "This is the guy?"

"I'm pretty sure. It looks like him, and the description says he has a tattoo of a dragon on his back."

She glanced at me over her shoulder. "You're not totally sure?"

"As sure as I can be. Ninety nine percent. It could be someone else, but I don't think so."

"That's too bad." She straightened.

"Why?"

"Because this guy is bad news."

I snorted. "Thank you, I know that. I met him."

"What I mean is, I was hoping the man you saw would turn out to be some two-bit hood with a grudge. Obviously that's not the case."

"No?"

She shook her head. "This is Jorge Pena. He's wanted in several states and foreign countries. Columbia. Venezuela. Brazil."

"An international hit man?" Surely they didn't exist in real life?

She hesitated. "It's mostly in books that you get the shadowy assassin with the sinister nickname."

"So what is he, then?"

She folded her arms across her chest. "Oh, he's a hit man. Of sorts. Someone who gets dispatched to take care of business. Mr. Collier must have pissed off some pretty bad people if it's come to this."

I felt a chill go down my spine, like a caterpillar with cold feet. "He'll be OK, won't he?"

"Mr. Collier? He's good. He can take care of himself." She hesitated. "Although I'm not sure he's this good."

The caterpillar moved, and settled like a clump of ice in my stomach. "You'll tell him, right?"

"That we've identified Mr. Pena? Of course. Or you can."

I shook my head. "I'm staying away from him."

Her mouth quirked. "Afraid you'll grab him and drag him back to bed?"

I blushed. "Something like that."

She smiled. "It might be just what you need. A couple of nights of sex hot enough to knock your socks off. Lose some of those inhibitions. Join the human race."

"I lost a few inhibitions already, thanks. And believe me, I'm very human." Human enough to regret the fact that I wouldn't be losing more. But the truth was that a couple more nights with Rafe wouldn't just knock my socks off and let me lose the rest of my inhibitions, they'd also ensure that I'd be hooked but good, and that I'd spend the rest of my life lamenting what I couldn't have. Sleeping with him once had given me something to remember; sleeping with him more than once would be self-indulgent and dangerous. No matter how much I wanted to.

Tamara Grimaldi shrugged. "Your loss."

"If you like him that much," I said, "go for it. He's available."

"You think?" She shook her head. "Thanks, but no thanks. I told you, he's not my type. I need someone steady, someone who doesn't court danger every day. He's all yours."

"I don't want him," I said, but we both knew I was lying.

I LEFT THE NEWS ABOUT JORGE Pena for Detective Grimaldi to tell—she'd warn Rafe, and he'd take proper precautions—and then I went to the office. I still hadn't heard anything from Gary Lee and Charlene's loan officer about the results of the appraisal, and after several days, that had me a little worried.

Brittany was behind the front desk as usual, her blonde hair in a cute little ponytail, her cute little face in its habitual pout. "What's the matter?" I asked when I stopped inside the front door to check my mailbox.

Brittany tossed her head. She's in her early twenties, barely out of college, and still has the teenage attitude down. "Tim's driving me crazy."

Tim drives everyone crazy. Of course, I didn't say so. "What has he done now?"

She sniffed. "He thinks I forgot to set the alarm last night."

"What makes him think that?"

"It was off when he got here," Brittany said with an annoyed shrug. "And it wasn't me. I had a date with Devon yesterday—" Devon was the boyfriend, a long-haired musician type, "so I left right at five. And I set the alarm!"

The last person out the door at night is supposed to set the alarm. We all have the code; I keep mine in my wallet and on a piece of paper tacked to the bulletin board in my apartment. Along with a spare key.

Brittany rolled her eyes. "One of the agents probably came back after hours to pick something up or drop something off, and forgot to set the alarm again when they left. It happens all the time."

"It wasn't me," I said.

"Wasn't anyone else, either. Or no one who's come in this morning." She shrugged. "He probably turned it off himself, and just forgot."

"Maybe so." I gathered up my mail—nothing exciting, just some postcards and fliers. "Any messages?"

"I would have sent any calls directly to your cell," Brittany said.

"Of course. Thanks." I headed for my office.

While I waited for the computer to boot up, I checked my voicemail and found I had none.

Sometimes I really wonder why I bother coming in to the office. I mean, there's nothing here that I can't do from home with my laptop and my cell phone. There's just something official about going to the office as opposed to working from home, I guess. It's more legitimate, somehow. Even if I do exactly the same work. And in any case, Officer Slater was living in my apartment, so I felt a little weird being there.

I opened the file on Gary Lee and Charlene Hodges—the only file on my desk; clients have been hard to come by in this tough economic time—and dialed the number for the mortgage broker who was working on the Hodges's loan.

"Brandon? This is Savannah Martin with... um... LB & A." I was still having problems remembering the most recent name of the company I worked for. It started out as Walker Lamont Realty, then became Lamont, Briggs & Associates, and now that had been abbreviated to just the initials. Tim was doing everything he could to make people forget that Walker Lamont was a murderer, yet without actually dropping Walker's name from the company he still owned.

"Yes, Savannah," Brandon's smooth voice said, "what can I do for you?"

"I was wondering if there was any news on the appraisal for Gary Lee and Charlene's place. I let the appraiser in three days ago. He should have filed his report by now."

"Let me see," Brandon said and put the phone down. I could hear him rustle through papers, and click on the keyboard, and I could hear him mutter—and I probably wasn't supposed to hear that, since I think he was muttering about me bothering him. After a minute he came back on. "I got it. Yesterday."

'And you didn't call me, *why*?' trembled on the tip of my tongue. I bit it back. "Any problems?"

"Actually, yes. It didn't appraise."

Uh-oh. "What do you mean, it didn't appraise?"

"Mr. Cobb looked at it and determined it isn't worth the amount the bank has been asked to loan."

"Thank you, Brandon." My voice was rather heavy with sarcasm, I'm sorry to say. "I do, in fact, know what the expression means. I was hoping you'd explain how that could be. I followed Mr. Cobb around the place. I pointed out all the upgrades. I told him what the other units in the development sold for. I provided comps for the area."

"I don't know," Brandon said.

I took a breath. And another. "How far apart are we?"

Brandon dug through his papers. I could hear the rustle. "The contract price is $145,000. The appraisal came in at $139,000."

"So six thousand dollars difference."

"Uh-huh," Brandon said, not sounding if he cared.

"What happens now?"

"We can't loan."

Thank you, Einstein. "I mean apart from that."

"There is no apart from that," Brandon said.

"You mean the deal is dead?!" After all my work? And all this time? I *needed* this commission! I was close to hitting bottom in the savings account, and there were no other transactions lined up behind this one.

"Afraid so," Brandon said, without sounding like he meant it.

"What can I do?" I opened the top drawer in the desk and fumbled for a pen while Brandon told me my options. The first thing I pulled out was a knife, and I put it aside, my entire focus on the phone call.

"You can try to talk the seller into dropping the sales price by 6K. Or you can ask your clients if they can come up with six thousand more in cash." His tone of voice said as clearly as words, *fat chance.*

I had to agree with that. The sellers wouldn't want to drop their price, and Gary Lee and Charlene didn't have six thousand dollars sitting around. Six thousand *more* dollars, on top of the money they were already putting down. However, I had another concern now.

"Thanks, Brandon. I'll have to call you back, OK?" I hung up without waiting to hear his reply. And then I pushed my chair back, as far as it would go, away from the desk.

There was a knife on my desk. A sharp one. One I recognized from my kitchen.

It could have been worse, I suppose. I could have touched the blade instead of the handle and cut myself. There could have been blood on it—mine or someone else's. Or if this was a Barbara Botticelli novel, the knife could have been rigged, via some intricate mechanism, to embed itself in my throat when I opened the drawer. It didn't. And it was singularly bloodless. It was, however, big and scary. And sharp. And here, where it had no business being.

I dialed the phone again. "Detective? Savannah Martin. There's a knife in my office."

"I beg your pardon?"

My voice started shaking. "A knife! In my desk drawer. At work. A chopping knife! Mine. I recognize it."

"The knife that disappeared from your apartment? Are you sure you didn't just bring it to work sometime and forget?"

"Of course I'm sure," I said, my teeth chattering. "There are knives in the kitchen here; it isn't like I'd have to bring one from home. And even if I did, I wouldn't keep it in my desk drawer. This is a threat. From whoever broke into my apartment and slashed my nightgown. The Hispanic guy. Jorge Pena. There's even a thread caught in the handle!"

"All right. Calm down." She took a couple of deep breaths. I did the same. It actually did make me feel a little calmer. "How would someone get into your office to leave it there?"

"The code to the alarm was hanging on my bulletin board at home. Along with a spare key. Just in case I lost mine. I didn't think about it in the excitement the other day. I mean, I still had my key in my purse, you know? And someone was here last night. Brittany set the alarm when she left yesterday. This morning it was off."

"Fine," Detective Grimaldi said. "Bring me the knife. Don't touch it. Wrap something around it when you pick it up. Like a handkerchief or a scarf."

"Kleenex?"

"That'll work. Hold it by the blade, that way we may be able to get prints off the handle. And be careful not to cut yourself. Put it in a bag or something. And bring it to me."

"OK." My hands shook as I followed the instructions. "I'll be there in twenty minutes."

"Just leave it downstairs at the desk. I'll have someone from the lab pick it up and dust it for prints. I'll call you as soon as I know something, OK?"

"OK," I said.

I was just about to hang up when she added, "Oh, by the way. We've released Mrs. Johnson's body. Her husband will be burying her tomorrow. In Sweetwater."

"Cletus?"

My surprise must have been clear, because— "They're still married," Tamara said.

I supposed. And then, of course, there were the children to consider. They didn't need to know about the problems their parents were having, if they didn't already know. Cletus probably didn't have much of a choice but to bury the wife who had left him and her kids.

"Are you going?" I'd seen Grimaldi attend funerals before. Brenda Puckett's, Lila Vaughn's.

"Not this time. I figure I'll leave that to the locals."

Bob Satterfield would probably be there. To support Cletus, Cletus being a deputy and all.

"I may go," I said. If I went back to Sweetwater, I could pick up the rest of my belongings from the mansion at the same time.

"You'll let me know if anything interesting happens, won't you?"

"Like, if Jorge Pena shows up?"

"That, of course. Or anything else."

"Sure," I said. "If anyone throws themselves into the grave, I'll be sure to take notes."

"I appreciate it."

"Um..." I waved to Brittany as I walked past the desk and out the front door, clutching the bag with the knife inside, "did you tell Rafe about Jorge Pena?"

"I did."

"How did he take it?"

She hesitated. "He didn't seem concerned, if that's what you mean. Just said he'd keep an eye out."

"Oh."

"And asked what'd happen if he killed Jorge."

"What?!"

Her calm voice didn't change. "I told him it would depend on the situation, but would likely be considered self defense. Depending on the circumstances, of course."

"You don't think he'll try to find Jorge, do you?" Or stake himself out as bait? It was something he'd do. It was pretty much what he'd done last night.

"I have no idea," Detective Grimaldi said cheerfully. "But if he does, and if Jorge ends up dead in the process, I don't think anyone will grieve."

Except me, if Rafe ended up going to prison for murder.

"Don't worry," Tamara Grimaldi said, reading my mind, "he's been inside before. He's not going to do anything to land there again. If he kills Jorge, he'll make sure it looks like self defense. He doesn't want to go back to prison."

"Good to know." And I couldn't believe what I was saying. After just two months of hanging out with Rafe, I was already talking about cold-blooded murder without batting an eye! "I'm getting in the car. I'll drop the knife off in the next ten or fifteen minutes."

"I'll let you know as soon as I know something," Grimaldi said, and hung up.

GARY LEE AND CHARLENE WERE not happy about the news from Brandon. They didn't have an extra six grand sitting around to make up the difference between the sales price and the appraised value of the townhouse they wanted to buy, and they weren't sure they'd want to pay more for it, anyway, if they'd had the extra money.

"I mean, really, Savannah," Gary Lee told me over the phone, "why would we pay more than it's worth? What happens in two years, if we decide to sell it?"

"You're planning to sell again in two years?"

"I don't know," Gary Lee said, "but what if we did? We wouldn't be able to get our money back, would we?"

"Probably not," I admitted. "If you overpay now, there are no guarantees that in two years, or whenever you're ready to sell, the market will have appreciated enough that the house will be worth more. Or even worth what you're paying now."

"So what are our options?"

I squeezed my eyes shut. "If you can't come up with the money to make up the difference, and you're not sure the house is worth 145K to you anyway, now that you know it won't appraise for that..." When, dammit, it had been worth 145K to them yesterday! "...the only other option is trying to talk the seller into lowering the price. The loan is contingent upon the appraisal..."

"What's that mean?" Gary Lee said.

"That if the appraisal doesn't match or exceed the sales price, you won't get a loan. Right now, the bank can't lend you the money you need to buy the house, because they'll be lending you more than the house is worth, and that's not in their best interest."

"Uh-huh," Gary Lee said.

"Either you come up with the difference in cash, or the price has to come down."

"Can't you just tell the people who own the house?"

I smiled tightly. "I can try. But since that means they'll be making six thousand dollars less than they thought they'd make, I'm sure they won't be happy."

"Oh. Yeah." Gary Lee was silent.

"I'll talk to the other agent and do my best, OK? But we may have to start from scratch."

And wouldn't that be fun? Especially if Gary Lee and Charlene had to test-drive every bedroom the way they'd been doing when I first started showing them around. They'd been having quickies upstairs in every house I took them into, while I stood downstairs wondering what was taking them so long. They'd finally told me they'd been looking for the one that would give them the biggest bang for their buck.

"Really?" Gary Lee said now, in response to my warning that we may be forced to start the house hunting process over. He didn't sound as resigned as I felt.

"Let's hope it doesn't come to that. I'll talk to the other agent and see what we can work out. I'll get back to you."

"Sure," Gary Lee said.

I dropped off my carving knife for Detective Grimaldi and headed back to the office. Where I bearded Tim in what used to be Walker's office, and explained the situation. And heard what I expected to hear: Tim did not think his sellers would be willing to take six thousand dollars less for the townhouse.

"Why don't you ask your clients to make up the difference, Savannah?"

"I have," I said. "They can't."

"So you expect our clients to take the loss?" He glanced at Heidi, whom he'd asked to sit in on the conversation, as well. She was chewing, and couldn't contribute anything but a tight-lipped smile.

I arched my brows. "Considering that that's all the house is worth? I certainly do. It's not as if they'll be able to sell it to anyone else for more, is there? Not if it won't appraise."

Tim looked surprised. He leaned back in his office chair and folded his manicured hands across his flat stomach, baby-blue eyes bright as he looked me over. "You look different, Savannah. Did you get some last night?"

"None of your business." But I blushed, and that was all Tim needed. He straightened up and leaned forward.

"Oooooh! Tell all!"

Even Heidi stopped chewing for a second to look at me.

"There's nothing to tell," I said.

"There certainly is! If you rolled around in bed with that megalicious hunk of manhood...!" He smacked his lips.

"If I did, I'm not telling you about it." I got up. "See what you can work out with your clients, please. And call me on my cell phone when you have their answer. I'm going back to Sweetwater for a few days. There's a funeral I have to go to tomorrow."

"Meanie," Tim said, pouting.

I permitted myself a smile as I walked toward the door, since my back was to him anyway.

Fifteen

Sweetwater has two cemeteries, in addition to the private one behind the Martin mansion, where Martins—and their slaves—of old were buried. It's not in use anymore, of course; these days, people can't arbitrarily bury dead bodies on their property, even if they are the Sweetwater Martins. Mother makes sure the small plot is mowed and taken care of, although it's rare that anyone comes by to see it. Once in a while, an elementary school class will stop by for a lesson in history, but no one claims a kinship with any of the people who are buried there. Just us Martins.

These days, folks either get buried in the old cemetery on Oak Street, the one that was started in the 1880s, or the newer cemetery outside town, only in operation since the 1970s. As the town of Sweetwater grew, there became more of a need for burial space, and the powers that be grabbed a couple of acres of ground on the south side.

Since the 1880s, the Martins have ended up in the cemetery on Oak Street, and that was also where Rafe's mother, LaDonna Collier, was buried earlier this summer. Next to her father Jim, her mother

Wanda, and her brother James Junior, AKA Bubba. If your family's already there, you get to put your newly deceased next to—or on top of—them. But if you don't already have a family plot on Oak Street, you end up in the new cemetery outside town.

Marquita was going in the ground on the south side of Waterfield. Not too far from where she'd grown up, ironically. Down a different road from the Bog, but as the crow flew, no more than a half mile away.

I'd never spent any time in the new cemetery. My family's not buried there, and I'm not at an age yet where my friends have started dropping like flies. The only close friend I could remember losing was Lila Vaughn, and her mother laid Lila to rest in Detroit, where she was from. All the other funerals I had attended recently had been in Nashville.

It was a pretty place, as cemeteries go. Sloped and hilly, with groves of trees here and there to break up the monotony of gravestones. We were into October by now, but in Middle Tennessee, that still meant temperatures in the seventies and light clothes, and the leaves were just barely starting to turn from green to yellow. No bright oranges or reds yet. For that, we'd have to wait for the first frost.

Dix had insisted on coming with me. I don't think it was because he knew Cletus. Dix and Marquita had been in the same year in high school, so maybe he felt an obligation. He asked me to meet him at the office, and drove us both out to Hillside Cemetery in his Land Rover.

We didn't attend the actual church service, just the gathering at the graveside. I didn't think I'd known Marquita well enough to sit in a pew at her funeral, especially considering that we'd pretty well loathed one another. It was enough to loiter under a tree nearby during the graveside ceremony, I thought.

A whole bunch of other people must have felt the same way, because there was quite a crowd gathered. Cletus and his kids, of course, and his mother, and a handful of women who looked enough like Marquita to be relatives, with their own double handfuls of kids. Six or eight women, some of whom I recognized from high school; probably friends. A few couples clustered around Cletus; more friends or family. A skinny, bald guy I recognized as a journalist from the local paper. If Marquita had been someone more important, Aunt Regina would probably be here as well. She's the society columnist. But Marquita's funeral probably wouldn't feature in the society pages of the *Sweetwater Reporter*.

Sheriff Satterfield was present, naturally, along with a few of his deputies, all in uniform. I looked around—surreptitiously—for Todd, but couldn't see him.

"He's not here," Dix said.

"Who?"

He glanced at me. "Todd. That's who you're looking for, isn't it?"

I nodded.

"You're gonna have to talk to him sooner or later, sis."

"I know that." It had better be later, though. Much later. The idea of having to face Todd and to have to respond to his proposal while I remembered—vividly—being in bed with Rafe, was more than I could handle right now.

Sheriff Satterfield nodded at us from a distance, but didn't approach. He might prefer to stay with his deputies, although I thought there was a chance that Todd had told him about the other night, and that the sheriff was giving me a wide berth either out of consideration or because he wanted to grab me and shake me until my teeth rattled.

"Did you know that mom and Bob Satterfield are involved?" I asked Dix.

He looked down at me. "Who told you that?"

I said that it had been Todd, the other night. "You knew?"

"It was hard not to notice," Dix said apologetically. "I mean, I see them together all the time. They tried to hide it at first, but that's hard to do with people who see you regularly. It's a lot easier to hide a relationship from someone you only see once in a while."

Please, God, I thought.

"Well, I certainly had no idea. Not until Todd told me. I know they spend a lot of time together, but then they always did, didn't they? Except it used to be with dad and Todd's mom, too."

Dix nodded.

"Why didn't you tell me?"

"That our mother's having an affair with the sheriff? That's her business, don't you think?"

"She pokes her nose into mine often enough," I said. And added, "Although I agree. It's her business. Just like my love life is mine."

Dix glanced over. "You have a love life?"

"It was a figure of speech." I concentrated hard on not blushing, and luckily something happened to distract us both.

"Hi, Savannah!"

I turned, and looked into the bright face of Yvonne McCoy. She grinned at me, and turned to Dix. "Hiya, Dix!"

Dix blinked, and I could see him flipping through the index card file in his head. To his credit, it took less than five seconds before he hit on the right name. "Yvonne."

She smiled, obviously thrilled that he remembered her. "How are you?"

"Good, thank you. I didn't realize you two were friends." He looked from Yvonne to me and back.

"Yvonne works at Beulah's," I said. "I've seen her a couple of times lately when I've stopped in for lunch."

"At Beulah's?" Dix looked surprised.

"Best meat'n three in Maury county," Yvonne said. "Though your little sister usually orders salad." She nudged me. I smiled.

"I'm trying to keep my girlish figure. You know what it's like."

Or maybe she didn't, since Yvonne hadn't had a girlish figure even when she was a girl. She was one of those women who matured early, and who'd had full-blown breasts while the rest of us were still playing with Barbies.

"Do they know anything more about what happened to Marquita?" she asked now, looking at me.

I shook my head. "I haven't heard anything. Although I guess the investigation is ongoing." That's what they say on TV, isn't it? It was what Tamara Grimaldi had said the other day.

"The Sweetwater sheriff's department is working with a Metro Nashville homicide team," Dix added. "I spoke to Sheriff Satterfield yesterday. They're trying to learn whether this certain man has been in Sweetwater in the past week or two. Have they come to see you?"

Yvonne nodded. "One of the deputies stopped by during breakfast. Showed me a mug shot. Some Spanish guy."

"Jorge Pena," I said.

They both looked at me. "Excuse me?"

"His name is Jorge Pena. I've seen him once."

"Here in Sweetwater?"

I shook my head. "In Nashville. A few days ago. He was bothering Mrs. Jenkins. Detective Grimaldi thinks he might have killed Marquita. And broken into my apartment." I turned my focus back on Yvonne. "Have you seen him?"

She shook her head.

"Are you sure?"

"Sure I'm sure. How many good-looking strangers d'you think I get to see in a week, sugar? Not enough to forget any of 'em." She grinned.

Right. If Yvonne had seen Jorge Pena, she'd have remembered. He was good-looking, in a deadly sort of way. "Had anyone else seen him?"

"Nobody's seen him," Yvonne said. "If he's been in Sweetwater, he didn't eat at Beulah's while he was here."

Down at the graveside, the ceremony got underway, and Yvonne excused herself to join the crowd. Dix and I stayed at a distance. To be honest, I hadn't come to take part in the service, just to observe. Just in case something interesting happened, that Detective Grimaldi might need to know.

But it seemed to be just the usual sad little gathering of family, friends, and ghouls like myself, who hadn't known or particularly liked the dearly departed, but who were here out of curiosity, morbid or otherwise.

Although she had known Marquita, Yvonne was probably in that latter group. She'd told me they hadn't had much contact lately. Still, if they'd been friends once, she might have felt compelled to attend. Wes Lawrence from the *Reporter* was clearly here out of curiosity—and because it was his job. There'd probably be a mention of the funeral in the local paper tomorrow. Bob Satterfield and his crew were probably here in part to support one of their own, and in part to make sure that nothing happened. And maybe because they believed that old adage about the murderer returning to the scene of the crime, or attending the funeral.

Did that really happen? Or was it just in fiction?

I thought back. Walker had attended Brenda's funeral. Hell, he had stood up in front of everyone, including Brenda's husband and two kids, and lied through his teeth about what a wonderful person she'd been. And Lila...

No, Lila's murderer had not attended her memorial. Connie Fortunato had been there, but not Perry. And by the time Connie herself was laid to rest, Perry was dead, too.

So obviously it didn't always hold true.

And not today. I looked around, but could see no sign of Jorge Pena.

That was assuming Jorge had killed Marquita, of course. He certainly might have, but I still thought it was possible that Cletus was the guilty party. Or his mother. Maybe Marquita had become a threat to them, perhaps by wanting her kids back, and Cletus had whacked her. I mean, she was killed here in Sweetwater, and that had to mean something. And Cletus did have a gun, and knew how to use it. It was hard to imagine him driving all the way to Nashville late at night to take potshots at me and Rafe through the window, though. There was no love lost between the two of them—Cletus and Rafe—but I doubted that Cletus wanted Rafe dead. Much more likely that he'd frame Rafe and get him thrown in jail. And as the person who had found the body, Cletus had had every opportunity to do so, but hadn't.

If not Cletus, then who? Did she have a relationship with anyone else in Sweetwater, who might have called and asked her to drive down here?

Cletus's mother hadn't seemed too thrilled with her daughter-in-law the other afternoon, when mom and I stopped by. If Marquita was driving Cletus crazy, Cletus's mom might have felt compelled to intervene. Mothers do anything for their children. And then there was everyone else I was looking at. The rest of the family and the rest of her friends. There could be all sorts of reasons why any one of them might have wanted Marquita dead. Of course, I'd never know.

And then—I took a deep breath; Dix glanced at me—there was Rafe. It was his family's trailer her car and body had been found behind. Given that, he was the most likely suspect. Of course, he wouldn't have been stupid enough to leave her there if he had killed her, but I couldn't expect everyone to realize that. And Marquita would definitely have come running if Rafe called her. If he said he couldn't go home, perhaps, but he wanted an update on Mrs. Jenkins. Wanted to make sure everything on Potsdam Street was running smoothly. Or he wanted to hand her a wad of cash for expenses, to keep the household going while he was AWOL.

And then when she showed up, he slipped out of the trailer and into her car, they talked for a few minutes, and then he pulled out a gun and shot her.

And walked away. Got on the bike and drove off. Fairly secure in the knowledge that no one would see him, since the Bog was empty these days and nobody came out that way very much anymore.

I suppressed a shiver. Not because it was cold, but because the scenario I'd built up in my head gave me chills.

Down at the graveside, the preacher came to a full stop. After a few seconds, a low hum started, and then a squeaky sort of noise as the coffin was lowered slowly into the ground. Everyone watched until it disappeared. Then Cletus took a step forward, followed by his two small children. Two little brown kids, a boy and a girl, both with cornrows with beads on the ends. Both dressed in black; the little boy in black pants and white shirt, the little girl—slightly older—in a white blouse with a black pinafore over top. All three of them scooped up handfuls of dirt and flung it into the hole on top of the coffin.

Cletus's mom followed, then the group of women who looked like Marquita, and their children. Everything was silent, except for the sound of clumps of dirt hitting wood. Cletus was crying quietly; tears rolling down his cheeks. The kids weren't; they were probably too small to fully understand that mom would never come home. The little boy was sucking his thumb.

"Shall we?" Dix asked, gesturing to the crowd.

I squared my shoulders. "I guess we'd better." It would be rude not to join in.

He took my arm and guided me across the grass, difficult to navigate on heels.

I'd dressed for the funeral, of course—black skirt, black shoes, subdued blue blouse—and Dix wore a dark suit and a tie, so we didn't look out of place at all. I couldn't say the same for everyone, unfortunately. Yvonne McCoy, for instance, looked like she had come straight from work. Her black skirt barely covered the essentials, while the white T-shirt was skin tight and so low-cut that Yvonne's cups were close to running over. But at least she had sensible shoes on: black hightop sneakers that made walking across the grass easy for her.

We did our part in scooping up handfuls of dirt and tossing them into the hole on top of the coffin, and then we stood by for a few minutes waiting to offer our condolences to Cletus—again—while Sheriff Satterfield and the other deputies surrounded him. When they moved off (the sheriff with a rather pointed look in my direction), we moved into position next to Cletus.

I let Dix do the honors this time, since I'd already given Cletus my own condolences—along with a casserole—the other day. As Dix expressed everyone's deep sympathy, I looked around.

The party was definitely breaking up. The preacher was hustling toward the parking lot, robes flapping. Sheriff Satterfield and the other cops were headed in that same direction. And Cletus's mom was herding her grandkids toward the cars, as well.

Yvonne McCoy, meanwhile, was headed the other way, up the hillock toward a stand of trees. I squinted into the late afternoon sun. Was someone up there, that she was going to meet?

It seemed that way. If I shaded my eyes and strained, I could make out a tall figure between the trees. Dark pants, white shirt. Dark head.

Dammit, had Jorge Pena shown up after all?

I was just about to tug Dix's sleeve when the man stepped out into view, and I dropped my hand as my stomach twisted.

No, that wasn't Jorge Pena. That was Rafe.

Smiling as he watched Yvonne come closer.

I shifted a little so I wasn't looking straight at them. I wasn't afraid that they'd notice me staring, but I didn't want Dix or Cletus to realize that Rafe was here. Especially Cletus. The last time they'd come face to face, Cletus had given Rafe a black eye, while Rafe had returned the favor, and thrown in a split lip and bruised ribs for good measure.

I had no desire to see a repeat. Especially not in a churchyard.

So I watched out of the corner of my eye as I kept half an ear on what Dix and Cletus were saying, and the rest of my attention on what was going on up on the hillside. Rafe and Yvonne were much too far away for me to be able to hear anything they said, but I could see them and read their body language. And it spoke loud and clear.

As soon as she got close enough, Yvonne held out both arms to embrace him, and if he minded, I sure couldn't see any sign of it. He put his arms around her too, and when she tilted her face up, he bent to kiss her.

I felt like I'd taken a sucker punch to the stomach, and for a second I couldn't breathe. By the time my body had resumed normal functions, it was over. They had moved apart again—although not too far apart—and were just standing there talking. I concentrated on pulling air into and pushing it out of my lungs as I dug my nails into my palms and forced myself to stay rooted to the spot.

What I wanted to do, was to storm up that hillside and tell Yvonne to get her hands off him; he was *mine*. Of course I wouldn't actually do it, and not only because it isn't something a lady does. He really wasn't mine. I'd made sure of that by walking away from him. Granted, I couldn't have kept him anyway, but by leaving his bed yesterday morning, and walking out of his life without a backward look, I'd given up any rights I might have had. If he wanted to kiss someone else, even just a day and a half after kissing me, there was nothing I could do about it.

So I clenched my fists and bit my tongue and sank my heels into the soft ground while I waited for Dix and Cletus to finish their conversation.

It seemed to take forever. Long enough that Rafe and Yvonne finished talking before Dix and Cletus did. She came back down the hillside and walked past us with a wink and a grin. I managed a smile in return, as I thought about that phone number she'd given me a few days ago, that I'd never passed along to Rafe. Looked like he had her number now, without my help.

Cletus and Dix kept yapping. They'd moved into discussing business; Cletus was talking to my brother the lawyer about drawing up some sort of document to provide for his kids in case something happened to Cletus. Given Cletus's job, the possibility wasn't as remote as one might think. Most cops and other law enforcement types die of natural causes in their own beds, but enough die on the job, too. Or as a result of the job, like when some wacko comes after them with a gun. Some wacko like Jorge Pena.

I turned to the grove of trees.

Rafe was still there.

I looked around. Nobody else was left. Just Dix and Cletus, and they'd started moving slowly away from the grave, in the direction of the parking lot, still talking. Rafe watched them for a few seconds, to make sure they weren't coming back, and then he left the trees and came toward me.

Sixteen

I stood where I was and waited. Not because I didn't want to go meet him, but because I didn't want anyone, including Rafe, to know I did.

He stopped in front of me. At a safe distance. If I wanted to touch him, or wanted him to touch me, I'd have to step forward.

He didn't speak, just looked at me.

"I didn't expect to see you here," I said, not quite believing just how much I wanted to take that last step.

He glanced at the still open grave. "She was a friend. And she worked for me."

While I watched, he took a sideways step, scooped up a handful of dirt, and threw it into the hole. And didn't speak or turn back to me for a second, just stood there, looking down.

"I'm sorry," I said, clenching my hands so I wouldn't reach out.

He glanced over. "I feel responsible."

"You're not."

"If someone did it to get to me, then I am."

Unfortunately, there was nothing I could say to that. Whoever killed Marquita was ultimately responsible, but if it was done to get to Rafe, then of course he'd feel that some of the onus was on him. "Detective Grimaldi told you about Jorge Pena."

He nodded.

"The sheriff's department is canvassing Sweetwater to see if anyone has seen him."

"They ain't gonna find anyone." He must have read the question on my face, because he answered before I could ask. "Guy like Jorge moves like the wind. In and out, without nobody seeing."

"*I* saw him."

"That's 'cause he wanted you to see him."

"Why would he want me to see him?"

He shrugged, muscles moving smoothly under the thin, white shirt. I could see the dark outline of the viper tattoo through the fabric. "Guess he figured you'd give me the message that he's coming for me. Or maybe he just got off on the look on your face."

"It sounds like you know him."

He shook his head. "Never met him. Figure I prob'ly will soon, though."

And one of them probably wouldn't walk away from the meeting.

My voice caught. "You're being careful, aren't you?"

He flashed a grin. "Didn't realize you cared, darlin'."

I cared. More than I wanted to admit. "Just because I don't want to sleep with you again, doesn't mean I want you to die."

"Glad to hear it. I can take care of myself."

"I don't doubt that. But apparently this guy is very good at what he does, and..."

"I'm very good at what he does, too."

I felt myself go pale. "Have you ever... I mean..."

His eyes were steady. "You watched me kill Perry Fortunato. You know I have."

Right. And because I'd been there, I knew he hadn't had a choice. Between the gun and the insanity, Perry wasn't a good candidate for mercy. Not that Rafe had been inclined to show him any.

But there's a big difference between killing in self defense, in the heat of the moment, and cold-blooded assassination. Jorge Pena was a hit-man. I wanted to know if Rafe was too, or ever had been. But there were limits to what I thought I could get away with asking. I may have shared his bed, but he wasn't the type to confuse physical intimacy with emotional closeness, and this was clearly over the line. Plus, I was a little afraid of the answer. I changed the subject.

"I saw Yvonne McCoy found you."

He smiled. "She's between husbands, she said."

"That's what she told me. Last week, when she asked me to give you her number."

"The one you left in your pocket. Right."

"I told you," I said. "It was an accident."

"Sure," Rafe answered. "No worries, darlin'. I got her number now."

That's what I thought. "So are you going to stop by while you're in town?"

He looked at me for a second. "You think I'd go from screwing you two nights ago to screwing her tonight?"

I couldn't help the kneejerk reaction. "You're a man, aren't you?"

"You should know."

Damn him. I took a deep breath. And let it out slowly. "For the record, you can sleep with anyone you want. If you want to stop by Yvonne's tonight, be my guest. I couldn't care less."

"Funny," Rafe drawled, "for a second or two, seemed a lot like you did."

Right.

"You spending the night in Sweetwater?" he added.

I nodded. "My mom will be hurt if I don't."

"Hot date with Satterfield tonight?" He scanned the cemetery as he asked.

I shook my head. "God, no. Not after... I mean..."

He grinned, meeting my eyes again. "Afraid he's gonna read it on your face, darlin'?"

The fact that I'd slept with Rafe. "He won't have to. He asks about you. Always. And when he does—"

"You ain't gonna lie?"

"Oh, I'll lie. He just won't believe me. He never does." And under the circumstance, who could blame him? I'm a poor liar, and the guilt—not to mention the memories—would make me blush as red as a beet. And Todd never needed much encouragement to jump to conclusions.

I shot him a glance under my lashes. "So... um... are *you* staying in Sweetwater overnight?"

"I thought I might."

"Where?"

"You thinking you might wanna stop by for round two, darlin'?"

"In your dreams," I said.

His grin widened. "Better believe it."

Right.

I looked over my shoulder. "I should go." Before I said anything stupid. More stupid. Or before I fell into temptation and told him that yes, I wanted to do it again. Because I didn't. Much. At all.

Rafe nodded solicitously. "That's prob'ly a good idea. Your brother's been watching us for a while. I've been waiting for him to come over here and drag you off."

Oops. I'd forgotten all about Dix, at least for the past few minutes.

"Then I should definitely go."

"You do that, darlin'. I figure I'll prob'ly spend the night in the Bog. Just in case you change your mind about that second round once you've had some time to think about it."

"Don't hold your breath," I said.

He grinned. "No worries, I won't. There's always Yvonne, if I get desperate."

And wouldn't that thought wreak havoc with the rest of my day?

I turned on my heel. "I'll see you around."

"Glad to hear it," Rafe said behind me.

"THAT'S COLLIER," DIX SAID WHEN I reached him, "isn't it?"

I nodded, throwing a glance over my shoulder. Rafe had struck up a conversation with the grave diggers, two men who had loitered nearby until everyone else left, and who were now preparing to shovel all the dirt back into the hole on top of Marquita's coffin. As we watched, Rafe grabbed one of the shovels and began working.

"What's he doing?" Dix said.

Penance, I thought. What I said was, "Marquita worked for him. He feels bad."

"And so he's helping to bury her?"

"I guess maybe he feels it's all he can do. Too little too late, but something."

Dix didn't answer. "You ready to leave, sis?"

"Sure," I said, and turned away from Rafe, and from Marquita's grave, toward the Range Rover.

We drove out of the lot in silence. It was empty now, except for a couple of cars parked at the far end. Two of the women from the funeral were clustered near them, chattering, while their kids played hide and seek or tag, zooming around the cars and the adults. One little imp almost careened right into the Range Rover so Dix had to stand on the brakes. A few spaces farther over, I recognized Yvonne McCoy's tight skirt and read hair leaning into the passenger window of a small white foreign car. Maybe she was biding her time, waiting for Rafe to leave.

"I guess that's where Yvonne went, too," Dix said as he maneuvered the Range Rover out of the lot and onto the road. "Up the hill to talk to Collier."

"Maybe."

"They had a thing, you know. In high school."

I nodded. "I know. She told me. He did, too."

My brother glanced at me. "You talk to him about stuff like that?"

I glanced back. "I talk to him about all sorts of things. He's easy to talk to. I don't have to worry about what he'll think of me."

Dix didn't answer for a second. "That must be nice," he said eventually.

"You have no idea. You're a man; it's not the same. No one expects you to be perfect."

"Except Sheila."

"Well... maybe so. But I always have to worry about looking the right way, acting the right way, saying the right things, not saying the wrong things... it's exhausting."

"I thought you liked all the fuss. You know, the finishing school, the debut, the dresses..."

"I don't mind any of that. I mind not being able to say what I think, and that I'm not allowed to have dessert when I go out to dinner. I like cheesecake, dammit, and it's not fair that Todd gets to scarf it down while I have to settle for black coffee!"

Dix looked at me. "Is that why Sheila won't eat dessert when we go out?"

"Probably. Or maybe not. You two are already married. Sheila's probably allowed to eat dessert. I'm not. Don't want a prospective husband to think I'll be expensive to keep. Or that I don't care about my figure."

"Right," Dix said. "Does Collier let you eat dessert?"

"I'm sure he would. He made me take a piece of cheesecake home once, when I wouldn't eat it then and there. It's been too ingrained in me that I have to eat like a bird when I sit across the table from a man."

"But you can talk to him?"

"Most of the time. About most things. Like everyone else, there are some things that are off-limits. It's just not the things that most people don't like to talk about."

"What do you mean?"

"Well... most men like to talk about themselves. Their jobs, their hobbies. Rafe doesn't. He won't tell me anything about himself. But I can ask him about almost anything else, and he'll answer."

"Like?" Dix said, and then thought better of it. "Never mind."

"That's probably safer." Considering that the topics Rafe and I had tackled ranged from frigidity to bondage to murder to breaking and entering. And in the process, he had told me a fair amount about himself; he just hadn't realized he was doing it.

Of course, I'd told him a whole lot more about me, fully cognizant of what I was doing. Sometimes the words just fell out of my mouth, but it wasn't like I didn't know that he had that effect on me. If I really cared what he learned, I'd stay away from him, or at the very least keep my mouth shut.

"By the way," I added, since I wanted very much to steer the conversation away from Rafe, "Yvonne likes you, you know."

Dix looked at me, incredulous, and for a second the car drifted across the median, before he pulled the wheel back. "I beg your pardon?"

"She likes you. Or she used to, in school. She knows you're married, so it's not like you have to worry about her making a pass at you, but she told me she's always liked you."

"You're kidding."

I shook my head. "Please don't tell her I said so."

He gave me an exasperated look. "When am I going to talk to Yvonne McCoy again, sis?"

"I don't know," I said, "but if you happen to go into Beulah's for lunch or something, please don't mention it. She probably wouldn't mind, and it wasn't like she told me to keep it a secret, but just don't say anything, please. To anyone. Not even Sheila, the next time you two get into a knock-down, drag-out fight and you want to say something to upset her."

Yeah, right. Like my perfect brother and my equally perfect sister-in-law would ever get into a screaming and hair-pulling argument.

"Don't worry," Dix said, "I won't."

He dropped me off outside the office, and I got into the Volvo and headed for the Martin mansion. With, I admit, some trepidation. This would be the first time I'd seen mother since I'd declined—or didn't accept—Todd's marriage proposal, and I wasn't looking forward to the show-down.

Talk about knock-down, drag-out. Not that mother is ever anything but unfailingly polite and absolutely ladylike, of course. She doesn't raise her voice, she doesn't use bad language, and she isn't mean or rude. She was just very disappointed, and let me know it.

"I'm sure you know best, Savannah." Delivered with a sigh. "Of course it is important that you feel ready to get married again. I wouldn't want you to go against your conscience, darling."

"But...?"

"No buts. Just... I fail to understand how you cannot feel ready to marry Todd. You have known him your entire life. He adores you."

"I know he does," I said. The problem was that I didn't adore him. Not the way I should if I planned to spend the rest of my life with him.

"Are you afraid that he will—" Her voice dropped, "be unfaithful?"

I stared at her. "Todd? Of course not!"

"Oh." Mom raised her voice out of the delicate range again. "I just thought, since I know how devastating it was for you to discover Bradley's adultery..."

It had been. I'd been beside myself. An absolute basket case. Once the dust settled, though, I had realized that I was upset not so much because my husband had slept with someone else as because he'd found me wanting. It was the failure that was galling to me, not the loss of Bradley's love, of which there had been very little to begin with. It was my pride that was hurt, not my heart.

"I'm over that," I said. "It was his loss. And I'm not worried that Todd's going to cheat. He's not the type."

"What *are* you worried about, darling?"

At this point it was after dinner, and we were sitting in the formal parlor, on Great-Aunt Ida's uncomfortable turn-of-the-(last)-century sofa upholstered in peach velvet, sharing a post-dinner drink. Mother was having sherry, to my white wine.

I twirled the stem of my glass between my fingers, watching the pale wine swirl, wondering how mother would react if I told her the truth. If for once in my life I didn't beat around the bush or use pretty, inoffensive euphemisms, but instead spoke plainly. Like I did the other night. *I spent two years faking orgasms for Bradley. I don't want to do it for the rest of my life.*

Mother would likely faint.

I sighed. "Our marriage had problems before Bradley was unfaithful. It didn't come out of nowhere."

Mother sipped her drink. "What do you mean, darling?"

"He was dissatisfied with me. So he went and found someone else."

"What could possibly dissatisfy him?" mother sniffed. "You were a wonderful wife, Savannah. Beautiful, polished, gracious, a good hostess..."

"He was dissatisfied with our sex-life," I said.

For a second, mother gaped like a goldfish out of water, her cheeks flushed. She closed her mouth, then opened it again. Took a breath. "That's... I mean... Really, Savannah! That's rather personal, isn't it?"

"You asked," I said, taking a sip of wine. I wanted to gulp a mouthful, or better yet, toss back what was left in the glass, but if I did that, mother would have a reason to be shocked. "By the way, Todd told me that you and Bob Satterfield have been dating."

It was mother's turn to take a fortifying swig of her sherry.

"Dix said he's known for a while," I added. "I guess I'm the only one who didn't know. When did I stop being part of the family?"

"It's not that we didn't want you to know, darling," mother demurred. "We didn't make an announcement. It's just that the others are around more. If you had moved back here after the divorce..."

Instead of striking out on my own in Nashville. Yes, I knew the drill. It wasn't the first time I'd heard it.

"If you're dating Bob Satterfield, wouldn't me marrying Todd be sort of incestuous?"

"That's a horrible thing to say, Savannah," mother chided.

Perhaps. But... "That's how I feel about Todd, though. Like a brother. Not like a man I want to spend the rest of my life with. Or a man I want to share my bed with. If you're sleeping with Sheriff Satterfield, surely you can understand that."

Mother turned as red as a cherry, and came close to choking on her drink. "Savannah...!"

"Well, I'm sorry," I said defensively, "but it's important, you know. Bradley left me because of it."

"I'm sure it was Bradley's failing and not yours, darling," mother managed. She was still flushed, and looked like she'd rather be anywhere else right now, than here with me having this conversation. I took pity on her, and put my glass down on the table and rolled to my feet.

"I think I'll go out for a while."

"Now?" Mother glanced at the window, where darkness was pressing against the glass. "It's late."

"Not that late." Only just going on eight o'clock. "I'll be careful."

Mother got to her feet, too, and followed me into the hallway. "Where are you going, darling?" I could sense the hopeful question she didn't ask. *To see Todd...?*

"Just out. For a drive. I need some air."

"Oh," mother said, disappointed. "All right, darling. You have your key?"

"Of course. But I won't be long. I'm just going to..." I hesitated, "drive around town for a little while."

Mother nodded.

"I'll be back within the hour. And if I'm not, I'll call."

"All right, darling," mother said again. And this time she smiled.

AT SOME POINT DURING THE AFTERNOON, I had looked up Yvonne McCoy's address in the Maury County telephone book, and now I plugged it into the GPS navigation system and started driving.

After a few minutes, I passed Beulah's Meat'n Three. It was still open, but the parking lot was deserted. It's a breakfast and lunch place mostly, and doesn't get a big dinner crowd, and what dinner business they'd had was over now. I slowed down as I drove past, to peer through the lighted windows. All the tables looked empty, and the waitress who was leaning on the counter talking to the cook wasn't Yvonne.

She lived in small community called Damascus, not too far from Rafe's other teenage conquest, Elspeth Caulfield. I drove past Elspeth's house on the way to Yvonne's, as a matter of fact. A big, dilapidated Victorian house in dire need of some paint and new windows. It was dark except for a single lighted window on the second floor, sort of like the cover of a Gothic romance. All it needed was Elspeth in a flowing white nightgown running through the yard, terror etched on her face.

Yvonne's house was much smaller, a little 1950s crackerbox in a neighborhood of others. Vinyl siding, a flat facade, and a little carport off to one side with a small, white Nissan parked underneath. I slowed down. There was no sign of Rafe's black Harley-Davidson anywhere. Yvonne's lights were on, though, and with the windows rolled down, I could hear loud music, or maybe the television.

I hesitated, my foot on the brake. Should I drive past, or should

I actually stop and get out and sneak up to one of the windows to see if Yvonne was alone? Was it enough that I didn't see Rafe's bike, or did I want to make extra-sure he really wasn't here? Was it possible that he might have parked somewhere out of sight, so no one would know he was visiting, and that's why I couldn't see the Harley?

Would he bother to stay out of sight, when everyone knew Yvonne's reputation? Or was it his own he'd be protecting?

I made a slow circuit around the block just to make sure he hadn't parked nearby. There was no sign of the bike. No sign of any other cars, either, other than the ones parked in the driveways. Rafe sometimes drives a black Town Car that he borrows from his buddy Wendell. I didn't see that, either. Going past Elspeth's house a second time, I noticed the tail end of a light-colored car parked behind her house. Another white Toyota or Honda; there sure were a lot of those around. The light was still on in the upstairs window. Elspeth's bedroom, most likely. Maybe she was reading.

But at least Rafe wasn't there. He'd told me, in no uncertain terms, that he'd steered clear of Elspeth after that initial misguided occasion when he slept with her. She'd been hounding him forever—some need to save him from himself, Rafe thought, or maybe the preacher's daughter just wanted to walk on the wild side—and she continued to pursue him after the fact. I wondered, not for the first time, whether she really had gotten pregnant and had an abortion afterwards, like Todd had suggested. Or merely a nervous breakdown at the thought of never seeing him again.

Yvonne's house looked the same when I came back. Lights on, TV blaring, car in the driveway, no sign of Rafe's bike. I pulled the Volvo to a stop on the corner and got out. Looked around. Everything was quiet. Nobody else was out and about, and no one was looking at me through their windows. I started down the sidewalk, my heels clicking softly on the pavement.

Yes, I was still wearing my skirt and blouse and high heels from the funeral. Way to go, Savannah; go sneaking through someone's yard in Italian leather slingbacks!

Then again, the heels were pretty well shot already, from walking around the graveyard in them earlier. I wasn't too worried.

Yvonne's house was low to the ground, but not so low that I could see through the front windows. When I got to the backyard, though, the ground was a little higher, and I could see inside. The kitchen window was shorter than the rest, and too high, but I could see into the back bedrooms. There were two: one was pristine and clearly unoccupied, with the bed neatly made and the chair in the corner pristine with a needlepoint pillow.

The other bedroom was a different story. There, the big bed was unmade, and there were clothes on practically every surface, including the floor. Yvonne's work uniform from earlier was lying in a pile on the carpet next to the black hightop sneakers she'd had on at the funeral. There was a bra hanging from the drawer pull on the bureau—it was black and lacy—and piles of discarded clothes everywhere. The top of the bureau was littered with earrings and bracelets, hairbrushes and combs, cough drops, rubber bands, and all the other items a woman keeps in her bedroom. There was no sign of Rafe.

Yvonne was in the living room; I caught just a glimpse of her profile through the doorway. She was curled up on the sofa, a bowl of popcorn in her lap, and she was laughing, probably at the TV. There were fuzzy slippers on her feet, and she was dressed in sweats and a T-shirt, so I thought it safe to assume that she was alone. If Rafe had been here, or been expected, she'd either be stark naked or severely dolled up.

I got back in the car and turned the Volvo back toward Sweetwater.

Seventeen

From where I was, the Bog was a thirty minute drive. I had to go back down the Pulaski Highway to Sweetwater, then through Sweetwater and out on the south side. I spent the time talking to myself about what I was doing and why.

The last time I drove through the night, from Sweetwater to Nashville after Todd's proposal, I hadn't realized, consciously, where I was going until I found myself outside the house on Potsdam Street. This time I had no illusions about that. I'd gone to Yvonne's house to see if Rafe was there. Now that I knew he wasn't, I was on my way to see him.

Not to sleep with him. That was a complication I didn't need again. Not when the first time was still playing on a continuous loop in my head. I just wanted to see him. Talk to him. Make sure he was OK. After all, he was all alone in the Bog, in a trailer that didn't even have electricity or running water anymore...

I almost missed the turnoff in the dark, and had to stand on the brakes and then reverse a few yards before I could turn the nose of the

Volvo down the track that led to the cluster of trailers and shacks. I parked in the open space between the houses and looked around. Just like every other time I'd been here, there was no sign of life. And pitch black, once I'd turned the headlights off. Eerily so. There were no street lights down here, no moon tonight, and no lights in any of the trailers. Nor surprisingly, since no one lived here.

The Collier trailer was also dark, and my heart was beating hard as I closed the car door and picked my way across the rutted ground, around the corner to the carport and the back door. There was no sign of the Harley-Davidson, and also no answer when I knocked. I waited a minute, my breath stuttering the whole time, and knocked again. The skin at the back of my neck crawled; I felt like the dark was full of staring eyes, and I braced myself for the door to open like last time, and for Rafe to yank me inside.

He didn't. The door didn't open, and nothing else happened, either. I tried the knob. The place was locked.

So Rafe wasn't with Yvonne, but obviously he wasn't here either. Maybe he'd changed his mind and decided to head back to Nashville after the funeral. Maybe the thought of staying in this God-forsaken place where he'd grown up, had been too much to bear.

Or maybe I'd missed him somewhere along the way and he was rolling around in Yvonne's bed right now.

There was nothing for it but to leave. And although I was tempted to drive all the way back through Sweetwater to Damascus again, for one last check, I didn't. It was just too pathetic. Instead, I drove home, where mother was thrilled that I was back safely, and happy to turn the conversation away from both Satterfields and our relationships with them.

WHEN I CAME DOWN TO the kitchen the next morning, mom looked surprised. "You're up early. Are you driving back to Nashville already?"

"I was thinking of going out for breakfast," I explained. "To Beulah's. You're welcome to come if you'd like." *Please say no.*

"Beulah's?" Mother wrinkled her aristocratic nose. "I don't think so, darling. I have an appointment with your Aunt Regina later this morning, to discuss the Sweetwater Christmas Tour of Homes. And Beulah's food is rather heavy, don't you find?"

"I guess." I wasn't going for the food, so I didn't care. "I'm not sure I'll be going back to Nashville today. I wouldn't mind going to see Aunt Regina with you. Maybe talk about advertising in the home tour brochure, or something. I have to come up with a way to get some clients. And make some money."

"If you remarried..." mom said and thought better of continuing.

"I like what I do. And I'd like to be successful at it. Aunt Regina is good at writing newspaper copy. Audrey is good at running the boutique. You've built the Martin mansion into an events venue. Catherine is a lawyer. I'd like to have a career, too. One I enjoy and I'm good at."

"Sheila doesn't have a career," mother pointed out.

"She seems happy taking care of Dix and the kids, though. Doesn't she?" I rarely see Sheila, other than Thanksgiving, Christmas, Easter, the fourth of July, and birthdays. Maybe a dozen times a year.

"Wouldn't you be happy taking care of a husband and children?"

"I guess that would depend on who the husband was."

The words fell out of my mouth before I realized I had had the thought. Mother looked shocked, and I added, "I know you brought me up to be a good wife and a good mother and all those things. But these days, women like to have careers outside the home, too. I'm not ready to stay home and take care of a man. I tried it with Bradley, and it didn't work."

"If you had had children..."

"I'm not sure that would have made a difference. If the marriage is rocky, adding kids to the mix will probably just make it worse."

I'd realized that when Bradley and I broke up. And then I'd been grateful that my one and only pregnancy had ended in a miscarriage. "I'm going to run. When are you meeting Aunt Regina?"

Mother said she and my aunt were meeting at eleven, for an early lunch at the café on the square. "You're not planning to spend three hours at Beulah's, are you, darling?"

"Of course not," I said. "I'm just having breakfast. And touching base with an old friend who works there."

"One of your old friends works at Beulah's?"

"She's more of an old acquaintance. Someone I went to school with. I saw her at Marquita's funeral yesterday, and thought I'd go to Beulah's for breakfast this morning."

"Ah." Mother's face cleared. "Well, be careful, darling. A lot of riff-raff goes to Beulah's."

"I've been there before. And it's broad daylight. I'm sure I'll be safe." I ducked out the door and hustled down the hallway.

Fifteen minutes later I pulled the Volvo into the parking lot outside Beulah's Meat'n Three, and had to wait for someone in a rusty pickup with a gun rack to pull out before I could slot my car in. Picking my way across the graveled lot, treacherous for someone on three inch heels, I tried to compose my face and my thoughts so I wouldn't grab Yvonne by the lapels when I saw her and scream at her to tell me whether she'd spent last night alone.

Beulah's was buzzing. Filled to the brim; there were people at all the tables and ranged around the breakfast counter. Two waitresses were threading their way between the tables, trays with coffee pots and water pitchers held above their heads. Neither of them was Yvonne. Nor was she the waitress behind the counter, taking care of the eight or nine men perched there.

"We're full up, hon," she called out when she saw me. "It'll be a few minutes before we can seat you."

I nodded. I thought about asking if Yvonne was anywhere about, but she'd already turned away to fill someone's coffee cup. Instead, I looked around the restaurant. And felt my stomach clench when my eyes reached the table in the far back, the one I'd sat at last time I was here.

Rafe was sitting there. With his back to the wall, so he could keep an eye on everyone in the place. He'd seen me as soon as I walked in, of course. He'd probably seen me cross the parking lot, too.

He was alone, at a table for two. Maybe he was having breakfast with Yvonne, and she was in the bathroom or something. I hesitated.

He arched his brows, watching me dither, and the expression in his eyes was somewhere between amusement and malice, with a little challenge thrown in for good measure.

I suppressed a sigh. Talk about being caught between the rock and the hard place. There were people here I knew, or at least people who knew me. People who were familiar with Rafe, as well. The fact that Margaret Anne Martin's perfect youngest daughter sat down to breakfast with LaDonna Collier's good-for-nothing son, would raise some eyebrows and set tongues a-wagging in Sweetwater.

On the other hand, pretending I didn't know him would hurt his feelings. And it would make me feel ashamed of myself.

I took a deep breath and headed for the back of the restaurant, my head held high, nodding and smiling politely left and right to people I recognized. They followed my progress out of the corners of their eyes, in some cases with undisguised curiosity.

I stopped in front of Rafe, my heart beating hard. "Good morning."

He smiled. "Morning, darlin'." The greeting was accompanied by a leisurely once-over, from the top of my head to the bottom of my skirt and back.

"I didn't expect to see you here," I said, making sure my voice carried to at least the tables closest to us. Bad enough that they saw me talking to him; at least they should know we hadn't planned to meet.

"I told you I'd be spending the night."

"I know you did. But last night..." I bit my tongue, just before blurting out that when I'd gone looking for him, he hadn't been where he said he'd be. He knew what I didn't say, though; I could read it in his eyes. They narrowed with amusement. When he didn't comment, I could have kissed him. At least if we'd been somewhere else.

"Have a seat." He pushed the chair on the opposite side of the table a few inches with his foot.

"You don't have company?" I pulled it the rest of the way out and sank down.

He quirked a brow. "Who'd I be eating with, darlin'?"

"I thought maybe... Yvonne?"

He shook his head. "She ain't here."

"Did you come to see her?"

"I just came to eat." He glanced around the room and back at me. "Lots of people looking at us."

I folded my hands in my lap, demurely. "This'll be all over town by suppertime."

His eyes met mine across the table. They were serious. "You OK with that?"

"I'm sitting here, aren't I?"

He smiled. "Bet your mama ain't gonna be happy when it gets back to her, though." He paused a second before he added, thoughtfully, "Or Satterfield."

Oops. The thought of Todd hadn't even crossed my mind. And he'd have an absolute fit when he heard. "I'm not doing anything wrong."

"Didn't say you were, darlin'." Rafe leaned back against the wall, hands folded across his stomach. He was wearing a short-sleeved black T-shirt today, tight across the chest and shoulders, with that viper winking at me from under the sleeve. "So what are *you* doing here? This place ain't exactly Fidelio's."

"Same as you. Just looking for breakfast," I said.

"Uh-huh."

I grimaced. "Fine. I was hoping to see Yvonne."

The amusement was back in his eyes. No malice this time. "Checking up on me, darlin'?"

"Why would I be doing that?"

"Can't imagine," Rafe said, grinning. After a moment he added, "You're outta luck, though. Yvonne's not here this morning." He raised his voice, snagging the waitress's attention, "Hey, darlin'. Savannah here's looking for Yvonne McCoy. She coming in later?"

The waitress, a bubble-gum popping fifty-year-old with a beehive, someone who'd been working at Beulah's since I was a little girl, stopped beside our table. "Yvonne's supposed to be here right now. Didn't show up this morning. That's why we're running around like chickens with our heads cut off." She glanced over her shoulder as someone else tried to get her attention, and held up a finger. "What can I get for you, hon?"

"Nothing," I said. "I'm not staying."

"Suit yourself. You done, hon?" She turned to Rafe. He nodded. "Here you go." She handed him his check and moved off.

"They must really want the table," I said. Rafe nodded.

"You ready?"

"I'll wait outside." I knew I should just get in my car and drive away, especially now that the old biddies and gents probably thought I'd come to Beulah's specifically for a three minute conversation with him before the two of us left together. I couldn't bring myself to do it, though.

"Do you think something's wrong?" I asked two minutes later, when he came through the door, putting on a pair of mirrored sunglasses.

"With Yvonne?" He shrugged. "Why'd you think that?"

"Because she was fine yesterday. And she doesn't seem the type who'd just not show up for work without calling in. If she can."

"Maybe she had company last night," Rafe suggested with a grin.

It was my turn to raise my brows. Both of them, since I can't lift one at a time the way he can. "If you're suggesting that you stopped by her house yesterday and made her too tired to walk this morning, you can spare yourself the trouble. I've spent the night with you, and I could still get out of bed the next day."

I bit my tongue, a little too late. And looked around guiltily. Nobody was near enough to have heard me. Praise the Lord.

Rafe chuckled. "You know, darlin', one of these days you're gonna end up being practically human."

"I'm practically human now."

"Yeah?" He switched subjects. "I'm parked round back. You can follow me over there if you want."

"To Yvonne's house? I know where it is."

"Course you do." He walked away. I made my way over to the Volvo and got in. By the time I had the engine started and the car running, he was leaving the parking lot.

I got to Yvonne's house about thirty seconds after he did. He was still sitting on the bike at the curb, and as I pulled to a stop behind him, I was reminded of the first time we'd met. The first time in twelve years, anyway. It had been the first week of August, outside Mrs. Jenkins's house, and when I saw him, he'd been straddling this same motorcycle, wearing what looked like these same faded jeans and this same black T-shirt. As well as these same sunglasses. And back then, before I recognized him and realized who—and what—he was, I'd taken one look at him and been floored by that raw sex-appeal he exuded. Followed half a second later by apprehension: this was not someone a nice girl should be getting involved with. My instincts had been screaming at me to stay away from him, to stay in the car and get the hell out of there. If I'd listened...

But that was water under the bridge. I opened the car door and got out. Rafe swung his leg over the bike and stood, as well. "Almost like old times, ain't it?"

Obviously I wasn't the only one who remembered. "Let's hope the outcome is a little better this time. I'd just as soon not stumble over another bloody corpse."

Rafe didn't answer. Which told me more about his expectations than a response would have done.

We went up to the front door and knocked.

"There's a back door, too," I said after a minute, when there'd been no answer. "And the ground is higher. We can see in."

Rafe glanced at me, but refrained from comment. He pulled the bottom of his T-shirt out of the waistband of his jeans and used it to try the doorknob. When the door turned out to be locked, he agreed to check around back.

We walked around the house, past the small, white car that was still parked under the carport. If I looked closely, I could see my footprints from last night; the way my spiky heels had sunk into the soft ground. Thank God I was wearing heels again today; maybe nobody had to know that I'd been here last night.

The back door was locked, as well. "That's the guest bedroom," I said when Rafe walked toward the nearest window. He quirked a brow, and I blushed. "I... um... stopped by last night."

His voice was dry. "Since you've been here before and I haven't, you care to tell me where Yvonne's bedroom is?"

"There." I pointed.

He met my eyes as he walked past, to the window and peered in. And breathed a curse. "You'd better call 911, darlin'."

"The police?" I had my phone out and was already dialing.

"An ambulance."

"Oh, no." I could feel my stomach turn. "What?"

"No idea. Can't see much. She's in the living room, and there's a lot of blood." His voice was tight.

On the other end of the telephone, the 911 operator answered, and I had to pull myself together to tell her who I was and what had happened. Of course it took me a few seconds to remember where I was, but eventually I managed to get the right address out. "She's inside the house. We can see her through the window. The door is locked, though. Do we kick it in, just in case she's still alive and there's something we can do for her? Or wait for the ambulance?"

"We?" the 911 operator said.

"I mean, if she's dead, I don't want to mess up the crime scene. Bad enough that I've been walking all over the yard. But if she's alive, I don't want her to die while I'm standing out here talking to you."

"The ambulance will be there in less than five minutes."

I relayed this to Rafe, who shook his head. "Never mind," I told the 911 operator as I watched him put his foot to the door, right next to the lock. "Looks like we're going in."

The door exploded with a splintering noise, and Rafe tumbled through. I ran up the steps and followed, explaining to the 911 operator what I was doing as I did it.

"I'm in the kitchen. There's nothing here. I'm walking into the dining room. Nothing here either. The living room... oh, dear God..."

Rafe hadn't wasted any time, but had gone directly to where he knew Yvonne was, on the floor in front of the sofa. He was kneeling next to her, the knees of his jeans in what would have been a pool of blood had the floor been hardwood. Yvonne had wall to wall carpet everywhere, and he was on his knees in soggy carpet fibers.

Unlike Marquita, whom Detective Grimaldi had told me was shot in the head, Yvonne had been stabbed or shot in the chest. And she had bled a lot. The white T-shirt—the same one she'd worn when I caught a glimpse of her through the window last night—was soaked through, and there was blood all the way down to her thighs. Some on her knees and the palms of her hands too. Maybe she'd tried to crawl, or to drag herself to the phone for help.

"What do you see?" the operator prompted. I began to recite facts as I watched Rafe reach out and put two fingers against the side of Yvonne's throat.

After a few seconds he moved them, reaching for her wrist instead. His face was grim.

"I think she's dead," I told the operator. And stopped when Rafe shook his head. "No?"

"There's a pulse. Very weak." He glanced up, his eyes flat black. "How long before the ambulance gets here?"

"You should hear them any second now," the operator said when I asked. I went to unlock and open the front door and stepped out on the stoop, straining my ears. "Is this a crime, ma'am? Do you need the police?"

"Please." It was unlikely that her chest had exploded on its own, so yes, I was pretty sure someone had committed a crime. I breathed deeply of the fresh air outside. There was that coppery scent of blood in the air inside the house, that took me back to 101 Potsdam Street and Brenda Puckett's body. The world got a little woozy.

"You OK?" Rafe said. He'd gotten to his feet, as well, and come out on the stoop with me. There was blood on his knees, and on his hands, otherwise he might have steadied me. When we found Brenda's body, and again after he killed Perry Fortunato, he'd had to carry me out of the room.

I nodded, my teeth chattering.

"Sit. Put your head down." He nodded to the front step, but didn't move to touch me. I sat. And closed my eyes and concentrated on taking deep breaths. In the distance, I could hear the ambulance approaching.

It was the usual drill after that. Except for one very important thing. Yvonne was still alive, so instead of worrying about the crime scene, the paramedics hooked her up to fluids and put her on a gurney, before hurrying her out of there. While they were doing that, a police car arrived, and Bob Satterfield took one look at Yvonne going past before he turned to us.

He greeted me first, although I could tell that he was a whole lot more interested in Rafe. "Savannah."

"Sheriff." I was still sitting on the top step, woozy all over again from watching Yvonne go by.

The sheriff turned to Rafe. Didn't say anything, just watched him for a few moments. A few *long* moments. Just as I was about to break the silence, he finally spoke. "Been a while."

"Not that long." Rafe's face was composed. "Just a couple months since you and your son and Cletus Johnson came knocking on my door in the Bog. To talk."

This was the occasion when Cletus and Rafe had exchanged black eyes.

Bob Satterfield looked past him into the house. "What happened here?"

Rafe shrugged. "Don't know. Someone shot her, looks like. Sometime overnight. No idea who or why."

Sheriff Satterfield turned to me. "Savannah?"

"I went to have breakfast at Beulah's," I said. "Yvonne works there. I wanted to ask her something. But she wasn't there. The other waitress said she didn't come to work this morning. I thought something might be wrong, so I left there and came here."

"Alone?" Bob Satterfield's gaze skimmed over Rafe.

"We came together. Sort of. Separately, but together." I could tell the explanation made things worse, so I started over. "Rafe was at Beulah's when I got there. When I said I wanted to come here to check on Yvonne, he came along. On the bike. While I drove the Volvo."

Like I said. Separately, but together.

The sheriff turned back to Rafe. "How d'you know Yvonne McCoy?"

"We all went to school together," I said, "remember? Todd and Dix, me and Charlotte, Yvonne McCoy, Rafe... All in different years, but together."

The sheriff nodded, but continued to interrogate Rafe. "When was the last time you saw her?"

I could see a muscle jump in Rafe's jaw, but he answered calmly enough. "Yesterday. At the funeral."

"You were there?"

"Marquita Johnson worked for me," Rafe said, his voice tight. "I'd known her for fifteen years. Yeah, I was there."

"I saw him," I contributed. "So did Dix. And Yvonne."

The sheriff kept his eyes on him. "The two of you talked?"

"For a minute."

"What about?"

That muscle jumped in Rafe's jaw again. "She came over to say hello. I hadn't seen her for twelve years. She told me to stop by sometime, if I was planning to stay in town."

"And did you? Stop by?"

Rafe shook his head.

"Where were you last night?"

Rafe said he'd spent the night in the Bog.

"In the trailer? I don't suppose anyone can verify that?"

"Don't suppose anyone can," Rafe agreed. "I didn't see nobody, so I don't imagine anybody saw me."

I certainly hadn't, when I knocked on the door.

"I think you'd better come down to the sheriff's office with me, son."

"Wait a second," I said. "You're arresting him? For what?"

The sheriff turned to me. "I ain't arresting him, darlin'. I just have some more questions I need to ask. And I think we'd all be a lot happier away from here. Especially when the crime scene unit comes in."

"The Sweetwater sheriff's office has a crime scene unit now?"

"They're comin' from Nashville. Soon's I heard you were involved," he looked at both of us, but I think he directed it more to Rafe than to me, "I called'em in. Figured maybe there's a connection to Marquita's murder."

Oh, God. My mind hadn't quite put the pieces together yet, but I saw what he was getting at. Except he was getting at something totally different than I was getting at. As usual, the Sweetwater sheriff was perfectly happy to believe Rafe guilty of anything that happened anywhere in or around Sweetwater.

I was more concerned that Jorge Pena had struck again. What if he'd been at the cemetery after all yesterday? Just because I hadn't seen him, didn't mean he couldn't have been there. What if he'd seen Rafe and Yvonne kiss? Maybe that was his little white car I'd seen Yvonne lean into when Dix and I drove out of the lot. Maybe he'd come knocking on her door later in the evening, hoping that Rafe would be there and he could finally finish the job I assumed he was getting paid to do. Yvonne would have opened the door to him. Jorge was male and fairly good-looking, and Yvonne wasn't known for her good sense. And then maybe he'd told her what he had planned, or maybe she figured it out on her own, and when she tried to take the gun away from him, he'd shot her. And then he'd left, thinking she was dead.

"Come along, son," Bob Satterfield said, not unkindly. "Let's go."

He gestured for Rafe to precede him down the stairs.

"What about me?" I asked, as Rafe brushed by, holding my eyes for a second on the way past.

"You can go on home, darlin'. Tell your mother I'll call her later."

"This isn't fair," I said, watching as the two of them walked through the yard. Rafe got on his bike, over the sheriff's objections, and then headed down the street while the sheriff scrambled into the police car. By the time Rafe turned the corner where I had parked last night, the sheriff had caught up. They went off together.

Eighteen

For a second I just stood there, dithering. The door was locked—the sheriff had locked it behind him—although the back door was still open, since Rafe had kicked it in. The sheriff might not realize that, as none of us had told him. I had no desire to go back into the house. If there were any clues to be found, Tamara Grimaldi's team of crime scene investigators would find them when they got here.

After a moment, I sat back down on the stoop and dialed her number. "Detective? Savannah Martin."

I could hear from the background, the low buzz, that I'd caught her in the car. Her voice sounded far away. "Where are you?"

"Sitting outside Yvonne McCoy's house in Damascus."

"We're on our way. ETA thirty minutes. Tell the sheriff."

"He's gone," I said. "He took Rafe with him down to the sheriff's office. To ask him more questions."

I thought I was calm, but my voice wobbled on that last sentence. Tamara Grimaldi was silent for a second. "Sheriff Satterfield thinks Mr. Collier had something to do with this attempt on Ms. McCoy's life?"

"Sheriff Satterfield is perfectly happy to lay anything criminal that happens anywhere in Maury County at Rafe's door. It's a habit." From the days when Rafe lived here and was in trouble more often than he was out of it.

"You don't have to tell me that," Tamara Grimaldi said. "I've seen his record. Juvenile and adult."

"I didn't know he had a juvenile record."

"It's small stuff. Some joyriding and drunk and disorderly conduct. Misdemeanors, mostly. Nothing serious enough to land him inside."

Under different circumstances I might have tried to find out more. At the moment, I couldn't care less about Rafe's juvenile record. "What do I do now?"

"Sheriff Satterfield didn't want you?"

"He's got Rafe," I said, "so no. Of course not."

She sighed. "What do you want me to do, Savannah?"

"I'm not sure. I just feel like someone should do something. Should I call my brother? He's a lawyer. So is my sister. And my brother-in-law."

"Do you think Mr. Collier needs representation?"

"I have no idea. But I know he didn't do this."

"Maybe he can prove that," Detective Grimaldi said. "Maybe he has an alibi for last night."

"He doesn't. He spent the night in the Bog. The trailer park where he grew up. It's deserted now. The houses are all condemned. Nobody is supposed to be there. And when I stopped by at nine o'clock last night, he wasn't, either."

"Wonderful," the detective said grimly. "All right. I'll contact Wendell Craig and tell him what's going on. Between the TBI thing and this new development with Jorge Pena, there may be good reasons why Mr. Collier is safer behind bars."

An icy fist wrapped around my stomach and closed. "What new development?"

"Nothing you don't already know. That we've identified Mr. Pena and that he's a contract killer. Mr. Craig has put out some feelers and confirmed the contract, by the way. Jorge Pena is in Middle Tennessee to kill Mr. Collier."

The news didn't come as a shock. Even so, my voice was a little shaken when I asked, "Who wants him dead?"

"We haven't gotten that far yet. Let me get off the phone so I can call Mr. Craig, OK?"

"What do I do?"

"Just act normally," Detective Grimaldi said. "When I know anything, I'll call you." She hung up.

I did the same, groaning. Act normally. Great.

When a voice spoke out of the blue, I jumped. I'd been so involved in my phone call I hadn't noticed one of the neighbors sneaking across the grass toward me.

All right, so maybe I shouldn't say that she snuck. She was a big woman, with a friendly round face and a low, pleasant voice. "I'm sorry to bother you."

"That's OK." I tried to convince my heart rate to return to normal.

"I'm Millie Ruth Durbin." She held out a plump hand.

"Nice to meet you. I'm Savannah Martin." We shook.

Millie Ruth tucked her soft paws into the pockets of her capacious house coat. "From Sweetwater? Catherine and Dixon's little sister?"

I'm not that small anymore, but I nodded. "Do you know my siblings?"

"I used to teach high school, sweetie. At Columbia High."

"How come I don't remember you?" I said. If I hadn't been so rattled, I wouldn't have. Admitting you don't remember someone is very rude. Much nicer to pretend you do even when you don't.

"I imagine I left a year or two before you started. I just managed to see Dix through ninth grade science." Millie Ruth lowered her voice another decibel. "What's wrong?"

"You saw the ambulance?"

"And the sheriff. Who was that he left with?"

I suppressed a sigh. "That was Rafe Collier. Also from Sweetwater."

Millie Ruth nodded. "I remember him."

You and everyone else in these parts, I thought.

"Grew up to be a good-looking boy, didn't he? Not that he wasn't good-looking back then, too, of course. And a real charmer when he wanted to be. I used to see him around here sometimes when he was younger."

"He was friends with Yvonne. More than friends for a time."

"What's he doing back here?"

I explained that he'd come down from Nashville for Marquita Johnson's funeral. Of course Millie Ruth remembered Marquita too, and we discussed what had happened for a minute before she returned to the reason she'd come across the grass from her house next door. "Is Yvonne OK? What happened?"

"I'm not entirely sure," I said apologetically. "Someone shot her, I think. She's lost a lot of blood, but she's still alive. Hopefully they can keep her that way."

"Oh, dear." Millie Ruth's smooth, round face paled.

"I don't suppose you saw anyone hanging around late last night? Or anyone visiting?"

Millie Ruth shook her head. "I saw a woman walking down the street in the evening. It was dark, though, so I didn't see her real well. All I noticed was that she had long, fair hair. Like yours."

Big surprise. "That probably *was* me," I admitted. "I was here about eight thirty. Yvonne was fine then."

"Oh." Millie Ruth bit her lip. "I thought it was later than that, but OK. I didn't see anyone else."

"No men? A tall guy with black hair, maybe wearing a pair of jeans and a T-shirt?"

"The Collier-boy?" She glanced toward the street, where Rafe's Harley had been parked.

I shook my head. "Someone else. Someone who looks a little like him." Although if she'd seen Rafe around Yvonne's house last night, I'd like to know that too.

"Can't say I did, precious." She glanced over her shoulder. "Guess I'd better get back inside. The kitties are waiting for breakfast."

"There'll be a crime scene investigation unit from Nashville showing up within the next thirty minutes. Just so you know." And sooner or later, someone from either the Metro Nashville PD or the Sweetwater sheriff's office would stop by to ask Millie Ruth what, if anything, she'd seen last night. She'd mention having seen me, of course, and then someone would figure out the connection between me and Rafe and the connection between Rafe and Yvonne, and before I knew it, I'd be a person of interest in the case. Someone might think I'd been jealous enough to hurt Yvonne, just because she'd kissed Rafe yesterday. Just because I'd been jealous enough to drive all the way to Damascus last night, to make sure he wasn't here.

It wasn't a comfortable thought. And I don't mean the possible murder rap. Nobody in their right minds—and I included Tamara Grimaldi and Bob Satterfield among those—would think I would try to kill anyone. Especially over something like a kiss. No, it was the realization that I was jealous that was uncomfortable. I hadn't put a name to it yesterday. Now I did. And scared myself half to death in the process.

Millie Ruth said goodbye and wandered back toward her own house, her steps light in spite of her bulk. I sat on the stoop and watched her and tried to convince myself that I couldn't possibly be jealous and faced the fact that yes, jealous was exactly what I was.

And had been for quite a while, too.

As far back as August, the first time I met Marquita, that day in the Bog, when she'd stepped between me and Rafe and essentially laid claim to him... she'd been loud and obnoxious and very disrespectful, but my dislike had been at least in part because I didn't want her to be involved with him. And that slip of paper with Yvonne's phone number, that I had conveniently left in my pocket in Sweetwater when I drove to Nashville... I couldn't very well deny that I hadn't wanted to hand it over. And that white-knuckled, fingernails-into-palms reaction yesterday in the cemetery, when he kissed her... I hadn't called it jealousy then, even though I'd gone as far as to imagine storming up the hill and telling her to keep her hands off him because he was mine...

Really, how much more obvious could it be?

Jealous.

Of Rafe Collier.

Lord have mercy.

I was still sitting in the same spot when the crime scene van from the Metro Nashville PD pulled up to the curb. The passenger side door opened and Tamara Grimaldi's boots hit the pavement. She stood and looked around for a second, taking in the sleepy street and the general air of nothing at all happening that all small towns share, before turning toward the house.

And seeing me.

I must look about as rattled as I felt, because she hurried up the walk toward me, her aquiline face concerned. "Savannah? What are you still doing here?"

I managed a smile. "I realized that the back door can't be locked. Rafe kicked it in. I didn't want to leave the place open. Plus, I have something to tell you."

Her eyes came back to mine. "What?"

"I was here last night. At about eight thirty. I parked on the corner and walked down to the house. And then I walked around the house and looked through the windows." My cheeks burned and I had a hard time meeting her eyes.

Tamara Grimaldi tilted her head to the side. "Why'd you do that?" Behind her, a crew of three began unloading the crime scene van.

"I wanted to see if Rafe was here," I admitted.

She furrowed her brows. "What made you think he would be?"

"He and Yvonne were involved in high school. Yesterday, at the funeral, she told him to stop by if he was planning to spend the night in Sweetwater."

"And you thought he would?" Her tone supplied the question, *why?*

I squirmed. "He told me he might."

"He was lying," Tamara Grimaldi said. "OK. So you were here at eight thirty. Sneaking around looking through the windows. What did you see?"

"Nothing at all. The problem is that someone saw me."

"Ah." She smiled. "Who?"

I made a face. "The lady next door. Her name is Millie Ruth Durbin. She came over to ask what was going on, and I asked her if she'd seen anyone around the place last night. I was hoping maybe she'd seen Jorge Pena, but she hadn't. She said she'd seen a woman with fair hair walking down the street last night, though."

"And you're a woman with fair hair."

I nodded.

"Although there are other women with fair hair too, you know."

"I know that. But I was really here. And I was afraid that if I didn't tell you myself, it'd look like I'd come here to try to kill Yvonne."

"Because of Rafe Collier?" Tamara grinned. "However jealous you were, Savannah, I don't think you would have tried to kill anyone. Especially if he wasn't even here. And he wouldn't have been."

"Glad to hear it. I didn't, as a matter of fact. I just looked through the windows, saw that Yvonne was alone—she was sitting on the sofa with a bowl of popcorn watching TV—and then I walked back to the car and drove to the Bog."

"But Mr. Collier wasn't there?"

I shook my head.

"Guess I'll have to ask him about that. Are you headed back to Sweetwater now, by any chance? Can you drop me at the sheriff's office?"

"Sure. But don't you want to stay and work on the crime scene?"

She shook her head. "They'll take care of that," indicating the crew of three making their way toward us from the street. "I want to talk to Sheriff Satterfield and the doctors. See what they can tell me about what happened."

"In that case, I'll be happy to drive you." And maybe pick up a few tidbits of information along the way.

We exchanged few words on the way back to Sweetwater. Tamara spent most of the time on the phone talking to other people while I focused on driving the car. And on listening.

The first call was to Nashville to report the team arriving in one piece; I guess that one was to her boss. The second was to Sheriff Satterfield to tell him she was on her way to see him.

"Savannah Martin is driving me," she added, with a sideways glance at me, "but I'll probably need a ride back to the crime scene later."

Sheriff Satterfield allowed how that would be no problem. It would be no problem for me to drive her back either, for that matter.

"She tells me you took Rafael Collier in for questioning," she said next. "Has he admitted anything?"

I sent her a look. She sent me one back and half turned toward the window. "Well, don't let him leave. I'll want a word with him when I get there."

The sheriff's voice quacked, and Tamara rolled her eyes. Her voice stayed polite, though. "No, I don't really think he did it. I just want to talk to him."

The sheriff said something else, and Tamara responded. "Yes, sheriff, I've seen his record. In this case, though, I don't see how he can be involved. The caliber of the bullet they dug out of Ms. McCoy matches the one that killed Marquita Johnson, as well as the one that was fired at Mr. Collier earlier this week. He had a witness at the time, who testifies to the incident. He did not shoot at himself.

A ballistics test will confirm that the bullet that was used on Ms. McCoy came from the same gun as the others, but for now, we're going on the assumption that the same person fired all the shots. And it wasn't Mr. Collier."

This was news to me, and apparently it was news to the sheriff as well, because he quacked again, sounding a little frantic. I turned my attention to driving and waited for the conversation to end.

"You didn't tell me that," I said when Tamara Grimaldi had disconnected the call, and before she could dial again. "That you've matched the bullets."

She glanced at me, distracted. "Sorry. I've had a lot on my mind."

"No problem. So the bullet that killed Marquita and the bullet that came at me and Rafe were from the same gun? Probably the same gun that someone used to shoot Yvonne?"

Tamara nodded. "No fingerprints on any of the bullets, of course. Although we have confirmed that the knife you found in your desk drawer is the same knife that was used to cut up your nightgown. The fiber thread caught in the handle matches."

"Good to know." Or not. "Why do you think he left it there? Or she? Was it Jorge Pena, do you think? Or someone else?"

"No idea," Tamara admitted. "It was meant as some sort of warning, probably, but why Jorge would target you, and why he'd want you to know that he did—if he did... I can't explain it."

"Rafe said that Jorge either wanted me to convey the message to Rafe that he was coming, or it was because he got off on the look on my face. I'm sure it was entertaining."

Tamara suppressed a smile. "Scared you, did he?"

"He would have scared you too, if he was there to kill someone you..." I stopped.

She glanced at me, but didn't ask me to complete the sentence. I'm not sure I could have. "Did Mr. Collier have a suggestion for why the knife was in your office?"

"I haven't mentioned it to him." We had reached Sweetwater, and were on our way down Oak Street toward the sheriff's office. "Feel free to ask him when you see him."

"You don't want to wait?"

"I'm having lunch with my mother and my Aunt Regina," I said steadily. "We're talking about the Sweetwater Christmas Tour of Homes. You have my phone number if you need me. If you need a ride anywhere else."

I pulled the car up to the steps outside the sheriff's office. Tamara reached for the handle.

I snagged the sleeve of her jacket. "You'll call me, right? If anything happens?"

"Sure." She twitched free of my grasp and swung her legs out. "As soon as I know something. And in the meantime, your boyfriend's safe inside." She got to her feet.

"He's not my boyfriend," I said, but I don't think she heard me. If she did, she didn't respond, just shut the car door. I watched her lope up the stairs on long legs, and let herself in through the door, and then I drove away, white-knuckling the steering wheel the whole way.

"YOU'RE LATE, DARLING," MOTHER CHIDED when I walked into the café in the middle of lunch. Then she took a closer look at me, and her expression changed. "What happened, Savannah?"

"My friend Yvonne, the one who works at Beulah's?" I pulled out a chair and sat down. "She didn't come to work this morning. Hi, Aunt Regina. Nice to see you. So I drove over to her house to make sure she was all right, and found her on the floor. Someone had shot her."

"Oh, dear!" Mother waved for the waitress. "A sherry, please."

"I'm afraid we don't..."

"White wine." I managed a gracious smile. "Thank you."

She scurried off while I composed myself.

Truth be told, I wasn't as upset as I let on, since I'd had a little time to process what had happened and since so far at least, Yvonne was holding on to life, if only by her fingernails. She had been upgraded from critical to stable, and the doctors—along with Tamara Grimaldi—were cautiously optimistic. I, however, was late, and I was brought up to believe that keeping someone waiting is a sin. I knew I needed an excuse, and as it happened, I had one readymade.

"By the way," I added, "Bob Satterfield said to tell you he'd call later."

Mother flushed. "I hope you didn't subject him to the kind of third degree you gave me last night, darling."

"I had a few other things on my mind." I accepted the glass of white wine from the waitress and took a healthy swallow. For once, mother didn't tell me it was unladylike to guzzle.

"What happened to your friend, Savannah?" Aunt Regina asked in her soft Southern voice. "A robbery?"

I turned to her. She looks like an older version of my sister Catherine, who takes after our father, Aunt Regina's sister. They're both short and dark, with grayish eyes, although Aunt Regina's hair would be gray now too if she didn't color it. Dix and I, on the other hand, take after the Georgia Calverts, mother's family, with our fair hair and blue eyes.

"I don't think so. The place wasn't messed up, and I didn't notice anything missing. The TV and computer were still there. She was just lying on the floor in a pool of blood."

Mother shuddered delicately. "I don't suppose you feel up to eating, darling, but perhaps you should put something in your stomach with the wine."

"That's a good idea." I reached for the basket of bread and snagged a roll. She was right, I didn't have much appetite. But I hadn't managed to eat anything for breakfast, and the wine on an empty stomach would probably not help the situation.

"Who did it?" Aunt Regina wanted to know. "The same man who killed Marquita Johnson?"

I turned to her, but since I'd just taken a bite of roll, and since mother definitely wouldn't approve of me talking with my mouth full, I couldn't answer. Mother got in first.

"Bob told me his deputies have been canvassing for a tall, dark-haired man in his early thirties."

Aunt Regina tsked. "That Collier-boy again, I suppose."

I swallowed, just as mother opened her mouth to agree. This time I got in first. "Not this time."

They both looked at me. "Pardon?"

"Not this time. This is a guy named Jorge Pena. He's a couple of inches shorter than Rafe, and not as good-looking. Also very scary."

Mother and Aunt Regina exchanged a look.

"Good-looking?" mother said.

"How do you know this, Savannah?" Aunt Regina wanted to know.

I ignored mother to focus on Aunt Regina. "I met him once. In Nashville. He's a contract killer."

"And you met him?" Mother forgot all about my slip of the tongue in her shock that I'd met a hired assassin. She paled. "Darling, are you sure you shouldn't move back to Sweetwater, where it's safe?"

"Two women my age have been shot here in the past week. I'm not sure how safe that is."

There was nothing she could say to that, of course, but she looked unhappy. "What is a hired killer doing, going around shooting young women in Sweetwater? And what did he want with you?"

I explained that Jorge had been hired to kill Rafe. "I guess he thought I might know where Rafe was."

Mom's eyes narrowed. "And did you?"

At the time? "Absolutely not," I said.

Mother smiled, relieved.

Nineteen

Tamara Grimaldi called just before five, to give me an update on everything.

"I'd love an update." I smiled sweetly at mom across the parlor; we were having a pre-dinner drink while we waited for Sheriff Satterfield to pick her up for dinner. "Please tell me you've found Jorge Pena and locked him up, so we can all sleep safely in our beds tonight."

"No such luck. And I'm not sure he's who we're looking for, anyway."

"What do you mean?" I heard my voice turning shrill and focused on getting it back down to the low, sweet register that befits a Southern Belle. *Breathe, Savannah.* "How can he not be who you're looking for?"

"Remember those fingerprints we found on the romance novel in your apartment after the break-in?"

Yes.

"We found the same prints in Yvonne McCoy's house."

I felt my jaw drop. "Yvonne broke into my apartment?!"

Tamara's voice sounded exasperated. "Of course not. They aren't her prints. They're someone else's."

"Whose?"

"Unfortunately, I have no idea. Someone without a criminal record."

"So Jorge didn't break into my apartment."

"No."

"And Jorge didn't shoot Yvonne."

"Well..." She hesitated. "We don't know that."

"What do you mean?"

"Let me make it simple, OK? The same person who shot Marquita Johnson, shot Yvonne McCoy and tried to shoot you and Rafe. Or if not the same person, then at least the same gun. And the same person who tore up your apartment and left the knife in your desk at work, has at some point been in Yvonne McCoy's house. We have no idea whether that fingerprint was left last night or some other time. We don't know if this is one person or two. But we do know the person who broke in at your place isn't Jorge Pena. His fingerprints are on file."

"Maybe he has an accomplice," I suggested. "Someone who broke into my apartment while Jorge was stalking Marquita."

"That's possible," Tamara admitted. "I'll look into it. Known associates. Meanwhile, I thought you'd like to know that your boyfriend's out of jail."

"He's not my boyfriend."

The denial was automatic. If I'd thought about it, I would have kept my mouth shut. Mother looked at me, her eyebrows raised, and I flushed.

Tamara chuckled. "I got him out without giving away the fact that he's informing for the TBI, too. Wendell Craig was adamant about that. If I couldn't do it, I'd have had to let the sheriff keep him in jail overnight."

"That's good. I guess." I got up and wandered out into the hallway, away from mother, with an apologetic smile and the phone still stuck to my ear.

Tamara's voice turned serious. "Part of me wanted to keep him locked up until we have Jorge Pena in custody. The problem is, Jorge will just bide his time until Rafe gets out, and then it starts all over. It's a matter of putting off the inevitable."

A chill went down my spine. "When you say inevitable..."

"Don't worry. I won't let anything happen to him."

"Thank you." I wasn't sure I could believe her, or whether she could actually do anything to affect the outcome—and whether anyone could really keep Rafe safe with a contract killer on his tail—but her assurance made me feel marginally better.

"What are you planning to do tonight? Are you still in Sweetwater?"

I said I was. "I guess I'll just stay another night and go back to Nashville tomorrow. Mom and Sheriff Satterfield are going to dinner, so it's just me. I don't suppose you want to get together for a bite to eat?"

"I'm afraid I have plans."

"Oh." She was probably on her way back to Nashville already. "All right, then. Call me if anything happens, OK?"

Tamara promised she would, and we both hung up.

"Everything all right, darling?" mother called out from the parlor.

I walked back there and stuck my head through the door. "Fine, thank you. I think I'll go to the kitchen and make myself something for dinner. Since you're going out."

"Oh, no, darling." My mother is too dignified to jump to her feet, but she did get up rather fast. "Don't do that. Why don't you come with me and Bob tonight?"

"To dinner? I don't think so. I don't want to intrude on your date."

"Don't be silly, darling. Bob adores you, you know that."

I wasn't so sure. Bob had liked me for as long as he thought I'd end up being his daughter-in-law one day, but now that I'd turned down—or not accepted—Todd's proposal, I had a feeling he didn't like me quite as much anymore.

Mother was insistent, though, and wouldn't take no for an answer. When Bob arrived at the door, I realized why: Todd was with him.

By then it was too late to back out, although I tried. "I can't do this."

"Do not embarrass me, Savannah!" mother hissed. "Smile!" She pinched me.

"Ow!" I moved away, holding my arm.

"Are you all right?" That was Todd, of course, rushing to grab my elbow.

"I'm fine, thank you. Um... mosquito."

Mother smiled.

"I'm glad you decided to come," Todd said softly as he guided me toward the car in mom and Bob Satterfield's wake. Since I couldn't exactly say that I was here under duress, I kept my mouth shut. "I'm sorry my proposal upset you the other night. If I had realized..."

He trailed off.

"It's OK. It's just... I'm not ready."

Todd nodded. "I understand that now. And I promise I won't ask again until you let me know that you are. I guess I never realized how much your marriage to Bradley affected you."

I blinked. He'd been married to Jolynn for a couple of years himself, and yet he thought it strange that my failed marriage had affected me? It made me wonder what their marriage had been like. And how shallow it must have been if Todd could go through two years of it, and then through the divorce, without being affected at all. I mean, Bradley and I may not have had the greatest marriage in the world, and in the end I'd been more humiliated than hurt when it ended, but I hadn't felt *nothing*.

I had to fall back on the manners mother—and finishing school in Charleston—had drummed into me, in order to make it through dinner. Todd was unfailingly polite, and so were mother and Bob Satterfield. The only bad moment came when the sheriff mentioned, I'm sure innocently, that he'd had Rafe in his office most of the day. I could see Todd's mood change.

"He's in Sweetwater?" He glanced at me across the table. We were at the Wayside Inn, sharing a table for four.

242 | Jenna Bennett

"Came down for the funeral yesterday," his father grunted. "Stayed the night in the Bog."

"Oh, dear." Mother took a dainty bite of her salmon. "Isn't that place condemned?"

Bob Satterfield shrugged. "Supposed to be. I guess with the economy, the contractor's draggin' his heels. The place is just sittin' there."

Todd looked from one to the other of us, ending with his dad. "What was he doing in your office?"

"Found him at Yvonne McCoy's house in Damascus this morning," Bob said. "With Savannah. You heard about that, right?"

"Yvonne McCoy getting shot? Of course. Everyone's heard. How is she?"

"Seems to be doin' all right. Still unconscious. But the bullet missed anything vital."

"That's good." Todd turned to me. "What were you doing in her house this morning, Savannah? With Rafe Collier?"

"I went to Beulah's for breakfast," I said, concentrating on keeping my voice even. And it wasn't even because I was afraid of saying the wrong thing. I was angry, pure and simple. Bad enough that Todd talked to me in that tone of voice, and interrogated me like this, when it was just the two of us; but I didn't appreciate him doing it in front of my mother and his father. "I asked mother to come along, but she didn't want to." And if I mentioned that, at least they'd all know that I hadn't planned to run into Rafe. "He was there. Yvonne wasn't. When I drove to her house to make sure she was all right, he followed me."

It had been the other way around, technically, but I didn't think Todd needed the mental picture of me chasing Rafe. He was already upset enough about Rafe chasing me.

"You didn't mention that during lunch, darling," mother said.

"That I'd run into Rafe? It didn't seem important." In light of what had happened to Yvonne, I'd forgotten all about my worry that people had seen me and Rafe together at Beulah's and that they'd talk and mother and Todd would be upset.

Todd turned to his dad. "What did you talk to him about?"

Bob shrugged. "Just stuff. What he's doin' here, what he was doin' in Damascus, what he's been doin' with himself since the last time I saw him. How well he knew Marquita Johnson and how well he knows Yvonne McCoy. The detective from Nashville had some questions 'bout things that had happened up there, as well."

"Detective from Nashville?" Todd glanced at me.

"Tamara Grimaldi," I said. "She came down with a forensic team to go over Yvonne's house this morning."

"They got involved after Marquita died," Bob Satterfield explained. "Seein' as she died here, but lived there. We're sharin' information."

"Of course." Todd looked miffed. "Well, *she's* never going to arrest Collier. She likes him."

"If he did something she needed to arrest him for," I said steadily, "she'd arrest him. He hasn't."

Todd looked at his dad. Bob nodded. "Had to let him go at the end of the day. Wasn't nothin' I could do to keep him."

Todd sniffed. I devoted myself to my food.

We got back to the mansion a little after eight. Todd did not try to kiss me goodnight, and his father did not try to kiss my mother. I was grateful. Mom and the sheriff probably did kiss on their own time, but I had no desire to watch. That would just be too weird. And as for Todd... I had no need for him to kiss me, either. Our interactions were definitely feeling the strain of that unaccepted proposal, mixed now with the guilt I felt over having slept with Rafe.

I couldn't wait for him to leave, and take his father with him. As soon as the door was shut behind them, I turned to mother. "I did not appreciate that."

She tried to look innocent. "What?"

"You set me up. You knew Todd would be coming, and you knew I didn't want to see him."

"You know you had to see him sooner or later, darling," mother said reasonably.

I planted my hands on my hips. "I wanted it to be later. After we'd both gotten some perspective. He's upset with me. And disappointed. And I'm sure he was hoping that I'd tell him I'd changed my mind and wanted to marry him after all."

He'd had a very hopeful sort of look on his face when he first stepped out of the car. Keeping things businesslike had been like kicking a puppy, something I never do.

"I'm sorry if I upset you, darling," mother said, sounding not sorry at all. "But at least now it's over and done with. And you can get back to the relationship you used to have."

I doubted we'd ever get back to the relationship we used to have, but I didn't say so. "I'm going to take a drive," I said instead, turning on my heel. "I can't settle down to sleep after that. I need some time alone."

Mother nodded, although there was a tiny wrinkle between her brows. "Of course, darling. Be careful."

Fifteen minutes later I turned the nose of the Volvo down the rutted dirt track to the Bog. I had no idea whether Rafe would be there or not— he might have gone back to Nashville after Sheriff Satterfield let him go—but if he hadn't, I wanted to see him. Apparently having interaction with Todd made me want to see Rafe. The irony was immense, and if Todd had any idea of the way he affected me, he'd probably cry.

There were no lights on in the trailer, and for a second I thought about just turning around and going back. But no, I was here; at least I should check the door. And—yes!—unlike yesterday evening, Rafe's Harley was parked under the carport in the back.

After sharing his bed, I might have earned the right to walk in without knocking, but I knocked anyway. It was only when there was no answer that I tried the doorknob. It turned in my hand and I pushed the door in. "Rafe?"

There was a sound from the back of the trailer. A rustle and something that sounded suspiciously like a curse.

I let the door slam shut behind me and started making my way through the kitchen, shuffling my feet and keeping my arms out to feel where I was going. The interior of the trailer was almost pitch black. "Rafe? Are you here?"

There was more rustling. My heart stopped for a second when I realized that maybe he wasn't alone. Maybe he had company. Like... Tammy Grimaldi?

But no. Surely neither of them would do that to me. And she had told me, apparently sincerely, that he wasn't someone she'd ever be interested in that way.

Even so, the fear gave my voice an edge. "Rafe?"

He sounded resigned. "In the back." I heard more noises. One of them the scrape of a match, and a moment later a tiny light illuminated the dark hallway. I hurried toward it.

He was in the back bedroom, the one that had been his growing up. There was a bedroll on the floor, and that Penthouse-page of the almost-naked girl on the wall, and that was it. Except for Rafe himself, of course, sitting on the bedroll with his back against the wall, looking almost demonic with the light from an old-fashioned kerosene lamp flickering over his face and over the ridges and valleys of his upper body. The flame reflected in his eyes and created deep shadows under his cheekbones.

I swallowed. He looked breathtaking, but there was something forbidding about him tonight, something dark and unwelcoming. Like he hadn't wanted to be bothered with me and wished I'd just leave.

But at least he was alone.

"I wasn't sure I'd find you here," I said, my voice not entirely steady. He cut his eyes to my face, but didn't speak. "I thought maybe you'd driven back to Nashville after the sheriff let you go."

He shook his head. "Something I gotta do first."

"What?"

He looked at me for a second. "I was expecting someone else."

"Who?" And I admit it, my heart clenched. Not Yvonne; she was in the hospital. Not Tamara Grimaldi; she must be back in Nashville by now. Who else could he possibly...?

And then my breath stopped for an entirely different reason, and I felt myself turn pale. "Oh, my God! You're waiting for Jorge Pena to come find you. Rafe... no!"

His voice was even, calm. "He'll stick around until he catches me. This way I'll make it easy for him."

"But he'll kill you!" He wasn't even wearing a shirt, let alone something like a bulletproof vest. "Please, let Tamara Grimaldi try to catch him. She will! And then you'll be safe."

He shook his head, and I felt panic curl through my stomach. My voice shook. "Please, Rafe. Don't do anything stupid. I know you can take care of yourself, but he's a killer. And I don't want you to die. Not when..."

He looked up, a warning in his eyes. "Watch what you say, darlin'."

I blinked. But before I could speak again, there was a noise outside. Like the crunch of a shoe on the dry ground.

Rafe breathed a curse. "Someone's coming."

"I can hear that."

"I wasn't talking to you. *Now* I am. Listen..." He looked up at me, his voice coming faster, losing the lazy Southern drawl. "See the closet? The one in the corner? Get in there. *Stay* in there. Don't come out, no matter what you hear. Not until I tell you it's safe."

"But you'll be all alone out here..." With someone who was probably Jorge Pena coming around the trailer as we stood here arguing.

"I know what I'm doing. I need you to do as I say so we can both walk outta here."

His eyes were black in the low light. I swallowed. "Please be careful. If anything happens to you..."

"Hold that thought."

The doorknob in the kitchen turned and he pointed to the closet. I went. Ducked inside and pulled the louvered doors halfway shut behind me, as silently as I could. And then I squeezed as far into the corner as possible and stood there, shivering in my fancy cocktail dress and my high heeled shoes, waiting for the showdown.

Twenty

I couldn't see Rafe, but I could hear him. His breathing was slow and even, and if his heart was beating faster, it was impossible to hear from where I stood. Out in the hallway, slow steps were coming our way. I held my breath as they reached the door.

"Hello, Rafael," a soft voice murmured, and for a second, the world tilted; it was *so* not what I was expecting.

Not Jorge Pena, but a woman.

Jorge's hypothetical partner in crime? Or someone else?

I don't think she was what Rafe was expecting either, because it took him a second to find his voice. "Elspeth."

Ah. I had thought the voice sounded familiar, but I'd had a hard time placing it. Now I knew why; I'd spoken to Elspeth only twice in the past twelve years, and only for a few minutes.

What was she doing here? Surely Elspeth Caulfield wasn't working with Jorge Pena?

I heard her footsteps brush the carpet as she came into the room. "It's been a long time."

"I don't get back to Sweetwater much." Rafe shifted his weight on the bedroll. "What's with the gun, sugar? You planning on shooting me?"

Gun...?

Elspeth giggled. "Of course not. Why would I shoot *you*?"

After a second she added, her voice totally different; cool and businesslike, "Isn't that Savannah's car outside?"

Uh-oh. A lead weight dropped into my stomach.

Rafe's even tone didn't change. "I borrowed it. She didn't need it tonight. Hot date with Todd Satterfield."

"Have you been seeing her?"

The mix of emotions in Elspeth's voice was frightening, especially from my perspective. Hurt mixed with jealousy and threat of violence. Not a good combination.

Rafe laughed. "You think Savannah Martin'd have anything to do with the likes of me, sugar?"

"I saw you together," Elspeth said. "At your house."

The soft words fell into the silence like stones. My stomach clenched. And not only because of that crazy mixture of emotions in her voice, added to the undertone of chilling, clearheaded insanity— not to mention the gun—but because I realized that it really wasn't Jorge Pena who had shot at us that night. Just like it wasn't Jorge who had broken into my apartment and slashed my nightgown and lipsticked my wall. It was all Elspeth. And she hadn't been trying to shoot Rafe; she'd been aiming for me.

But she'd been crazy enough to risk hitting him in the process. Like he'd said, we'd been standing pretty close together, and it wouldn't have taken much to shoot the wrong person under the circumstances.

"Three, four days ago?" Rafe's voice was still level, conversational. "That was just sex, sugar. It didn't mean nothing. She was upset, and I thought I'd be nice to her and see if I couldn't get laid. That's all."

"Are you sure?" She sounded suspicious. But also pathetically eager to believe him.

"Course I'm sure. You think she's gonna wanna take me home and introduce me to her mama?" He chuckled cynically. "Nah, sugar. She woke up the next morning begging me not to tell anyone."

He waited a second before he added, "Wasn't like I didn't expect it, you know? She'd had too much to drink; wasn't like she'd'a wanted anything to do with me otherwise."

Again, the irony was almost too much to bear. Two months ago, I'd been playing this same scene, trying to get another nutcase with a gun—Perry Fortunato—to believe that there was nothing going on between Rafe and me. Now he was doing the same thing to Elspeth. And sounding very convincing, I might add.

Unless he really believed it...?

I *had* been upset the night I showed up at his house, and although I hadn't been drunk, I'm sure he'd figured he might get lucky if he played his cards right. He probably wasn't under any illusions about the possibility of a future. I'd made it pretty clear to him—before, during and after—that I wouldn't be talking about what had happened with anyone. I certainly wouldn't be taking him home to meet my mother; he'd hit that nail square on. It wasn't like I could object to what he was saying, or the way he was saying it, when he was just repeating the things I'd already told myself, multiple times. But somehow it sounded worse when he said it.

Did he really believe that the only reason I'd wanted him was because I'd been freaked out over Todd's proposal and had had just enough wine to lose some of my inhibitions?

Didn't he realize that I was more than halfway in love with him? That I would have to be, to do what I did? I may have talked a good game—I may have come close to convincing even myself—but the truth is that I've never had 'just sex' in my life, and I doubt I ever will. I would never have slept with him if I hadn't been emotionally involved.

I missed the next few sentences in my bout of uncomfortable self-revelation. When I got back to the conversation, Rafe had moved on.

He'd obviously made the same deductions I had, and realized that if Elspeth had shot at us that night on Potsdam Street, then it was Elspeth who had killed Marquita, and Elspeth who tried to kill Yvonne, as well.

"What did she ever do?" he wanted to know.

"You kissed her," Elspeth said, as if this was a perfectly reasonable explanation for why Yvonne had to die. "Yesterday. At the cemetery."

"You were there?"

Obviously. Although I hadn't seen her, either.

"In the parking lot," Elspeth said. "I watched you. You kissed Yvonne. And you talked to Savannah." She paused a moment and then she added, thoughtfully, "She looked like she wanted you to kiss her, too."

Rafe resisted the bait. Again. I could hear the effort it took for him to sound careless. "I kiss a lot of women, sugar."

"You can't do that anymore," Elspeth said, her voice tight.

"You gonna shoot every woman I kiss from here on out?"

"You belong with me," Elspeth said. "Now that you're back, we can be together again."

I recognized the undertone in her voice, that almost Joan of Arc-like serenity. Her eyes were probably glowing with semi-religious fervor, too. She'd looked that way the first time I talked to her, when she spoke about Rafe.

I'm sure he wanted to tell her that he wasn't back, and there was no way in hell he'd want to be with her kooky self. He didn't.

"If we're gonna be together," he said instead, calmly, "you can't go shooting nobody. I get into enough trouble without that. Why don't you gimme the gun, sugar?"

Silence. I'll never know whether Elspeth would have done it or not, because now a new voice entered the conversation.

"Better yet, why don't you give it to me?"

I jumped. I'd been too caught up in my own thoughts and the conversation to have heard Jorge Pena make his way into the trailer and down the hallway to the bedroom. Or maybe he was just really,

really good at sneaking up on people without making any noise at all. I wondered how long he'd been listening to their conversation before he made himself known.

It was horribly annoying to be stuck here in the closet, and not being able to see what was going on outside. On the other hand, I didn't want to risk moving just in case they heard me.

"No," Elspeth said. Her voice shook a little. I guess she was less brave looking down the barrel of Jorge's gun than she had been wielding her own. Still, she was brave enough to refuse to hand over her weapon.

"It would be best. That way I won't have to kill you." Jorge's voice was perfectly pleasant, but with an undertone of steel.

"I expected you a couple days ago," Rafe's voice said. "Took you long enough to get here."

"You turned out to be more difficult to find than I had expected." Jorge sounded irritated about that.

Rafe sounded amused. "Glad to hear it."

"Hiding behind your girlfriend isn't going to help you now I'm here, though. If I have to shoot her to get to you, I will."

Nobody spoke for a second.

"I'm not moving," Elspeth said. I rolled my eyes, even as I dug my fingernails into my palms deeply enough to leave dents.

"It's your funeral," Jorge replied. I wondered if he was trying to be funny, or whether he just didn't recognize the humor in what he'd said. It was impossible to know for sure without seeing his expression.

I could hear Rafe shift his weight on the bedroll, but no other movement. No words, either. And I admit I was a little surprised by that. He'd never struck me as the kind of man who'd hide behind a woman. Whenever we'd been together and something happened, he'd always put himself between me and it.

"I'm going to count to five," Jorge said. "If you haven't moved by then, I'm going to kill you. And then I'll kill your boyfriend. Is he worth dying for?"

Elspeth didn't answer. But she didn't move either, because Jorge started counting.

"Five."

I dug my fingernails into my palms, holding my breath.

"Four."

Was there anything I could do? Leap out of the closet and distract him...? If I did, maybe Elspeth would shoot him.

"Three."

Rafe would shoot him, given that opportunity. But Rafe didn't have the gun. Elspeth did.

"Two."

If I'd been Elspeth, I wouldn't have waited for him to count all the way down. I would have shot him long before he got to...

"One."

For a breathless second, nothing happened.

And then the world exploded.

One shot. Two. Three. Four...

I think I screamed, but it wasn't like anyone could hear me in the fusillade.

And then there was silence, apart from my ringing ears and my own rapid gasps of breath. No one spoke. No one made a sound.

I hesitated, torn.

Rafe had told me to stay in the closet until he said I could come out. But what if he couldn't talk? What he was bleeding to death outside, while I was standing in here doing nothing? What if he was already dead?

I pushed the louvered doors aside, my mouth dry and my stomach in a knot.

Nothing happened when I stepped out into the room. No one said anything. No bullets came my way. I looked around.

In just the last few seconds, the bedroom had turned into a battlefield. Jorge lay crumpled in the door, his body halfway into the hallway and his knees bent up at an uncomfortable angle. There was blood spray on the door jamb next to him, and he'd let go of his gun, which was lying next to him. He didn't move, didn't so much as twitch.

Elspeth was in the middle of the floor, still between Jorge and the bedroll, her pale blonde hair fanned out across the green carpet. She was wearing virginal white, and bright crimson stains blossomed on her chest, like Yvonne this morning.

Rafe...

I caught my breath on a sob. He was on the bedroll, but slumped down, his eyes closed and his body lax. A gun—a third gun—was still in his hand, held loosely.

I moved toward him, on legs that threatened to give out with every step.

"Oh, God, no..."

There was blood on his chest, too. Not as much as on Elspeth, though.

I sank to my knees in front of him, my hand shaking as I reached out. His skin was still warm, and his heart beat under my palm.

"God!" I sat back on my heels, tears running down my face. "Thank you!"

His eyelids fluttered and then his eyes opened. They were glassy for a second before they fastened on my face. He moistened his lips. "I thought I told you to stay in the closet." His voice cracked.

"You got shot," I said. "Did you really expect me to stay in the closet when you might be dying out here?"

He didn't answer, so I guess maybe he did. Instead, he tried to push himself up. It was hard to do with a bullet in his shoulder. I reached out to help, but he sent me a hard look, and I let my hands drop.

In the back of my mind, I'd been vaguely aware of sounds outside the trailer, and now the back door was wrenched open and running footsteps came pounding down the hallway.

Rafe was still fumbling to get upright, and in no position to protect himself. I snatched the gun—his gun—from beside him, and pointed it at the doorway, scrambling into position between him and whoever was coming.

In the back of my mind, I could fully appreciate the delicious irony in the situation. I was doing the same thing Elspeth had done: putting myself between Rafe and danger, and look what had happened to her. I didn't care, though. My hands were steady, and at that moment I would have shot anyone who threatened either of us.

It didn't come to that. Tamara Grimaldi skidded to a stop beside Jorge's body, followed a second later by Rafe's associate, Wendell Craig, a middle-aged black man with a gray military haircut. Both were holding guns. Both looked a lot more comfortable handling them than I felt about handling mine.

Rafe reached past me and took the gun out of my hand, a second before I dropped it. That probably wouldn't have been good.

Tamara holstered hers, with a wry look at me. "Way to go, Annie Oakley. How much of this carnage are you responsible for?"

Rafe answered for me. "None of it. Jorge shot Elspeth and I shot Jorge. Jorge shot me. Savannah wasn't here."

"He told me to hide in the closet," I muttered.

"I see." Tamara's lips twitched as she bent to check Jorge's pulse. She straightened again. "He's gone. Looks like two rounds in the chest."

"That's where I was aiming," Rafe confirmed, looking up as Wendell stepped over Jorge's body and around Elspeth's to reach us. The older man met my eyes for a second—I scrambled out of the way—before he bent to probe Rafe's shoulder. Rafe sucked his breath in, and my stomach twisted in sympathy.

"Doesn't look too bad," Wendell pronounced.

Rafe shook his head. "The bullet'll have to come out, and I'll be sore for a couple days. But I've been hurt worse before."

"You don't have to tell me." Wendell clasped Rafe's forearm for a second before he let go and turned to me. "Miss Martin."

"Call me Savannah," I said weakly.

"I guess it's time I call the sheriff." Tamara reached for her cell phone.

"Hold off just a second on that," Wendell instructed. "The fewer people who know about this, the better."

"We're in his town, though. And he needs to know that this young woman," she glanced at Elspeth, "killed Mrs. Johnson and shot Ms. McCoy."

Of course he did. That way he could stop bothering Rafe whenever something—anything—went wrong in Sweetwater, and Todd could stop throwing the horrible fate of poor Elspeth Caulfield in my face.

Except... how did Tamara know that Elspeth had killed Marquita and shot Yvonne? Elspeth had told Rafe that inside the trailer. While Tamara and Wendell were outside.

And then I realized: Rafe had said, "I wasn't talking to you," earlier. I'd assumed he'd been talking to himself, since no one else was here. But he'd also told me to be careful what I said. I had thought he was warning me not to say anything I'd regret, but what if he'd been telling me not to say anything I didn't want anyone else to hear?

I turned to Tamara. "Are there microphones in here? Were you guys listening in?"

She nodded. Rafe met my eyes for a second but didn't say anything.

"Surely you could just tell him that?" Wendell suggested, back on the subject of the sheriff again.

"I could," Tamara agreed. "But why?"

"I had this idea." He glanced at Rafe, who looked resigned, as if he already knew what Wendell was thinking.

"Before you get to that," he suggested, "maybe we should let Savannah leave? I think she's prob'ly had enough for one day."

I opened my mouth. "I want to stay with you," hovered on my lips. I swallowed it. "I should probably get back. Mother will worry about me."

No one said anything to stop me. "I'll walk you out," Tamara Grimaldi said, when I had navigated around Elspeth and over Jorge, who stared up at me with dead, glassy eyes.

"Thanks." I glanced over my shoulder one last time before I headed down the hallway. Rafe was sitting on the bedroll, holding a handful of fabric—probably his wadded-up T-shirt—against his shoulder. He was paler than usual, and there was some blood, but he didn't look like he was in imminent danger of dying.

"You'll make sure he gets to a doctor and gets that bullet out, won't you?" I asked Tamara when we had reached the kitchen and were out of hearing range of the bedroom.

"Mr. Craig will take care of him. And like he said, he's been hurt worse before." She didn't sound worried.

"So nothing bad will happen as a result of him not getting to the hospital right away?"

She shook her head. "He'll be fine. I won't let anything happen to him. Neither will Mr. Craig."

"Thank you."

We stepped out into the cool October evening, and I wrapped my arms around myself as goose bumps broke out on my naked shoulders.

"Drive carefully," Tamara said.

"You too."

"I'll call you tomorrow. When I get back to Nashville."

I nodded. "I'll probably be going home tomorrow, too."

"No reason why you can't go back to your apartment. And your regular life."

Exactly. "Make sure Rafe gets to a doctor. I don't want anything to happen to him."

She looked at me for a second. "Have you told him that?"

"He knows." How could he not? Everything I'd done inside the trailer had been a great, big, honking giveaway.

Tamara didn't argue. "I'll give you a call tomorrow. Until then, don't talk to anyone about what happened tonight, OK? I'm not sure what Mr. Craig's plan is, but I have an inkling that it'll be radically different from what really happened."

I nodded. "I won't say anything to anyone. Just let me know the party line when you figure it out. That way I'll know what not to say if anyone talks about it."

She promised she would. I resisted the need to tell her—again—to make sure Rafe got to the hospital and got taken care of, and then I walked through the dark to the Volvo, got in, and left the Bog.

Twenty-One

Dix called just as I was heading out the next morning. It was around ten. Mother had been asleep when I got home, and with everything that had happened—gunshots, confessions, revelations, not to mention the fact that I'd realized I was in love with Rafe, and no halfway about it—I had found sleep elusive. The result was that I woke up bleary-eyed, and didn't get my act together until quite late. But at least mother was already out and about, and I didn't have to worry about her interrogating me.

And then, just as I was putting my overnight bags—both of them; one from last time I was down here, one from this trip—in the trunk of the car, the cell phone rang and it was my brother.

His greeting was unusually abrupt. "Where are you?"

I told him I was standing outside the mansion, about to get in the car to drive home.

"Don't move. I'm on my way."

He hung up. I arched my brows, but did as he said. It was a nice day, crisp and sunny, and it was nice to be alive. Not so nice to be in love with a man I couldn't introduce to my family, but you can't win them all.

It took Dix less than five minutes to pull up next to me in the circular drive. He leaned over and opened the passenger side door. "Get in."

"How lovely to see you too," I said pleasantly, nevertheless doing as he said.

He gunned the engine as soon as the door was shut behind me. I fumbled to fasten my seatbelt as his tires spit gravel down the driveway. "Where are we going in such a hurry?"

He glanced at me. "Damascus."

"Why?"

"Long story. First I need to tell you something."

"OK." He sounded serious. I folded my hands in my lap and waited for him to lay the bad news on me.

"Todd called me this morning. His dad had called him. To say that there was a shoot-out in the Bog last night."

"Wow." I should probably act like I didn't already know that.

"A couple of people died."

"You're kidding."

He shook his head. "I'm sorry, sis. But Rafe Collier was one of them."

"No," I said.

"I'm sorry. But yes, he was."

"No, he wasn't." He'd been shot, but not killed. I'd seen him. I'd touched him. Talked to him. He'd been alive when I left. And Tamara had assured me he'd be just fine.

Unless she'd been lying? If he'd been hurt worse than I'd realized, maybe she'd had to, to keep me from having hysterics. Maybe there was a reason they couldn't get him to a hospital right away, and so he'd died. And it was all my fault, for leaving him there, for not making sure that he was safe.

My eyes filled with tears.

"I'm really sorry, sis." Dix fumbled between the seats and came up with a box of Kleenex, which he dumped in my lap.

I pulled one out and dabbed at my eyes. "Maybe Todd misunderstood. Maybe he doesn't have all the information. Maybe Rafe was shot but he's still alive. Maybe..."

"I really don't think so, Savannah." Dix alternated between looking at the road and looking at me, concern on his face. "Todd had it straight from his dad. And the sheriff ought to know, don't you think?"

"I suppose." I'd passed the sheriff's car on Main Street last night, just after turning off the Pulaski Highway, so they must have called him pretty much as soon as I left the trailer. But I'd seen Rafe. He'd been alive when I left.

"He said it was some kind of ambush. Apparently someone has been gunning for Collier for a while, and last night they found him. With a woman. I'm sorry, sis."

I shook my head.

"Elspeth Caulfield," Dix said. "Remember her? They had some kind of fling in high school. Apparently they were there together, in the trailer in the Bog, when this guy showed up. José somebody. Or maybe it was Jorge. Anyway, he killed them both."

"No."

"The sheriff told Todd there's no doubt. He's dead. And so is Elspeth."

"No." I shook my head, tears spilling down my face faster than I could mop them up. Dix reached over and squeezed my hand.

"I'm sorry, sis. D'you want me to pull over?"

I shook my head. "Just... don't talk for a while. Give me some time to get myself together."

He nodded. "Sure."

"Or maybe you could talk about something else."

"Like what?"

"Like..." I sniffed into the tissue. "Why are we going to Damascus?"

"Oh." Dix flushed. "That's something else I have to tell you."

"God." Sounded like more bad news. Although it couldn't possibly be as bad as the last thing he'd said. I still had a hard time believing it. I mean, I'd *seen* Rafe. Felt his heartbeat. Talked to him. How could he be dead?

"Well..." Dix said, "Elspeth Caulfield died."

"And?"

"Her father was a client of dad's. When dad died, the account went to Jonathan, Catherine, and me. Since Elspeth inherited the house and a good bit of money from her parents, and since she wasn't married and didn't have any close kin, she made a will. She asked Jonathan to draw it up. Probably because she remembered me and Catherine from school and didn't want us to know too much about what was in it."

I nodded. That made sense. I didn't want anyone to know too much about what was going on in my personal life, either.

"I hadn't read it before today. But when Todd called to say she'd died, we pulled it out."

"And?"

He looked over at me. "She left everything she owned to her son."

"What?"

"She left everything she owned to her son."

It sounded the same this time. "I didn't know she had a son," I said.

"Neither did I," Dix answered. "Neither did anyone. And that's why we're on our way to her house. To see if we can figure out who he is."

"Yikes." I dabbed my face with the soggy tissue. "No offense, Dix, but why are you involving me in this? I don't work for Martin and McCall. I didn't know Elspeth. And to be honest, I think I'm probably the last person she'd want going through her things."

"What makes you say that?" Dix wanted to know.

"Because she's spent the past week trying to kill me. Just like she killed Marquita and tried to kill Yvonne."

Dix stared at me. For long enough that I had to remind him to watch the road.

He focused forward again. "You're kidding."

I shook my head. "Tamara Grimaldi told me."

"Wow." Dix didn't say anything else for a moment, just concentrated on driving. "Um... why? Why did Elspeth kill Marquita and try to kill you and Yvonne?"

I sighed. "Because of Rafe. She wanted him for herself. Apparently she thought we were all a threat to their happily-ever-after."

"She and Collier had a happily-ever-after?"

"In her mind they did. She hadn't even seen him for twelve years, but I guess she never got over that one-night-stand in high school."

"Huh," Dix said.

"Marquita lived with Rafe, to take care of Mrs. Jenkins, so Elspeth thought they were involved. Marquita may even have intimated that they were. Wishful thinking, you know? And Elspeth was at the cemetery the other day, and saw him kiss Yvonne, so Yvonne had to die."

That was probably Elspeth who Millie Ruth next door had seen walking down the street that night. Instead of me.

"What about you?" Dix asked, in a weird echo of my thoughts. It took me a second to figure out what he wanted to know.

"I talked to Elspeth a couple of months ago, after Todd told me about her and Rafe. She wouldn't tell me what happened between them in high school, but since I drove down here to ask, I guess she formed the impression that there was something between us."

"Something?"

"I was sort of..." I swallowed, "...falling for him, a little." And now he was dead. Before I'd had the chance to tell him how I felt. My eyes filled with fresh tears.

Dix muttered something. He was obviously lost for words, so he just reached over, fished out another tissue, and handed it to me. I sniffed.

Neither of us spoke again until we pulled up in front of Elspeth's big, white house in Damascus. Dix got out and walked around the car. I waited for him to open the door for me. He's been trained well, plus, I was really, really reluctant to do this. Going through Elspeth's things; Elspeth, of all people...

"You go ahead inside," I told Dix as we stood on the wraparound porch and he fumbled the key into the lock. "I want to make a phone call."

He looked at me for a second, but then he nodded. I waited until the door was closed behind him before I pulled out my phone and dialed.

And got Tamara Grimaldi's voice mail.

Of all the mornings for her not to answer her phone...! Of course, it had been a late night for her. Later than for me, since she'd had to deal with the—my heart squeezed—bodies.

Still, I needed her. She ought to be there.

"Detective? This is Savannah Martin. It's about ten thirty. I'm still in Sweetwater. At Elspeth Caulfield's house, actually. With my brother. He's her lawyer. We're trying to figure out where her next of kin lives. Anyway... Dix told me—"

My voice broke, and I had to stop and get myself under control before I could continue.

"Dix told me that Rafe... that Rafe didn't... oh, God!" I couldn't force myself to say the words out loud. "Just call me, OK? Please? As soon as you can." I hung up, and spent another few minutes sobbing into a tissue. Before I squared my shoulders and walked into Elspeth's house.

And stopped inside the door like I'd walked into an invisible wall.

The interior of the house was almost surreal.

It's not that I'm not used to old houses. The Martin mansion is antebellum, 1839, so fifty or sixty years older than this place, and full of antique furniture, including some of the original pieces from when the house was first built. Mrs. Jenkins's house is another Victorian, with dark woodwork and immensely tall ceilings. And I've seen my share of other old homes too, in the three or four months I've had my real estate license. But this, this was freaky. It was like stepping into the 19th century. Heavy, dark furniture, lamps with fringe, tchotchkes everywhere. Waxed flowers under glass, ceramic kittens, old books with their distinctive leathery smell.

Except for the painting above the fireplace mantel. I would have expected some Victorian monstrosity of dead birds and lemons, or maybe a reproduction Renoir or Monet; the impressionists would fit the time period of the house. Instead, what I got was the cover of a Barbara Botticelli romance. Blown up to thirty times its paperback size, and stuck in an ornate gold frame.

I blinked. Why would Elspeth Caulfield have the cover art for a Barbara Botticelli romance on display in her house? Maybe it was just a painting, or a photograph, that looked a little like it.

But no, I was pretty sure it was the real thing. I even knew which Barbara Botticelli novel it came from. The debut, released about four years earlier. I'd read it, of course. In one sitting.

As with all the BB books, the plot was a variation on the blonde and beautiful, well-bred heroine and the dark and dangerous, not-at-all-well-bred, bad-boy hero. It was called "Slave to Passion" and was set during the Civil War. In the Deep South. With a Southern Belle heroine named Elizabeth, who was irresistibly drawn to a man she couldn't have, not only because she was engaged to someone else, but because Benjamin was a Yankee, and a soldier for the North, who was occupying her family's land, and most of all because he was colored: the product of a union between Elizabeth's fiancée's father, the owner of a neighboring plantation, and the father's slave, who had run away and made it all the way to the North before giving birth to Elizabeth's fiancée's half brother.

The cover was the usual confection: the swooning heroine, her long blonde hair undone and the bodice of her hoop-skirted gown ditto, clasped in the hero's brawny arms, her soft white hands clutching his muscular shoulders and his dark head buried in her neck. He was naked to the waist, of course, the way Union soldiers always were. The two of them were up against a background of glossy-leaved magnolia trees, obviously hiding from Elizabeth's family in the big white plantation house in the distance.

She—Elizabeth—looked a lot like Elspeth.

I took a couple of steps closer and squinted.

She looked *a lot* like Elspeth. Funny I hadn't noticed that when I read the book.

Then again, I hadn't seen Elspeth for years at that point, so maybe it wasn't that funny, after all.

I noticed now, though. And my brain hiccupped.

There was a sound from the room to the left of the front hall, and I went over to a pair of sliding pocket doors and peered in. It was an office, and Dix was sitting at the desk busily sorting through paperwork. Of which there was plenty. Papers everywhere. Stacks and folders on the desk, piles on every flat surface, including the floor. Built-in bookshelves on one wall, floor to ceiling, and along the wall next to them, some sort of clothesline with a row of small colored index cards held up by clothes pins. There were also more Barbara Botticelli covers, small ones this time, framed and hanging on the wall. Along with what looked like—I squinted—awards?

Definitely awards. Given to Barbara Botticelli for excellence in the romance genre.

"Holy cow," I said.

Dix looked up from the paper sorting. "What?"

"I think she's Barbara Botticelli."

"Who?"

"Elspeth. I think she's Barbara Botticelli." Or was.

"Who's Barbara Botticelli?" Dix wanted to know.

I stared at him. "Only my favorite romance author. Doesn't Sheila read Barbara Botticelli?"

"I have no idea," Dix said, and went back to his papers.

Maybe his and Sheila's sex life was exciting enough without the aid of romance novels, but speaking for myself, I'd found them a great comfort during my short-lived marriage to Bradley. Who was about as far from a dark and dangerous Botticelli hero as it's possible to get.

If Elspeth was Barbara Botticelli, it explained why all her books were variations on the theme 'sweet, innocent, blonde good girl falls for dark, dangerous, mysterious bad boy,' anyway. If she'd been obsessed with Rafe since high school, he'd obviously been the hero of every book she'd ever written. I guess she'd been imagining herself redeeming him. Over and over and over. Rewriting their story so they got their happily ever after.

It also explained why I'd pictured every Botticelli hero—at least recently—with Rafe's face. I truly wasn't going crazy.

Or maybe that was just because I had fallen in love with him.

And now he was gone.

I blinked back another round of tears and turned to Dix. "Anything?"

"Not yet. There's a lot to go through here. Would you mind walking through the rest of the house, just to see if anything jumps out at you? Most likely any information would be here in the office, but have a look around."

"Sure." I left the room and wandered back into the hallway, sparing Elizabeth/Elspeth and Benjamin/Rafe a glance on the way past.

Unlike the Martin mansion, which is symmetrical with a central foyer and long hallway straight through to the back door, Elspeth's house was a Queen Anne Victorian: asymmetrical and quirkily charming. The foyer was in the front right corner of the house, with the parlor to the left, and a short hallway down the middle, ending in the master bedroom. On the right side, beyond the foyer, the house widened, and another room—the dining room—flowed into the kitchen. I walked through it all, but didn't see anything of interest. The dining room was pristine, with dark, heavy furniture, while the kitchen was updated with stainless steel appliances and a tile floor. There were no kid drawings fastened to the fridge, the way there were in many of the houses I'd seen over the past few months. There were a few photographs, but they were of Elspeth herself. Hidden under a big picture hat, wearing some kind of fairy costume, maybe from a party or something. There were no telephone numbers or addresses tacked to the fridge, either; the only thing worthy of note was the books everywhere. There was at least one bookcase in every room, including the kitchen. They were stuffed full, and the small bedroom between the master and the parlor had been turned into a library, with shelves on all four walls.

Upstairs was mostly unused, it seemed. Several of the rooms had dust covers over all the furniture. The room where I'd seen the light on the other night, when I drove over to Yvonne's house, was Elspeth's bedroom, just as I had suspected. And like my bedroom in the mansion, it didn't look like it had changed since she was a teenager. Mine hadn't either, but that was because I didn't live there anymore. And because it hadn't changed appreciably in the past hundred years before I was born, either.

Elspeth's bedroom was sweet and girly: pale blue walls, white canopied bed, frilly lace curtains. White furniture and a fluffy rug on the floor. Like she hadn't grown or changed since she was fifteen.

There were books here, too, and a stack of paper next to the bed. A manuscript, I saw when I got closer. A new Barbara Botticelli. I'd have to make sure Dix sent it back to the publisher in New York on Elspeth's behalf.

It was called "Prisoner of Love," which seemed a worthy follow-up to "Apache Amour" and "Pirate's Booty," not to mention "Highland Fling" and "Slave to Passion."

I couldn't resist sitting down on the bed and leafing through a couple of pages, and before I knew it fifteen minutes had passed. I put the manuscript down, guiltily, and looked at the rest of the room. And froze.

There were a couple of photographs on the night table, next to the stack of printed pages. I'd been so busy honing in on the manuscript that I hadn't noticed them. There was Elspeth, with her big, black dogs. She owned a half dozen of the beasts, which must have been removed to a facility somewhere before we arrived, probably by the sheriff's department. Two months ago, when I was here, they'd tried to lick me to death. Another framed picture showed an older couple, probably Elspeth's parents, on the porch outside. Her mother was small and blond and looked harassed, with a tense smile and worried eyes, while Elspeth's father was big and beefy with an uncompromising look to his thin lips and straight brows.

Those were not what interested me, although a closer study of the picture of the parents might give some insight into Elspeth's psyche. At the moment I didn't care. I reached for the last photograph with a hand that was shaking.

For a moment I thought I was looking at Rafe. Not Rafe the way I'd ever seen him; Rafe long before we ended up at Columbia High together. Nine or ten years old, maybe. With a couple of oversized front teeth and a big grin, dancing eyes and a boyish face.

And for a second it hurt, and I thought I might start crying again. But then I saw the car in the background, behind the boy. An SUV. Fairly new. This picture had been taken within the last few years. Not twenty years ago, when Rafe was this age.

"Your phone rang," Dix said when I came back into the office, photograph in hand.

I glanced at my purse, which I had left on the chair next to him. "Why didn't you answer it?"

"I did. It was Detective Grimaldi from Nashville."

God. "What did she say?"

"She didn't say anything," Dix said. "Just that she was returning your call and to try her again later."

"That's it?"

"I asked her if it was true that Rafe Collier had died."

My heart stuttered. "And?"

Dix shook his head, his eyes somber. "I'm sorry, sis. She said yes." He caught sight of the photograph I had put on the desk and added, "Whoa. Where did you find this?"

I struggled to get myself together as I told him it had been on the night table upstairs, next to Elspeth's bed.

"This isn't Collier, is it?"

I shook my head.

"Looks like him, though."

I nodded. "But the car..." My voice was barely audible.

"I see it. This could be the son. If Elspeth did get pregnant in high school, after that one-night-stand with Collier, her son would be... twelve or so now?"

I nodded. "In that case, this picture would be a couple of years old."

"And that's about the time Chrysler started making these cars. This could be him."

"Did you find anything down here?"

He shook his head. "Not so far. This picture is our best clue."

"Glad to help." I looked around. "This is going to be a big job."

Dix nodded. "The information is here somewhere. Someone knows what happened and where this boy is. We can check Elspeth's financial records and her travel itineraries and her phone records. Whatever it takes to find this kid."

I nodded. "Do you have to do it now?"

He looked up at me. "You ready to go, sis?"

"I'd like to get home. To my apartment. To Nashville." Where I might be able to corner Tamara Grimaldi. And where I could hibernate in bed with a box of Kleenex and cry my heart out without worrying about what anyone would think. I knew Dix loved me, and he hadn't seemed too surprised at my reaction to the news that Rafe was dead, but I had been more subdued than I would have been had

I been alone when I found out. I wanted to be by myself, to howl and mourn in peace.

"I'll take you back to your car," Dix said. "I can always come back here later." He looked around, and added, "I'll have to. There's enough work here for a couple of days, at least."

"I can stay and help if you want."

He shook his head. "Go home. Take care of yourself. Do you want me to let you know what I find out?"

"Please," I said. There was no Rafe to tell anymore—Elspeth hadn't told him she was pregnant, and now he'd never know he had a son—but I'd still like to know. At least that the boy was well taken care of and happy. Although what I'd do if he wasn't, I didn't know. "I'd like a copy of the picture, too, please. If you don't mind."

"I'll send it to your phone," Dix promised and put his arm around my shoulders. "And keep you posted about everything else. Including the funeral."

"Funeral?" What made him think I'd want to go to Elspeth's funeral?

"For Collier? He'll probably go in the ground up on Oak Street, don't you think? Where his mother is buried?"

I shrugged. I didn't want to think about it. And Dix, bless his heart, must have realized it, because he kept his mouth shut on the drive from Damascus back to Sweetwater.

Twenty-Two

I cried most of the way back to Nashville. Not loudly, not in a way that made me a menace to the other people on the road, but quietly, softly, with tears running down my face. By the time I reached Nashville, my eyes were puffy and sore, and my face was swollen. I looked awful. That didn't stop me from driving directly to 101 Potsdam Street to knock on the door. Somewhere in the back of my mind, I had this crazy hope that once I got there, maybe it would all be OK. It would turn out to have been a misunderstanding, and Rafe would be there and everything would be all right.

But of course he wasn't. There was no answer to my knock, and the house was locked up tight while the driveway was empty. I got back in the car and drove downtown to Police Plaza, where I demanded to see Tamara Grimaldi.

The guard on duty seemed a little leery of letting me upstairs, and paid extra special attention to the contents of my handbag—including confiscating my lipstick pepper spray and miniature lipstick knife—but eventually he let me in. By the time the elevator opened on Tamara's floor, she was standing in the hallway waiting for me.

And she looked almost as bad as I felt. Her eyes weren't red from crying, but they were bloodshot and puffy from lack of sleep. Her face was drawn, her color was bad, and she was still wearing the same clothes she'd worn last night. I deduced she hadn't been to bed yet.

She was on the ball, though. One look at my face, and she dragged me into an empty interrogation room away from everyone else, pushed me down on a chair, and sat down across the table from me. "What's wrong?"

"You told me he'd be OK. You said you'd take care of him."

"What?"

"You told me he'd be OK. You said you'd take care of him." My mouth seemed to be stuck on instant replay.

She shook her head, not in negation but to clear it. "What are you talking about?"

"Rafe. You told me he'd be OK. You said you'd take care of him. That nothing bad would happen if he didn't get to the hospital right away."

"So?"

So?

"So you lied." My voice was shaking, and I grabbed the edge of the table to steady myself. "And I can understand why. I really can. I mean, if you'd told me the truth, I would have had a gibbering meltdown right there; I realize that. So I understand why you did it. But I didn't get to say goodbye. And now..."

I was crying again. Tamara looked at me for a second before getting up and leaving the room. When she came back, she was carrying a can of Diet Coke and an economy-sized box of Kleenex. She put both on the table in front of me. "Listen."

I sniffed into a tissue.

"I have no idea what you've heard, or from whom—"

"I left you a message," I said.

"I know. I tried to call you back. Your brother answered."

"You told him Rafe was dead."

"Of course I did. I..."

" You told me you'd take care of him. You said he'd be OK!" I snatched another tissue.

"Whoa! Whoa!" She was waving her hands. "Of course he's OK. I told you he would be. Did you think he died?"

She looked at me, and her face changed. "You did think he died."

"You mean he didn't?"

"Of course he didn't! I told you he wouldn't. *He* told you he wouldn't. He took a bullet to the shoulder. The doctor dug it out and slapped a Band Aid on the hole. You thought he died?"

"Dix told me he died!" I said. Shrieked, really. "He said Todd told him, and that the sheriff had told Todd. And then he asked you, and you said Rafe had died!"

"Ah." She nodded.

Ah? What the hell? "You sound like that makes sense to you."

"That's because it does. See, it's like this..."

She explained. By the time she was finished, I had to admit it did sort of make sense. If word got out that Rafe was dead, that would protect him from whoever had sent Jorge after him, as well as from anyone else who might be tempted to take him out in the future. And if Rafe was dead, then Jorge would have to be alive. But...

"Sheriff Satterfield doesn't know? How did you manage that?"

"Told him that Mrs. Jenkins would want the body taken to Nashville to bury next to his father." Tamara shrugged.

"And... that was Jorge Pena's body?"

She nodded. "We made sure the sheriff didn't get a good look at it. There's a resemblance, but not so strong that someone who knew Mr. Collier wouldn't have been able to tell the difference."

"Oh, believe me, Sheriff Satterfield knows Rafe. He arrested him often enough as a teenager."

"That's what you said. Mr. Craig had thought ahead and brought a van, so we loaded the body in there and he took it with him. Along with Mr. Collier, of course. We picked him up on the road; he walked through the woods from the trailer so the sheriff wouldn't see him. Ms. Caulfield's body we left for Sheriff Satterfield. To give him something to do to keep him busy."

"I'm sure he appreciates that." My voice was a little weak, both from the crying and from the relief. "So where is he now?"

"The sheriff is in Sweetwater. Mr. Pena's body is at the morgue, with Mr. Collier's name on it. As for Wendell Craig..."

"You know that's not what I meant."

Tamara grimaced. "He's in Jorge's motel room."

"Where?"

She shook her head. "I can't tell you that."

"Why?"

"Because if we want people to believe that he's dead, he can't have you showing up at his motel."

"I'll dress up as a hooker," I said. "And pretend that Jorge called for some company."

She looked at me, up and down, for a second, before her mouth quirked. "It'd be worth it, just to see that. I'm almost tempted to let you."

"Please. I really need to see him. He's going to be leaving town again, isn't he?"

She nodded. "For a week or two. Just until we can figure out who sent Jorge after him and put them behind bars."

"And you don't think that'll take more than two weeks?"

"I doubt it. A month at the most."

"If he's going away again," I said, "I definitely need to see him before he goes. It doesn't have to be at his motel. It doesn't even have to be in private. I'll take a phone call, if it's all I can get. But I want to hear his voice and know he's all right."

She arched her brows. "Don't you trust me?"

"I trust you. I just want to hear it for myself." I hesitated for a second. "There's something I have to tell him."

"Ah." She didn't argue with that. "All right. I'll see what I can do. Where are you headed when you leave here?"

I glanced at the clock on the wall. It was going on three o'clock. "I'm going back to my apartment. And I'm staying there. Unless you call and tell me to get my hooker-clothes on."

"You own hooker-clothes?" She got to her feet without waiting for my answer. And no, I don't.

Although I could put on my new red dress again, I supposed. It was more suited to an expensive call-girl than a hooker, but it was as close as I could get. And springing it on Rafe a second time might prove... interesting.

"Pack up anything of Officer Slater's that you come across and I'll send her out to pick it up later. I'll be in touch."

I walked out of there, got in my car, and went home.

IT WAS NICE TO BE BACK. Nice not to have to worry about people breaking in or gunning for me. Nice to know that Rafe wasn't dead after all.

Damn Tamara Grimaldi and Wendell, though, for not calling and telling me right away what their plan was. And damn Rafe most of all. How could he not know that I'd freak out if I heard he'd died? He should have called me and told me himself, dammit. It was the least he could do.

Unless he really had no idea that I cared. Maybe I'd somehow succeeded in convincing him that I ran to him just for sex the other night. Maybe he thought, when I showed up again yesterday—in another skimpy cocktail dress, straight from another date with Todd—that I wanted more of the same. *Just* more of the same. Not that I wanted to see him because I—so help me, God—was in love with him and being with him made me—so help me, God—happy.

Was that a good thing, I wondered as I moved wet clothes from the washer to the dryer.

Maybe it was. I couldn't have a relationship with him. No matter how happy being with him made me. I couldn't bring him into the family. It would be uncomfortable for him as well as for them, not to mention for me, stuck in the middle. And honestly, it was still a little uncomfortable to go anywhere with him. In public, I mean. Here in Nashville it wasn't such a big deal; people here are used to seeing mixed couples. Nobody stared at us at Fidelio's or that other place he'd taken me to once, the Short Stop Sports Bar. But at Beulah's the other morning... it had been like walking a gauntlet. All those eyes, and whispers. All that avid interest in what really ought to be just between the two of us.

How can you have a relationship with someone, if you're too embarrassed—or too afraid—to be seen in public with him?

You can't. And shouldn't. So maybe it was all for the best that he didn't know. Maybe, if I was too embarrassed and afraid to be with him, openly, I didn't deserve him anyway.

BY THE END OF THE WORKDAY, Megan Slater had stopped by to pick up her bag of possessions; she *did* look rather a lot like me, if in much better shape physically. I'd never make it through the police academy. Also, Dix had emailed the picture from Elspeth's night table to my cell phone, along with the news that he had no further information. He was confident he would discover the truth, though. Elspeth's house was full of paperwork and old journals, and somewhere in the mess, there was sure to be something helpful. I emailed back to ask that he please let me know what it was when he found it and then I left it at that.

Tamara Grimaldi called at seven. "Get your hooker-clothes on. He's staying at the Congress Inn on Dickerson Pike. Room 116. And he won't be there for long, so you'd better hurry."

She hung up, before I could express my thanks.

Ten minutes later I was on my way, red satin dress, silver sandals, and all.

The Congress Inn is a fifteen minute drive, roughly, from my apartment, but it's in a part of East Nashville that's nowhere near as nice or safe. In fact, it's not too far from Apple Annie's Motel, which rents rooms by the hour. It's also not too far from the Stor-All facility that Rafe and I had burgled two months earlier, when I was trying to figure out who killed Brenda Puckett. And finally, it's only a few blocks from Potsdam Street.

In other words, it was the perfect location for Jorge.

I had noticed the place before, driving past. It's right at the intersection of Dickerson Pike and Hart Lane, and the main building must have been a beautiful house once upon a time. Long ago now, but the traces of old beauty are still there. It's an Italianate Victorian, late 1800s, two stories tall, painted white.

That's not where the motel rooms are, of course. They surround the main house in long, low brick strips. Rafe's—AKA Jorge Pena's—room, 116, was close to the front.

I took a deep breath before I opened the car door and got out onto the pavement, on legs that shook. And then it took me a second to adjust the red satin dress—up, not down—before I made my way toward room 116. Accompanied by shrill whistles from a couple of gentlemen on the other side of the parking lot, sitting outside their own rooms sharing a six-pack or two of beer. I'll spare you the remarks they directed my way, but basically they ran to the suggestion that if I didn't find what I was looking for on my side of the motel, I should try theirs.

Oh, and how much did I charge?

At first when I knocked on the door to room 116, there was no answer. I could hear rustling from inside, though, so I knocked again. And stood back when the curtain fluttered, so he could see me.

Then the door opened, and I took another step back.

He looked different, and it wasn't just the gun he let me see for a second before stashing it out of sight behind his back. His eyes were hard and his jaw tight, and his hair was styled in a way I wasn't used to, but that I'd seen on Jorge. He was unshaven, too, with the beginnings of Jorge's little goatee. There was a small silver cross in his ear, that he hadn't had yesterday, and I didn't doubt that when he turned around, I'd find a copy of Jorge's dragon tattoo on his back. Just above that gun tucked into the waistband of his jeans.

There was a piece of gauze taped to his shoulder; quite small considering that it was covering a gunshot wound. Yet it was considerably larger than the Band Aid Tamara Grimaldi had told me about.

And he looked like he was ready for a visit from a hooker, with his shirt off and his jeans zipped only halfway up and the button at the waistband open. He was wearing no underwear that I could see.

I swallowed.

"Hey, man!" one of the inebriated gentlemen from across the parking lot hollered, "when you're done with her, send her over here, huh?"

Rafe's response was pithy and crude and very graphic, even the parts of it I didn't understand because he spoke Spanish. I blushed. He looked at me, with a grin that was hot enough to sizzle metal. "C'mon in, *querida*. I ain't got much time, so you're gonna have to work fast."

He even sounded a little like Jorge.

I took a steadying breath before I stepped through the door. The room beyond was awful. Small and dark and smelly, with stained 1970s shag carpet on the floor, and a bare bulb under the ceiling. There was a single bed, unmade, and through an opening in the back wall, I could see a dingy bathroom with black mold around the tub.

I shuddered. You couldn't pay me enough to spend the night here.

Unless he asked me to stay. Then I might be able to get over my squeamishness.

"You shouldn't be here, darlin'."

I turned to look at him. His eyes were sober now; that raunchy heat gone along with the flinty hardness, and he'd finished zipping and fastening his jeans. It was almost disappointing.

I moved my attention back up to his face. "I had to see you before you left town again."

"What's going on?"

Aside from the fact that I think I'm in love with you? "They told me you were dead. I wanted to see for myself that you weren't."

He looked surprised. "Who told you I was dead?"

"My brother Dix. Todd Satterfield told him—" unable to contain his glee, no doubt, "and the sheriff told Todd."

He nodded. "And nobody told you." He reached out to run a finger down my cheek. "Sorry, darlin'. Guess we all figured you'd know."

"It's been a rough day," I said, blinking to stave off the tears that threatened.

"C'mere." He reached out a hand. I stepped into his embrace and put my head against his shoulder. The uninjured one. He wrapped his arms around me, and we stood like that for a minute, while I enjoyed the warm softness of his skin against my cheek and the steady movement of his breath against my hair.

When I lifted my head to look up at him, he kissed me. Softly. And then he smiled. "I'd ask you to stay awhile, so I can prove that all the parts still work, but I don't have the time."

I nodded. "It's becoming almost a habit, isn't it?" Having to say goodbye before he hightailed it out of town again. "How long will you be gone this time?"

"If I'm lucky, just a few weeks."

"And if not?"

"Could be another month, maybe."

I nodded. "Before you go, I have something to show you."

His eyes crinkled. "I've already seen what you got, darlin'. And if you think showing it to me again is gonna make me change my mind and stay in Nashville—"

"Lovely as that sounds, this is something different." I pulled my cell phone from my purse and flicked it open.

"That's a shame," Rafe said, "cause I was just about to let myself be talked into it."

I ignored him while I hunted through my pictures for the one Dix had sent earlier. And then I put the phone in Rafe's hand and watched his expression.

For a second, his face turned absolutely blank, and I don't think he remembered to breathe. When he found his voice again, it was carefully neutral, but not without the slightest of tremors. "Looks like me."

I nodded. "He does."

"Who is he?"

"I'm afraid I don't know. It's a picture Elspeth Caulfield had on her nightstand."

I explained, quickly, about the will, and how Martin and McCall were the executors, and that Dix and I had gone to Elspeth's house looking for information. "There's no name on the back of the photo, and Dix hasn't been able to find anything else yet, either. It could even be a coincidence."

"How d'you figure that?"

"She was a little crazy, you know? Delusional, or whatnot. She might have seen this boy somewhere and taken a picture of him just because he does look so much like you. He might not be anybody."

Rafe shook his head. "Look at him. He's mine. And probably hers. Fuck!"

I didn't answer. After a second he glanced at me, "Sorry."

"No problem." I'd expected a few bad words. He was actually being pretty calm, everything considered.

"But I have a kid! A kid that nobody bothered to tell me about. A kid who's…" He calculated in his head, "eleven years and eight or nine months old. And he doesn't know who I am!"

"He probably has a family," I said.

He looked at me, his eyes a little wild. "You think?"

"Look at him. He looks happy, healthy, well-fed, clean…" All the things Rafe hadn't been at that age. "If the car in the background is theirs, they're reasonably well-off, and the shirt he's wearing looks like part of a uniform. See the logo? He probably goes to private school."

"Yeah." Rafe looked down at the screen again. The boy smiled back, his dark eyes shining and his smile brilliant.

"I'm sorry to spring it on you like this, especially with everything else you have to worry about right now. But if you're not coming back for weeks, or even a month, I didn't want you to leave Nashville without knowing. Dix is trying to track him down. I'll let you know what he finds out."

He nodded.

"Do you have a phone number or an email address I can use to reach you?"

"Call Tammy. She'll call Wendell and he'll get a message to me."

"Do you want a copy of the picture? To take with you?"

I could see he was tempted, but he shook his head. "Better not." He handed the phone back, after one more look. I tucked it into my bag.

We stood in silence for a second.

"You should go," Rafe said.

I nodded. I didn't want to, but I should. The sooner I left, the sooner he could leave, and the sooner he'd be back. "Do you think enough time has passed for the guys across the parking lot to believe that we've… um… finished our business?"

"We can take a couple minutes to make it look convincing. C'mere, darlin'."

He reached for me. Drove his fingers into my hair and mussed it. Yanked my skirt up a couple of inches. Kissed me, hard. Made sure

I looked breathless and roughly used before he opened the door and pushed me through the opening. "Thanks, *querida*. I'll call you next time I'm in town."

The door slammed shut behind me. The guys across the lot laughed uproariously. I stood there for a second, straightening my dress and smoothing down my hair, before I walked to the Volvo with as much dignity I could muster. And then I drove away, without looking back.

ABOUT THE AUTHOR

Jenna Bennett writes the *USA Today* bestselling Savannah Martin mystery series for her own gratification, as well as the *New York Times* bestselling Do-It-Yourself home renovation mysteries from Berkley Prime Crime under the pseudonym Jennie Bentley. For a change of pace, she writes a variety of romance, from contemporary to futuristic, and from paranormal to suspense.

FOR MORE INFORMATION, PLEASE VISIT HER WEBSITE:
WWW.JENNABENNETT.COM